HIDE & SEEK

BRANTLEY WALKER: *Off the Books, 3*

DEAD HEAT RANCH
Boots Optional
Betting on Grace
Overnight Love

DEVIL'S BEND
Chasing Dreams
Vanishing Dreams

MISPLACED HALOS
Protected in Darkness
Salvation in Darkness
Bound in Darkness

OFFICE INTRIGUE
Office Intrigue
Intrigued Out of the Office
Their Rebellious Submissive
Their Famous Dominant
Their Ruthless Sadist
Their Naughty Student
Their Fairy Princess

PIER 70
Reckless
Fearless
Speechless
Harmless
Clueless

SNIPER 1 SECURITY
Wait for Morning
Never Say Never
Tomorrow's Too Late

SOUTHERN BOY MAFIA/DEVIL'S PLAYGROUND
Beautifully Brutal
Without Regret
Beautifully Loyal
Without Restraint

STANDALONE NOVELS
Unhinged Trilogy
A Million Tiny Pieces
Inked on Paper
Bad Reputation
Bad Business

NAUGHTY HOLIDAY EDITIONS
2015
2016

HIDE & SEEK

BRANTLEY WALKER: OFF THE BOOKS, 3

NICOLE EDWARDS

Published by Nicole Edwards Limited
PO Box 1086, Pflugerville, Texas 78691

Hide & Seek
Brantley Walker: Off the Books, 3
Nicole Edwards

This is a work of fiction. Names, characters, businesses, places, events and incidents either are the products of the author's imagination or used in a fictitious manner. Any resemblance to actual persons, living or dead, business establishments, events, or locals is entirely coincidental.

COVER DETAILS:

Image: © Galyna Andrushko (44902864) | 123rf.com
Design: © Nicole Edwards Limited

INTERIOR DETAILS:

Formatting: Nicole Edwards Limited
Editing: Blue Otter Editing | BlueOtterEditing.com

ISBN:
Ebook 9781644180327 | Paperback 9781644180334 | Audio 9781644180341

SUBJECTS:
BISAC: FICTION / Romance / Gay
BISAC: FICTION / Romance / General

Chapter One

Monday, November 9, 2020

"DONUTS AND COFFEE," JJ SAID. "BREAKFAST OF champions."

"Coffee, yes. Donuts, no," Baz insisted. "Tacos are a key morning staple."

"Key?" Reese snorted. "Coffee's the staple. Take or leave the rest."

Brantley Walker looked up from his desk at the three members of his task force. Well, technically, it was Governor Greenwood's task force, but Brantley was the man in charge, overseeing the work, which involved solving missing persons cases, both cold and current, so he figured he had the right to call it his. The very group formed by a horrific ordeal that had directly affected Brantley's family when his five-year-old cousin was abducted by a crazed bitch hell-bent on revenge. The team had been officially inaugurated when they solved a decade-old case of a missing girl from their hometown of Coyote Ridge, Texas.

It had been nearly two months since Kate Walker was snatched from a field trip at the state capitol, and during that time, they'd accomplished quite a bit, including solving three major cases, one of which had resulted from their digging into that cold case, but it counted as far as he was concerned. And the hub of their operation? A four-thousand-square-foot old horse barn that Brantley had repaired and converted back before he could've known any of this would happen. The barn, dubbed HQ, had gotten a few updates in recent months, including a new set of stairs leading up to the old hayloft and some furniture to make it usable.

Seeing his team there, all hard at work on a Monday morning—arguing about their breakfast preferences—made him smile.

Been a good couple of months, he would say.

And he had them to thank for it.

Jessica James, a.k.a. JJ, was his hacker extraordinaire. They'd grown up together, their friendship surviving the seventeen years he'd served in the US Navy and her on-again, off-again relationship with the town douchebag. Although she was pretty with her auburn hair and light green eyes, the woman's wit was her most charming feature. Plus, she was a whiz with a computer. Didn't matter what they needed, JJ could ferret it out of the deepest, darkest corners whether by weeding through data or a little cyber B-and-E. She was damn good at what she did. Oh, and JJ found old cases daunting and she had a penchant for donuts.

Sebastian Buchanan was the newest member, an APD detective who'd been brought in during the last case. When the governor's daughter had gone missing, Baz was the one who stepped in to handle for the Austin Police Department. Blond hair, blue eyes, chiseled everything, the guy would've come off as one of those uppity frat boys if it wasn't for his laid-back charm. Since Brantley tended to do things his own way, he figured it was good to have Baz there to keep them walking that fine, legal line. The guy claimed he had a problem with authority, but it was his willingness to adapt to the situation that had made Brantley bring him on board permanently.

And last but certainly not least: Reese Tavoularis. Six feet, five inches of prime sin, Reese was Brantley's partner in every sense of the word. The man he'd fallen in love with, the man he now shared a bed with every night. He was the one Brantley trusted his life to, the guy he wanted to have his back from now until the day he took his last breath. It had been a rocky transition to this place in their lives, mostly due to the fact that, before Brantley, Reese had never been with a man, much less fallen in love with one. Brantley was honored to hold that title.

Now that they were all there and the day was underway, Brantley was ready to tell them what their next assignment was. An important task they had to knock out before they could do much of anything. Their objective? Decide on a fucking name for their task force. He hoped like hell at least one of them could come up with something, because if they had any hope of establishing a reputation with law enforcement agencies across the state, they had to be something other than "the governor's task force."

"First order of business," Brantley said, getting to his feet.

"Breakfast?" JJ replied. "Yes, please. But not donuts. Unless they're Round Rock Donuts. But that's too far, so…"

"I nominate tacos," Baz chimed in, leaning back in his chair and propping his booted foot on his desk.

"You always nominate tacos," JJ grumbled. "What's wrong with sausage biscuits?"

"What do you want, Tavoularis?"

"Already ate. Omelets and bacon this morning. Just need more coffee." Reese got to his feet, looked at Brantley. "Want some?"

Unable to turn down more caffeine, Brantley nodded, tossed back what was left in his mug, then passed it to Reese.

"Would it hurt you to make a couple extra omelets in the mornin'?" JJ whined with a smile. "The rest of us gotta eat, too."

"Cereal's a healthy part of a day, but this ain't about breakfast," Brantley told her, cutting them off before they could take this down the rabbit hole.

"You suck," JJ said, tacking on a "boo" for good measure.

Brantley rolled his eyes, unable to hide his smile. "We need a name."

"Um…" Baz frowned, scratched his forehead. "Brantley's not good enough?" Baz asked, deadpan.

JJ laughed. Proving she thought the six-foot, one-inch Adonis was hot, because his jokes were certainly lackluster.

"Not for me. For the task force."

"Why?" Baz asked, holding up the badge they'd been given as proof they were technically law enforcement. "I figure this is good enough."

"Maybe, but either we come up with a name or we're nothin' but glorified PIs."

"Like Magnum," JJ said.

"Who's Magnum?" he asked, knowing he would regret it.

"You know. Magnum, P.I. Ex-Navy SEAL turned private investigator? Originally played by the uber-sexy Tom Selleck? Now by the delicious Jay Hernandez?" JJ sighed when he simply shook his head. "Come on, Brantley. Don't tell me you don't watch any TV."

Baz barked a laugh, pinned his eyes on Brantley. "You really are our very own Magnum."

"He doesn't," Reese said, bringing Brantley his coffee. "Watch TV."

"Thanks."

"Yep." Reese glanced over at JJ. "Unless it's the news, or somethin' I happen to have on, he doesn't watch."

"Surely you're makin' headway there, Tavoularis." She cocked an eyebrow at her empty coffee mug.

"Might I remind you, we don't have a couch," Reese said, "so our living room's useless."

"Where's your TV?" Baz asked, his brow furrowed as though he couldn't believe it was even possible for someone not to have one.

"In the bedroom," Brantley said, looking directly at JJ. "And there're far more important things to do in the bedroom than watch TV."

JJ's eyebrows bounced. "So I've heard. Maybe I could take a peek sometime. See what all the fuss is about."

Brantley narrowed his eyes. "Watch it, woman."

A laugh was her response.

"Back on topic," Reese said, his face an interesting shade of crimson.

"Yes. Task force name." Baz cleared his throat, looked down at his desk. "Please, God, let us get back on topic."

Brantley smirked. "So? Suggestions?"

"Well, we've already decided Five-O is out of the question," JJ said.

He found it amusing that there was a hint of a question in that statement. "We're not gonna be Five-O."

"Fine." She huffed. "What number is Texas?"

"Twenty-eighth to join the union," Reese noted.

"Paid attention in Texas History, did you?" JJ teased.

Reese winked.

"Nothing remarkable about Two-Eight. Doesn't have a ring to it," Baz mused. "But we are the Lone Star State. Maybe we're the Lone Star Task Force."

"Next thing you know, we'll be called the Lone Rangers," JJ said. "No way."

A buzzer sounded, signaling someone was at the door, drawing the conversation to a halt and all eyes in that direction.

"You expectin' someone?" Brantley asked no one in particular.

"It's Travis," JJ said.

Brantley glanced back to where she'd projected the camera image onto the TV. Sure enough, the man was standing outside, holding a paper sack and likely his patience.

Reese headed for the door, unlocked it.

Travis Walker was one of Brantley's many cousins. His daughter Kate's disappearance was the first case they'd taken on, although it hadn't been in an official capacity. However, it was the one that had resulted in the governor assigning a task force.

Brantley watched as Reese shook Travis's hand, gestured the guy inside, and closed the door behind him.

"What brings you by?" Brantley asked, curious as to what would've drawn the man their way first thing on a Monday. Considering he owned and operated Alluring Indulgence Resort, he probably had more pressing issues to deal with.

"I brought tacos," he said, holding up a white paper sack.

"Oh. My. God!" JJ launched herself up and raced over to him. "If you weren't married, I'd kiss you right now."

Travis chuckled. "Yeah. My husband and wife might get a little upset about that."

"I know, right?" JJ grinned, snagged the bag, and trotted toward the kitchen.

Travis's attention shifted to Baz, and it was then Brantley realized the true reason Travis had come by. He was here to scope out the new guy.

"Travis, meet our newest task force member. Former Austin PD Detective Sebastian Buchanan. Baz, meet Travis Walker."

The two men shook hands.

"I've heard quite a bit about you," Baz said with a grin. "Mostly good."

Travis chuckled. "If it's all good, you know they're lyin'."

There was so much truth in that statement.

Although Travis had no authority over the task force, he was a silent member. His father's friendship with the governor had played a part in the task force being formed, and Travis had vowed to assist from a financial perspective if necessary. He was a staunch supporter since it was his daughter who'd been kidnapped from the state capitol.

"How's it goin'?" Travis asked, glancing around the space. "Looks official in here." He peered over at Brantley. "I see you've got a couch."

Brantley grinned. "Not in the house."

"I'm lookin' to change that," Reese said.

Now that Reese had officially moved in, they were still trying to decide what to do with all the extra square footage in the house. Including the dining room and living room, which Brantley had never bothered to furnish. In his defense, he hadn't needed furniture when it was just him. And for some reason, it offended Travis's sensibilities that Brantley didn't have somewhere to plant his ass in the living room.

"Well, I know a guy," Travis said.

"You know all the guys," Reese countered.

Travis chuckled. "Not all, but many."

"We were just tryin' to come up with a name for the task force," JJ said when she returned, two foil-wrapped breakfast tacos in her hand. She passed one to Baz, then addressed Travis with, "Got any ideas?"

"What're my choices?"

"We got nothin'," Baz informed him.

"OTB," Travis said easily.

"You down with OTB, yeah, you know me," Baz sang, loud and off-key.

Brantley stared, confused.

"Christ. This guy doesn't listen to music, either?"

"Not unless it's country," JJ stated. "Definitely not Naughty by Nature."

Brantley shrugged off the peanut gallery, glanced back at Travis. "I'll bite. What does it mean?"

"Off the books," Travis explained as though it was obvious. "OTB keeps it simple."

"And it sounds official-like," JJ noted. "O. T. B. Hmm. Doesn't suck."

Seriously? They'd spent a couple of months introducing themselves as the governor's task force and Travis Walker waltzes in here and gives them a name within thirty seconds of arriving?

Was there anything this guy couldn't do?

"And it'll be easy to add to the badge. Texas OTB," Travis stated.

"And when someone wants us to explain it?" Baz asked.

Travis's grin was slow. "You tell 'em it's none of their damn business."

Baz laughed. "I like this guy."

"Everyone does," Reese said under his breath.

"Now that you've scoped out the place, seen the new guy, and named the task force, what else you got for us?" Brantley asked Travis, putting him on the spot.

"I didn't come by for any of those things. I actually came to tell you I got you some wings."

Again, Brantley was stupefied. "What?"

"For lunch?" JJ asked, eyebrows lifted, hope radiating on her face.

"Is that all you ever think about?" Baz asked her.

JJ shrugged.

"Not food," Travis clarified.

"You bought a plane?" Reese asked, clearly the smarter one.

"I did. Private jet. And a helicopter."

"You're shittin' me." Brantley stared, slack-jawed.

"I am not." Travis held up his hands to calm Brantley before he argued. "Don't worry, it wasn't a spur-of-the-moment decision. I've been thinkin' about it for a while. They're not just for you, but they are there if you need 'em. When you need 'em."

Well, shit.

This was a hell of a way to start a Monday.

Travis hung around to chat with the team for a few minutes, then announced he was leaving.

"I'll walk you out," he offered, knowing Travis hadn't simply stopped by to deliver breakfast tacos and the news about a private plane at their disposal.

Outside, the cool November morning breeze sent the leaves dancing down from the trees that surrounded the barn. The grass was brittle from the cooler weather, beginning to wither as it usually did this time of year.

"You consider puttin' in a walkway?" Travis asked as they trudged through the soggy ground toward the house.

"On my list of enhancements," he said snidely. "You know, bottom of the page, right after find all the missin' people."

"Smart-ass."

Brantley smirked. "Family trait. I come by it naturally."

"That you do."

"So where's your sidekick?" he asked, keeping the conversation casual.

"You mean my husband?"

Brantley grinned, tucked his hands in his pockets. "Live together, work together, play together. Figured y'all were closer than that, but yeah. Where's Gage?"

Travis shrugged. "At the office, probably."

Where Travis should've been, Brantley figured. And would've been if it weren't for this detour.

They reached the back of the house, continued around to the side.

"Spill it, Travis," he said curtly. "I know you've got another reason for bein' here."

As he expected, Travis didn't argue. He wasn't a man to make excuses for what he did or his reasons for doing them.

"Looks like you've settled in nicely."

However, he wasn't above beating around the bush, apparently.

"We have," Brantley confirmed, pretending the small talk was necessary. "Not completely up to speed, but we're gettin' there."

They stopped at the driveway, directly in front of the fancy blacked-out Cadillac Escalade that sat alongside the other vehicles parked there. It was Travis's most recent acquisition. The man usually rolled around in his Chevy Silverado, like a third of the population of Coyote Ridge.

"I need your help."

"You got it," he said without a second thought. "What can I do?"

"Find Juliet Prince."

The adamance in Travis's tone wasn't abnormal. Travis Walker was one of those men who took control of the situation, manned the team from the front. He was used to being large and in charge.

Unfortunately for Travis, Brantley had spent too many years leading his SEAL team to take orders from anyone other than the top brass. And while many saw Travis as exactly that, Brantley did not.

"She's in the wind," Brantley said, keeping his tone level. "The FBI's workin' the case now."

"They're doin' a shit job," Travis said, his blue-gray eyes sparking with fire. "I want her found now."

Brantley studied Travis's expression, noticed the tension lines around his mouth and eyes. If he had to guess, Travis wasn't getting much sleep these days.

"These things take time. You know that. They will find her, Trav."

His lips pursed. "Not good enough."

The anger rolling off the other man was palpable.

"Look," Travis said, turning to face him fully. "I need help findin' her. I was hopin' you'd help."

"You know I will," he said quickly. "Of course I will, Travis."

"Good." Travis gave a curt nod. "Because I'd hate to have to convince JJ to come work for me."

Brantley frowned, hearing a hint of a threat in his cousin's voice. "What did you say?"

"You heard me. I'm not above usin' money to get what I want, Brantley. You should know that about me by now."

Before he could argue, Travis strolled around to the driver's side of the SUV, climbed inside.

Brantley was still standing there as Travis drove down the long drive, heading back the way he'd come, when JJ came out to join him.

"Somethin' wrong?" she asked, stopping at his side.

"I don't know," he admitted, glancing over at her. "You talk to Travis lately?"

Her dark eyebrows lowered. "No. Why would I?"

"Don't know."

"Brantley?"

Turning to face her more fully, he explained the conversation that had just taken place.

"Work for him?" She snorted. "Why in hell would I work for him? I mean, he's a nice guy and I like him just fine, but I'm not all that into the kink he's got goin' on at that resort."

"It's your skills he wants," Brantley told her.

JJ smiled, bringing her hand up and breathing on her fingernails before polishing them on her chest. "What can I say, B? I'm good like that."

She was good like that. Brantley wouldn't argue that point. But she wasn't a hacker-for-hire.

"You're worried about him?" JJ said softly, her humor disappearing.

"Yeah." He was definitely worried.

The man who had just threatened him was not the Travis Brantley knew.

16

"Well, since you're just standin' around, holdin' down the dirt, come help me."

"With?"

"I brought a few things from home. For my desk."

Shaking off the weird conversation with Travis, Brantley followed JJ over to her little hybrid SUV. She popped the hatch, motioned for the bag and the box.

"A few things, JJ? This looks like you're movin' in."

Her laughter was enough to get his head back in the game.

"Quit complainin', Walker. Just carry it."

He did.

Ensuring she knew how put out he was the entire trek back to the barn.

Chapter Two

LATER THAT EVENING, REESE WAS STANDING AT the stove when Brantley strolled into the kitchen, fresh out of the shower. Even over the aroma of marinara and garlic, he could smell the fresh, musky scent of the man, and like usual, it went right to his head. To say it was odd that he would ever think that way was an understatement. Reese had spent his entire thirty-one years finding perfume appealing over cologne. At least on his partners, anyway. Yet here he was, infatuated by the sexiest man in existence.

Stirring the sauce, he smiled to himself, wondering if he would ever get over this obscene need that made his blood run hotter. Rather than settle, it seemed to intensify day after day. Didn't matter that they'd already taken their relationship to the next level.

Nine days ago, Brantley had asked him to move in with him. Eight days ago, they'd started moving his things. Seven days ago, he'd officially changed his address. On paper, at least. And now here they were, settling into a routine that was both relatively mundane and oddly exciting. Reese had never lived with a lover before. At times, he had wondered if he ever would.

"Did Autumn get moved into your apartment?" Brantley asked, grabbing two glasses out of the cabinet and moving to the refrigerator.

Reese cast a sideways glance, admired the man from the back, the charcoal gray T-shirt formed nicely to his muscular torso. "She did. The lease'll transfer to her in December. She was thrilled. Said it'll cut down on her travel time quite a bit."

"How's she likin' Walker Demo?"

Knowing it was a sensitive subject, he turned his attention back to the sauce. "I didn't ask."

"You can, you know," Brantley said, pausing as he was pouring tea into the second glass. "It doesn't bother me."

"I know." And he did.

Although Reese had damn near fucked their relationship nine ways to Sunday when he panicked after Autumn Jameson, his replacement at Walker Demo, had caught on to the fact Reese and Brantley were exploring this thing between them, it seemed Brantley held no ill will toward the woman. Reese didn't, either. She'd done nothing wrong by accepting his offer of drinks one night. Completely platonic, of course. The conversation had stayed on the topic of work mostly, but still. Reese had fucked up, more so by ignoring Brantley than asking a woman to have drinks.

"If she has work questions, I'll be happy to help her out." Otherwise, he saw little reason for him to interact with Autumn. It wasn't like he'd known her before she had taken over his position so he could move on to the task force. He saw no reason for them to get chummy now.

Brantley carried their tea glasses around to the other side of the quartz-topped island, then returned to grab silverware while Reese dished their food onto two plates.

"Can you get the bread outta the oven?" Reese asked, grabbing the Parmesan cheese from the fridge.

They moved around the kitchen like they'd been in sync all their lives. When they had settled onto the barstools for dinner, Reese let the conversation lull. He knew Brantley. When it came to food, the man ate with gusto, and Reese had learned not to interrupt until Brantley had dished his second helping.

"What's on your mind, Tavoularis?" Brantley asked around a mouthful. "I can hear your brain workin'."

Reese chuckled, wiping his mouth with a napkin. "I talked to Z again today."

Brantley reached for his tea. "Yeah? What'd your brother have to say for himself?"

"They want us to come to Dallas for Christmas."

"Breakfast or dinner?"

Reese glanced over. "What?"

"Do they serve breakfast or dinner for Christmas?"

"Dinner."

"Perfect. My family does the breakfast thing. We can swing through my folks' place in the mornin', then hit the road. We'll be in Dallas in time for dinner."

Well, that seemed relatively easy, Reese thought.

"What about Thanksgiving?" Brantley asked, picking up his fork.

"What about it?"

Brantley chuckled, chewed. "You haven't given me an answer."

Reese filled his own mouth with spaghetti, felt his nerves begin to churn in his stomach.

"They don't bite, Reese."

"I know." He piled in more food. "It's just..." Chew. Just chew.

"I'll invite them over here," Brantley stated. "This weekend. Saturday night. You can cook."

Reese's jaw stopped working and the damn rioting bullets began pinging around in his stomach. He grabbed his tea, washed down the mouthful, and cleared his throat.

This wasn't the first time they'd had the conversation about Reese meeting Brantley's parents. In fact, he was pretty sure they'd discussed it at least once a day since he moved in, and somehow Reese had managed to avoid giving him an affirmative. Didn't look like Brantley was going to let him get by with it this time.

"It's settled then," Brantley said, reaching for his phone.

Reese set down his glass, then snapped his hand around Brantley's wrist, making the man laugh.

"I've never met the parents before," Reese said on a rush of air, his gut suddenly churning the spaghetti in a not-so-friendly manner.

"I fuckin' love that about you."

A strangled laugh escaped. "Brantley."

"It'll be fine. We'll make it a casual thing. Just my mom and dad. No brothers or sisters."

Reese knew it was going to have to happen sooner or later. And the truth was, he would rather meet them before Thanksgiving. Talk about a truly awkward situation for him to be introduced to the fam over a major holiday. He could see it now, Brantley walking him into his parents' house, announcing his live-in boyfriend was there to meet all twenty-whatever of them there probably were. Oh, and by the way, Reece only recently realized he's gay for me and me alone.

No, thank you.

While Reese was having a miniature panic attack, Brantley was staring at him, a huge grin on his face.

"Have I told you how hot you are when you're tongue-tied?"

Reese glared.

Brantley laughed. "Okay, I'll make you a deal."

That got his attention.

"If you'll agree to meet my parents, I'll buy a couch."

Reese glanced over at the sparse living room then back to Brantley. "And a TV."

"Fine. And another TV."

"And a dining room table."

"Okay." Brantley chuckled. "You drive a hard bargain, Tavoularis."

"Plus some furniture for upstairs."

Brantley's eyes narrowed, then he shook his head, turned back to his food. "Nope. Never mind. No couch, no TV, no parents. We'll continue to live in this empty house, just like it is. My folks'll keep right on wonderin' why I'm hidin' you. And my nephew'll think of you as candy from here on out."

It was Reese's turn to laugh, and this time he felt lighter than before. "Fine. But a couch, TV and a dining table. I pick them out."

Brantley peered over, gave him a quick once-over. "You're kinda new to this whole gay thing. You think you can color coordinate?"

Reese smiled so hard his cheeks hurt. "I'm sure I'll figure it out."

Brantley winked. "Deal."

Reese wasn't sure what it was about this man. Since the day he met Brantley Walker, he'd been in way over his head. The fact that he'd fallen for the guy when he hadn't even realized he was interested in men said a lot. Then again, he got the feeling he wasn't interested in men. He was interested in this man. Only Brantley.

"You want more?" Brantley offered, snatching his own plate before heading back to the stove.

"I'm good. Thanks." Reese watched him. "You're not at all worried about meetin' my family?"

Brantley turned around with his plate full once more. "Why would I be?"

Reese shrugged. "It's not weird?"

"No. What's weird is the fact that we live together and neither of us has met the other's family."

He had a point there. Not that Reese regretted the fact they'd decided to move in together. It felt right to him. Or it would once he managed to convince the man to actually go out and buy some furniture. Maybe a pool table for the upstairs game room. Probably wouldn't hurt if they had a guest bedroom.

Baby steps, he reminded himself.

An hour and a half later, Reese was crawling into bed beside Brantley.

"You're not mad at me, are you?" he asked, feeling a tad vulnerable after their dinner conversation.

Brantley clicked the remote to turn off the television, the weather guy's face disappearing in an instant. "No. Why would I be?"

Reese shrugged, then flipped off the lamp on his side of the bed. It pitched the room into darkness, not making his insecurities any better.

He flopped back on his pillow, stared up at the ceiling although his eyes hadn't adjusted and he saw only black.

"I want to meet your parents," he said, hoping to reassure Brantley that this wasn't some fucked-up crisis he was undergoing. God knows he'd had enough of those lately.

"No, you don't," Brantley teased, his big arm sliding over his chest as Brantley eased up to his right side. "But that's normal."

As usual, he let the foreign sensations wash over him. The man was big and hard, a far cry from the women he'd been with in the past. Reese could feel the hair on Brantley's leg as it brushed his, the scent of his musky body wash. Initially it had been awkward, this insane attraction he had to Brantley. Now it settled around him, comforting in its familiarity.

"Is it?" Reese turned his head toward Brantley. "Normal?"

"You said you've never met the parents before, right?"

"Yes."

"So what stopped you before?"

"Never felt like the right time."

"Does it now?"

"Yeah." Reese relaxed again, staring up at the ceiling. "It does. Now it's just nerves."

"They're gonna love you." Brantley's lips brushed his shoulder. "As much as I do."

Warmth churned through him, filling his chest. Ever since they had declared their love for one another, it had gotten a bit easier for Reese. Sure, he was still uncertain of himself, but he figured that was to be expected in any relationship. However, there was the comfort of knowing they had something real between them.

No, he wasn't quite comfortable with the whole PDA thing. Then again, Brantley wasn't the lovey-dovey sort, so he didn't have that to worry about. They also hadn't gone out on another public date after the epic failure that was their first and only. Reese still felt ill when he thought about it, but it seemed Brantley had put it behind them.

"Relax," Brantley whispered, his lips trailing upward toward his neck. "Let me have you, Reese."

Oh, how he loved to hear that coming out of Brantley's mouth. He wasn't sure what it was, but he definitely enjoyed submitting to this man, giving himself over and not having to worry about anything but the pleasure that came from their bodies coming together.

"Can I have you?" Brantley taunted, his leg hooking over Reese's, his big hand sliding down Reese's stomach, making the muscles contract.

"You've got me."

"Mmm."

With little effort, Brantley shifted and was over him, Reese's legs gripped between Brantley's knees. That wicked-hot mouth blazed a fiery trail across his skin from his neck downward, over his chest. The man paused to tease Reese's nipples, making his entire body harden from the exquisite sensation. He'd never felt anything like what he felt when Brantley touched him.

"Get the lube," Brantley urged. "I'm gonna need it in a bit."

While Reese twisted his torso, reaching over to open the nightstand drawer, Brantley's warm mouth circled his cock. He groaned long and low, forgetting for a second what he was doing as he pumped his hips, pushing into the blessed wet heat working him into a frenzy. Somehow he managed to remember his mission, retrieving the lube from the drawer, tossing it in Brantley's direction.

"Fuck, yes," he hissed, cupping Brantley's head, loving the way his hair tickled his palm. "Suck me."

Brantley moaned, sending vibrations up through his shaft, which ignited a tingle in his spine.

Reese sank into the pillow, letting the pleasure consume him, the heat gliding up and down his cock. Every so often, Brantley would lick his balls, that wicked tongue stirring to life every nerve ending in his body.

It seemed to go on forever until Reese was hanging by a thread, seconds away from detonating.

As though he sensed it, Brantley stopped, moving over him again, their mouths melding together briefly. Reese thought that Brantley would take him then, but the man seemed to have other plans, because he broke the kiss and crawled up Reese's body until he was straddling his chest, those muscular legs pinning his arms to his sides.

"Suck me," Brantley ordered. "Let me feel that fuckin' mouth on me."

Eager to give Brantley what he wanted, Reese opened his mouth around the thick head, licked the pre-cum from the tip before sucking him in deep. From there, Brantley took over, his hands gripping the headboard as he pumped his hips, fucking Reese's face. His arms were trapped, so it was Brantley who controlled the pace, the depth of his cock in Reese's throat. His eyes had adjusted enough to see Brantley above him, staring down, watching.

"Oh, yeah. God, you're good at that," Brantley hissed. "So fuckin' good."

While he continued to lick and lave Brantley's cock, Reese was barely aware of the man moving, the sound of the lubricant being opened. He waited, not sure what was going to happen. Once again, he was surprised when Brantley eased out of his mouth, sitting on Reese's chest.

"Lube me up," Brantley instructed.

Dragging one arm out from under Brantley's leg, he held out his hand so Brantley could fill it with the cool liquid. He then proceeded to stroke Brantley's rigid cock, enjoying the way it pulsed against his palm. That and the sounds of Brantley's groans had his body throbbing, his blood reaching a boiling point.

"Fuck me," Reese pleaded, still stroking Brantley as he stared up that incredible body.

As was the case anytime they were together, the overwhelming intensity of his lust slammed into him, made him desperate. It was a feeling he'd never known before Brantley. Heat and light seemed to replace his insides, churning and boiling, his muscles tensing, his cock throbbing as the ache overtook him.

"I need… Fuck, Brantley, I need you inside me."

A tormented groan escaped Brantley before the man moved once more, inching down Reese's torso, then shifting between his thighs.

Brantley did all the work, shoving Reese's legs wide, draping them over his arms, pushing his knees toward his chest as he began prodding his asshole with the head of his cock. Time for foreplay was over, the need too great to ignore any longer.

Helping him along, Reese reached down, guided Brantley where he wanted him, and breathed in deep when he pushed forward, impaling him in one intense thrust.

Reese grunted when Brantley folded him in half and retreated slowly, a wicked-slow glide out, then in. Out once more.

"Oh, fuck," Reese moaned.

"You ready, baby?"

Fuck, he loved when Brantley called him that and he had no idea why.

"So fucking ready," he growled. "Fuck me."

That was exactly what Brantley did. He fucked him. Hard, deep. So fucking deep.

They maintained a leisurely pace with Brantley jerking his hips to fill Reese impossibly full on every downstroke. It wasn't long before sweat broke out over his skin, his cock so hard it hurt.

Brantley held himself over him, those all-seeing eyes staring down. "Tell me, Reese."

"More," he bit out through clenched teeth, accepting the pleasure that coursed through him every time Brantley drove deep inside him. "Make me come."

Brantley kneeled upright, his hands shifting to Reese's knees as he held him there, using him as leverage as his hips once again surged forward and back. He began to slam into him. Faster, harder.

"Oh, fuck." Reese was panting, his chest heaving as he gripped his cock, stroking in time with Brantley's thrusts.

"I'm gonna come," Brantley warned. "You better come with me, Reese."

Reese groaned, tightening his fist on his cock, jerking roughly. He was so damn close but it felt so fucking good. He didn't want to come yet, he wanted it to last for—

"Oh, fuck!" Reese's cock jerked in his fist as he came in a rush, his body shuddering from the near-painful blasts of ecstasy that rocketed through him.

Brantley groaned a second later, following him right over.

Chapter Three

THE NEXT MORNING, BRANTLEY FOUND HIMSELF ONCE again sitting at his desk in the barn, feeling antsy.

"What do we have that's local? Or relatively close?" Brantley prompted, feeling the need to get up and move around.

He wasn't sure how they could all sit there so serene, behind a desk, noses buried in their computer screens. It was the one thing Brantley never understood. He needed to be out and about. Give him a mission and he was on it, head in the game, no questions asked. Tell him to search something on the internet and he'd rather shoot himself in the foot.

"Take your pick," JJ said, sitting up to peer at him over her computer monitor. "We got another box yesterday afternoon."

"From where?"

She shrugged. "No idea. Haven't had time to start goin' through them."

"What are you workin' on?" he asked, realizing too late that it had come out wrong.

Her eyes narrowed. "Just twiddlin' my thumbs, B. That's what you pay me for, right?"

"Shit," he grumbled. "Sorry. I didn't mean it the way it sounded."

"You sure about that?" JJ bit out. "I mean, you're more than welcome to deal with these expense reports if you'd like. Not sure if you know this, but someone's gotta pay for all the equipment, and Rhonda's breathin' down my neck daily to get it done."

"Who's Rhonda?"

JJ shot him that are you serious right now? look. "The governor's secretary."

Her duh was implied.

"She's not happy that she's been tasked with gettin' the task force set up, either. But we do what we have to."

Effectively put in his place, Brantley took a deep breath, headed for the storage area where they were keeping the boxes of case files the various departments and agencies had started sending their way.

"I've pulled out a few," Baz said, holding a folder high in the air to get his attention.

Pivoting, he headed over to Baz's desk, where he had a stack of manila folders.

"Let me start this by sayin', I haven't had time to actually look over the notes, but I was lookin' for those that might result in us findin' the victim alive. Figured those were worth prioritizin'."

Made sense to him, only there were quite a few files on Baz's desk. If there were that many who could potentially be saved versus recovered…

Picking up the first file, Brantley skimmed the pages. Two-year-old boy abducted from front yard eight months ago. Suspect that convicted-felon father kidnapped. Case went cold after four weeks of searching.

Next folder. Woman last seen jogging at a lake in downtown Austin back in January of this year. Body never found, no clues. Case cold after three months despite active parent participation.

Next. Thirteen-year-old girl disappeared. Had been talking to someone online. Believed to be older man who lured her out. Six weeks of investigating led nowhere.

Brantley looked up from the last file, glanced at Baz, JJ, then Reese.

How the fuck were they supposed to tackle all of these? These were just three of many, and if he was asked to prioritize which of these specific three was more pressing, no way could he. They were all critical as far as he was concerned.

"We need more people," he said, slapping the file down on the desk and heading outside.

He needed air, needed time to think, to plan, to...

"You okay?"

Brantley nodded, but he didn't look back at Reese. Couldn't. How was he supposed to tell his partner that he felt incompetent to lead this team? Searching for bad guys was what he did. Well, terrorists mostly. That was what he was good at, strategizing a takedown, breaching a compound filled with tangos, slipping into enemy territory undetected, neutralizing a threat. Hell, he could do that shit blindfolded.

But this...

"Hey. Stop for a minute."

He did but he didn't look up when Reese appeared before him.

"How the hell do we find all those people?"

"One person at a time," Reese said softly. "Trust me, I know it's overwhelming. I've skimmed those files, too."

Brantley did look up then and right into those bottomless dark brown eyes. "We need more people," he repeated.

"I won't argue with you there. I figured we were gonna wing it for a bit, tackle what we could."

"And here I was proud that we'd solved three already," he grumbled, turning away to pace.

"Don't discredit what we've done," Reese stated, his tone hard. "We've worked hard, Brantley. And we'll continue to do so. Even if it's just the four of us."

It couldn't only be the four of them. One case at a time, prioritizing those that were active. How the fuck were they going to make a dent like that?

No, they did need more people.

"You want a bigger team?" Reese asked.

Brantley turned to look at him. "Yeah."

"Okay. Then we put together the reasons why and we present it to the governor. He's got the power to approve or deny, right?"

"It's his team," Brantley confirmed.

"So let's do that. Let's sit down and write it up. How many people, what they'll be workin' on. That sort of thing."

And just like that, the anxiety was past him. Reese was right. Brantley couldn't let emotion cloud his judgment. No matter how much he wanted to, he couldn't save them all. He accepted that. However, he did have the means to make a difference, and creating a task force that could at least make a dent was his objective. Had been since the day the governor presented him with the idea.

"We'll get JJ to determine the cost of expanding HQ to accommodate. Baz can provide us with a high-level list of cases that he feels should be looked into first. We can research how many active investigations there are at a few agencies, provide those numbers." Reese stepped forward. "If you want to do this, we will."

Brantley stared back at Reese. He was usually the one talking Reese off the ledge, so it felt a bit foreign for the roles to be reversed. However, he liked this aggressive side to the man. The take-charge, get-shit-done side.

"Okay," Brantley agreed.

"Then let's do this. Time's a wastin'."

He breathed deeply, exhaled his relief.

And just like that, they were moving in a new direction.

WHEN REESE AND BRANTLEY WENT OUTSIDE, JJ carried her laptop up to the loft and plopped down on the leather sofa that had been added to the minimal space. There still wasn't much of anything up here that would make it a viable break area, but it hadn't really been a priority. In fact, she knew the stairs had been a spur-of-the-moment decision, a way for Brantley to deal with some of the feelings Reese had stirred up in him. Now that they were in, the area left much to be desired.

That didn't necessarily explain why she preferred it so much. Well, okay, it was probably because there was a window. The only one in the entire building, at that. And after spending hours and hours in the barn, sometimes she just needed to see the sun. Or she was simply trying to put some distance between her and Baz. Her pride liked to think it was the former because the latter would mean she was a chickenshit. And JJ was no chickenshit.

She wasn't. Really.

However, she knew Baz liked her, and as much as it pained her to admit it, she liked him, too.

Good thing was, they worked together, which made him off-limits. Of course, there were no rules regarding fraternization within the task force. If there was, Brantley and Reese would've been up shit creek from the get-go. No, this was more of a personal decision. JJ was no dummy when it came to relationships. Statistics showed they didn't last, certainly not between co-workers. Not that she'd looked it up or anything; her data was based solely on personal experience. And what she'd seen in others.

Did she think it was possible for those relationships to survive? Sure. Just not one that involved her.

The outside door opened, so she listened carefully. She knew Brantley was on edge, though she wasn't sure why. It was rare for him, the man whose patience seemed endless. But she had witnessed a change in him a few minutes ago. Possibly for the first time in all the time she'd known him, Brantley's countenance had reflected doubt.

Reese's resonating voice penetrated the otherwise silent space. He was talking to Baz, although she couldn't quite make out the words. Being nosy as she was, JJ got to her feet, carried her laptop back downstairs.

She arched a surprised eyebrow, pretending she hadn't known they'd returned. "You're back." No sense giving away all her secrets.

The three men continued their conversation while JJ grabbed her cup, headed to the kitchen to refill it with water. She let the sounds of their voices relax her, listened to the inflection. Brantley's tone was smooth and even, not quite as deep as Reese's. Baz's voice held less of the Texas drawl than Brantley's and Reese's, but there was a raspy quality to it she was fond of. She had to admit, it was rather nice to work with three incredibly hot guys. It meant she always had something nice to look at.

And no, that wasn't her objectifying them. She merely had to find a way to pass the time or to clear some of the rather unpleasant images from her mind. After all, she had seen some of those crime scene photos, heard the horror story about them finding Kate Walker, and she'd dug deep enough into some of their suspects to know that the world was a very wicked place. No better way to stay positive than to check out hot guys who just so happened to be ridiculously smart and kinda lethal.

Despite the fact Baz was the only blond in the building, he fit right in with the perfection of Brantley and Reese. Perfectly contoured face, nice square jaw, beguiling blue eyes. And that body… She suspected beneath the jeans and polos there was a nicely chiseled rest of him.

Not that she was thinking about Baz that way. She simply suspected because she had danced with him at Moonshiners. They'd been up close and personal. Nothing romantic.

Well, except for that kiss.

Okay, not going there.

"What's goin' on?" she asked when she returned to find Brantley standing at the whiteboard while Reese perched on the top of Brantley's desk.

Baz was in his own chair, leaned back, hands behind his head as he watched Brantley write something in what could only be described as chicken scratch.

"Nope," she said, depositing her cup on her desk. "No way. We can't read that."

"You wanna do it?" he asked, spinning around and holding the marker out.

"So kind of you to offer." She plucked the marker from his hand. "What is it that we're writing?"

"A list," Brantley said.

"Of?"

"All the things that'll justify quadrupling the size of this team."

JJ stared at Brantley. No way she'd heard him right.

REESE AND THE REST OF THE TEAM spent the next few hours chiming in as to how they saw the team expanding and ramping up productivity in the process. The best use of time and resources was taken into account, as was travel now that Travis Walker had donated the use of his private jet and the helicopter. They documented what they'd done to date, from the cases they'd worked to the supplies and equipment they had acquired. JJ went so far as to draw up a new floor plan, which involved a couple of minor changes to the layout, mostly rearranging.

When they were finished, they had a three-page document prepared for the governor, which they decided would be presented by Brantley and JJ. Brantley because he was the face Governor Greenwood recognized and JJ because she had a way with persuasion. Reese didn't argue, because who in their right mind wanted to present to the governor of Texas? Damn sure not him.

JJ used her powers of persuasion to manipulate their way onto the governor's calendar that same day. Once it was set, they ran through their presentation once more, then headed for the state capitol.

And that left Reese and Baz back at HQ.

"She's somethin', huh?" Baz said, his gaze swinging to the whiteboard, which was still covered in JJ's loopy handwriting.

"She is."

Reese knew Baz wasn't merely referring to the woman's brains, although, like the rest of them, Reese figured he was in awe of JJ's intelligence as well. The woman was damn smart. Sometimes too smart but that wasn't necessarily a bad thing.

"You wanna grab some lunch?" Baz asked, pushing to his feet.

Without a thought, Reese said, "Sure. Where to?"

"The diner in town? I'll drive."

"Just how often do you eat there?" Reese asked with a grin as they stepped out into the warm November day, Baz's keys jangling as he twirled them on his finger.

"Couple times a week. Had I known it was there before I met y'all, I'da been a resident of Coyote Ridge a long time ago."

"You live here now?"

"No. From what I hear, that's quite the feat."

"It is that. When I moved in here, I sublet my apartment to the woman who took my previous role at Walker Demo. She'd been lookin' for a while."

"I've been thinkin' about movin' closer," Baz said as they climbed into his truck. "Takes me a good twenty-five minutes to get here and that's if I utilize the toll road and manage to bypass traffic."

Reese didn't envy him there. He'd gotten used to his daily five-minute drive to the demolition office. Now he could get to work in under a minute. Walking.

"Is it true JJ was datin' the governor's son?"

Reese glanced over, surprised by the question. "Uh… yeah. From what I heard."

"You meet him?"

"Once."

"And?"

"Wasn't impressed."

"Because he's the douchebag Brantley accuses him of bein'?"

Reese stared out the window and smiled. Brantley really did not like Dante Greenwood, who Brantley had recently nicknamed Dante the Douche. Reese wasn't one for gossip, but he knew that Baz was curious about the rest of them. Since JJ's relationship with Dante was in the past, he decided he would share what he knew.

"He's one of those who doesn't necessarily want the woman but doesn't want anyone else to have her, either. Kept her on a string for a while, then purposely sabotaged the relationship."

Of course, Reese suspected JJ hadn't been invested any more than Dante, but for whatever reason, they'd continued to do the dance again and again.

Baz turned into the nearly full lot, parked, got out. Reese followed suit.

"You said purposely?" Baz asked, walking alongside him toward the door.

"Yeah. Brought his new assistant—a leggy redhead—to Moonshiners."

"Not sure I understand."

"The guy doesn't live in Coyote Ridge anymore," Reese explained, holding up two fingers to show the hostess how many in their party.

"But he brought her to a small-town, backwoods bar."

"Yep. And as you know, we're not exactly a direct route to and from anything. I think he figured JJ'd be there so he could sabotage himself again."

"Was she?"

Reese shook his head. "But Brantley was. Guy's lucky he made it out of there with both legs intact."

They took a seat at the table the waitress directed them to, were offered drinks, both opting for water.

Reese didn't need to look at the menu, selecting the daily soup special and a salad.

Baz grinned after Reese rattled it off, then asked for the same. "Figured it's best to make up for some of the crap food JJ likes to eat."

"Brantley, too," Reese noted. "He's got the culinary skills of a teenager, eats whatever's easiest and fastest. Helps that he's got a metabolism that keeps up with him. Unfortunately, I don't."

"They're a pair, huh?"

"They are."

"What part does Travis play in all this?"

Finally a question that didn't make him feel uncomfortable. "Travis is Brantley's cousin."

"Kate's his daughter," Baz stated. "The little girl who was kidnapped two months ago?"

"Yes. When the governor approached Brantley with the idea of the task force, it was with Travis's backing."

"He a good guy?"

"The best. Good intentions."

"What about the woman who kidnapped his daughter? JJ told me she was gone by the time y'all found Kate."

"She was. Still is. In the wind, as they say."

"The FBI have anything?"

"No." Which was a sore spot for Reese. It pissed him off to no end that Juliet Prince was still out there.

"I know JJ's still lookin' into the case."

"Yeah. We're still hopin' to track her down."

"Daunting task."

"We'll find her."

"Maybe if Brantley and JJ can convince the governor to expand the team, we can dedicate someone to it full-time."

Reese knew that expanding the team was the right thing to do. What few cases they'd worked on, it took tremendous resources.

"I think that's his plan."

"Well, let me know how I can help. Not sure what I can contribute just yet, but I get the feelin' I'll find my place soon enough."

They all would, Reese knew. It would take some time, but this was a good start.

Once they returned, Reese spent the better part of the afternoon looking into what JJ had on Juliet Prince. He figured since he was waiting for Brantley to give him word on the governor's decision, it was a good way to spend his time.

He was surprised to see how much information she'd collected on the woman. Not to mention, the things she was tracking. JJ kept detailed notes in an online document, outlining the searches she had set up, including one on Juliet's ex-husband and the daughter they had together. There were very few leads she'd traced since they'd returned Kate to her parents, but it was maintained daily.

He was reading her latest entry when his phone buzzed on his wrist.

"They're back," Baz said as they both turned to the television mounted on the wall, which reflected a view from the cameras overlooking the driveway.

Reese hoped it was good news. And if it wasn't, he hoped they could come up with an alternative that would suit Brantley. He'd been a bit surprised by Brantley's reaction that morning, but when he thought back on it, he understood it. Brantley wanted to save the world. His reaction spoke to the type of guy he was, and if he could accomplish his goal in a day versus a year, he was going to take that route, no matter how impossible it might seem.

They both turned toward the door as it opened.

JJ's beaming grin was their answer.

"I take it we've got work to do?" Baz asked.

"We do. Lots."

Reese met Brantley's gaze as he removed his sunglasses. The smirk he received had his blood humming under his skin.

Yeah, this was the Brantley he'd come to love.

Chapter Four

THURSDAY ROLLED AROUND AND THE TEAM WAS in the process of sorting through interviews on a case from one of their cold files when Brantley got a call from a detective with the Houston Police Department. Evidently, a memo had gone out from the governor's office to all law enforcement agencies, encouraging the use of the OTB Task Force.

It seemed that by expanding, they were also increasing their workload.

Not that it made any difference to Brantley how someone had gotten his number. A case was a case, regardless of how they'd come by it.

"Wait. You said social media?" Brantley asked the detective who was rambling on the other end of the line. "Hold up a sec. Let me put you on speaker."

While he hit the button on the phone, Brantley walked over to JJ's desk and set it down.

"All right, Detective Gallegos. I've got the rest of my team here. I'd like them to hear this, too."

"No problem. I'm not sure if you've heard about it elsewhere, but there's a scam taking place on social media. In groups, specifically."

Brantley recalled the governor mentioning something along the lines of social media, but he'd yet to get any additional details as to what it pertained to. Since Brantley didn't have any social media accounts, nor did he have any desire to, it wasn't something he was familiar with. However, he had to wonder if this was related to that.

"What are groups?" Brantley asked, not caring that JJ looked at him like he'd been living under a rock.

"A lot of communities and schools have these online groups where neighbors, parents, teachers, whatnot can congregate in cyberspace, get to know one another, help out when necessary," the detective explained. "There's rarely any security to monitor who joins, and if there is, it's left to a person to make a judgment call. Unfortunately, people tend to trust their neighbors to be who they claim to be. And that's where we've started seeing the issue across the nation. These scammers are inserting themselves into the groups, pretending to be members of the community. They're looking for various things like borrowing a saw or a ladder, as well as offering services when parents are seeking them."

"Services?" Reese inquired.

"Lawn care, babysitting, carpool."

"Holy shit," Baz muttered, clearly seeing how bad that could be.

"Exactly," the detective replied. "When parents are seeking someone to help out with their kid, maybe by picking them up from school one day or meeting them at the bus stop, these scammers are in the group already, pretending to be their neighbor. They've established a rapport with those in the group, so no one thinks twice that Betty Sue is offering to pick up their kid from school or even take them to dance."

"But Betty Sue doesn't exist," Brantley mused.

"More than likely, Betty Sue's really Jimmy Don Bad Guy," Gallegos noted. "We've gotten a couple of reports in the past few months, but thankfully none of the parents have taken these people up on their offers."

"This sounds more like something cybercrime should be handling, does it not?" Baz said, speaking to the detective.

"They are, yes. Across the nation, there are various law enforcement agencies looking into this because they believe it to be a specific group of people."

"There've been no kidnappings yet?" JJ asked.

Gallegos cleared his throat. "There's one that they had initially logged as a potential up in Washington State, but they were able to locate the five-year-old boy who went missing within half an hour. They noted it as carpool confusion, but it came across the wire anyway."

"Why aren't we seein' anything about this on the news?" Reese asked.

"Depends on where you're at," Detective Gallegos said. "It's only recently made national news but it hasn't yet become a priority."

"What is it you need my team to do, Detective?" Brantley asked, staring down at the phone.

"I need you to find the young man who went missing early this morning."

Brantley planted his hands on JJ's desk, leaned down closer to the phone. "What? I thought you just said there was only one related incident. Alleged."

"Officially, there is," he said solemnly. "But I can't shake the feeling that this young man's disappearance is related."

"How long has he been missing?"

"Since last night at eight. The young man, his name's Tanner Wright, supposedly went on a date with a girl he met through his school's social media group. The parents reported him as a runaway after the school called them, so there isn't a missing persons case open on him. I've done my best to relay my concerns to my boss, but I'm getting no traction. I'm being told there are more important issues to tackle."

"And the girl he went to meet? Did you find her?"

"From what we can tell, she doesn't exist. Which is what raised my hackles."

"That's where we come in," Brantley said.

"That's my hope. Maybe it's a long shot, but like I said, I can't shake this feeling. Based on what the parents have told me, Tanner's the type of kid to run away because he's disrespectful, yada, yada. They're a piece of work, mind you."

"You've been called out there before?"

"Not for this, no. And not me, but they do have a sheet. Drunk and disorderly, public disturbance, things like that."

"Fantastic," Brantley said, "So we've got a sixteen-year-old who could or could not be a runaway, parents who don't seem too concerned, and no girl to ask if she's seen him?"

"That's the gist of it, yes," the detective replied.

"Give me a couple of hours, Detective. My partner and I will head that way."

There was a relieved sigh on the other end followed by, "Thank you."

"Yep." Brantley disconnected the call, tucked the phone in his pocket.

"You think this is the same thing the governor mentioned?" Reese asked, his brown eyes narrowed with concern.

"You can bet your ass we're gonna find out." He headed to his desk, retrieved his gun from the biometric safe he kept it in, holstered it, then turned back to JJ and Baz. "While Reese and I head that way, I want you two to dig up anything and everything you can find on this scam. If it's nationwide, Washington's not the only state that's been affected. They just haven't put two and two together yet."

"You gonna take the private jet down there?" JJ asked with a smirk.

"Damn straight we are." No way was Brantley going to pass that opportunity by.

"I'll call Travis," she offered. "Get the jet ready." JJ chuckled. "God, that sounds so official and shit."

"And I'll call Gallegos back," Baz said, his tone somber. "Get all the details I can from him on what he knows about the Washington incident. Then I'll start diggin'."

"Keep us updated on what you find."

"You do the same."

Two hours later, Brantley and Reese had made it to Houston and secured a Chevy Tahoe to get them to and from. Because you had to start somewhere and there was no better place than someone's home, he opted to head to Tanner Wright's house first. His first order of business was to interview the parents, find out why they were adamant their son was being rebellious rather than a potential victim. Perhaps they knew something they hadn't shared yet and this case could come to a quick close.

"You think Gallegos is right?" Reese asked after keying Tanner's address into the navigation system. "That this case is related to that social media scam?"

"Twenty years on the force? I have to believe he's been doin' this long enough, he can see things others don't."

"Could also be he's jumpin' the gun. Maybe the kid got lucky last night and stayed with the girl he went out with."

"Maybe." Brantley kept his eyes on the road. "But why wouldn't Gallegos be able to get ahold of—or better yet, identify—the girl if that was the case?"

"They're in a seedy motel doin' what teenagers long to do?"

And grown men, Brantley thought while he said, "You were one horny teenager, weren't you, Tavoularis?"

"Probably not nearly as horny as you were."

Brantley chuckled. "Yes, that's probably true. Sad, but true."

"Were you a horndog in high school, Brantley?" There was a teasing tone to Reese's voice but there was some curiosity mixed in.

"I had a steady boyfriend," he admitted. "And we were both horny all the damn time. So no to bein' a horndog. But I was gettin' laid on the regular."

"Of course you were."

"Oh, don't go pretendin' you were a prude. Have you looked in the mirror lately?"

Reese ran his hand over his short hair. "Would you believe me if I told you I was a nerd in high school?"

Brantley cut his eyes to Reese, considered it. "No."

Reese laughed. "Okay, fine. I wasn't. But I already told you. I spent all my energy workin' on one girl. By the time I realized she wasn't gonna put out, I'd invested so much damn time."

"Poor thing. I guess we'll have to make up for that lost time, now won't we?"

"I thought that's what we've been doin'."

"Yeah?" Brantley grinned again. "I could turn up the heat if you'd like, because once a day ain't nearly enough."

"You've been holdin' back on me, Walker?"

"Takin' things slow like I promised."

"No one ever said I need slow." Reese turned his attention out the passenger window. "Not anymore, anyway."

"Careful what you wish for, baby."

Of course, this conversation wasn't helping things in that regard, either. From the moment he'd woken up to find Reese had already headed for work, Brantley had regretted not sleeping lighter last night. If he'd known Reese would've snuck out on him, he would've set an alarm.

But he wasn't lying when he said he was taking things slow. It wasn't easy pretending he wasn't walking around with a hard-on twenty-four seven. The man made him ache in ways he'd never expected, wishing like hell for some privacy more than just when they called it a day. If he had his way, he would have Reese naked and on every horizontal surface he could find. Hell, some vertical ones, too.

Knowing he had to get his head in the game, he mentally re-dressed Reese and shook off the thought. "Get anything from Baz yet?"

Reese pulled out his phone, tapped the screen. "He's got some information on the kid. Nothin' we don't already know."

"Hopefully the parents can enlighten us," Brantley said, taking a turn into the neighborhood the navigation directed him to.

"My question is," Reese began, "if the only known case was a five-year-old, what would this group want with a sixteen-year-old? Big difference in age there."

"Depends on what they're after," Brantley stated, winding his way toward the Wrights' house. "If it's human trafficking, age won't necessarily matter."

"Gender?"

"Perhaps. Or they could be grabbin' whoever they can, whenever they can." Brantley glanced over. "You belong to any of these online groups?"

"Yeah."

"Seriously?"

"Sure. Why not?"

"Which ones?"

"Coyote Ridge has one."

Of course they did. "That the only one?"

"Yes."

Brantley wanted to ask what sort of interactions took place, but he wasn't sure he cared to know. Plus, he was pulling up to Tanner Wright's house, which gave him something more pressing to deal with.

When Reese followed Brantley into the Wrights' house, he wasn't sure what he'd been expecting. From the outside, it appeared to be a decent neighborhood. Nothing fancy, probably mid- to low-income area, but well-maintained.

It certainly wasn't to watch Tanner Wright's father march his wife-beater-and-shorts-wearing ass over and plant it in front of the television and continue playing a video game. Or for the young man's mother to be sitting at the kitchen table playing slots—or so he assumed based on the noises coming from that direction—on her electronic tablet while smoking a cigarette. Neither seemed at all concerned that Tanner wasn't home, or that he hadn't been seen since he left their house last night.

"Whaddya want?" Mrs. Wright called out, blowing a stream of smoke toward the ceiling. "We already talked to the cops."

"Ain't got nothin' more to tell 'em," the father said, eyes glued to the TV.

"Mr. Wright, would it be possible for you to pause the game for a moment?" Reese requested, attempting to be polite when what he wanted to do was punch the fucker in the mouth.

"I'm in a tournament right now," the older man grumbled back.

Why were these people not at work?

"Mrs. Wright, would you please join us in the living room?" Brantley stated, his tone a bit firmer than Reese's had been.

"If you boys wanna talk, you can come in here," she said snidely, stabbing her cigarette out in an ashtray. No, wait. That was a plate.

When Brantley cast a look his way, Reese nodded toward the kitchen. Might as well get it over with.

They strolled through the dingy living room, past a table holding an ashtray filled to overflowing with butts, and an empty bowl with God only knew what caked around the sides. It was orange, that was all he knew.

Reese stepped into the kitchen, pausing to take a look around. Besides the disgustingness of the whole place, the kitchen wasn't in bad shape. Countertops had seen better days, but the cabinets were level, the refrigerator running.

That was a good sign, right?

Continuing toward the mother, Reese circled the small breakfast table, peered out the window into the backyard.

Just outside on the chipped concrete porch was a bowl of water that was so grimy it would've likely been toxic if it had a drop of water in it, beside it a chewed-up bowl that probably held food every now and then.

He cut his eyes over to the woman. "Do you have a dog?"

Mrs. Wright nodded toward the window. "He's an idiot, that mutt."

Reese moved to the other window, squinted beyond the plastic blinds that were cracked and bent to find…

"Fuck," he muttered under his breath.

Nope. No fucking way.

Outside, chained to a stake in the middle of the yard, was what was supposed to pass as a dog. There was no shade, and though it was November, he doubted the reason for the lack of shelter had anything to do with the season. The poor dog—it almost resembled a German shepherd but not quite—looked to be a good ten, maybe fifteen pounds underweight, its ribs protruding beneath the dull brown and black fur. From what Reese could tell, the hair was relatively short but matted in a few places. It looked like it hadn't been tended to in—he glanced over at the mother— well, probably never.

The dog was in bad shape and these people didn't give a shit.

"Why's your dog chained up out there?"

"Can't let the fucker in the house," she snarled. "Pisses on the carpet every chance it gets."

"How long've you had it?"

"Too damn long if you ask me."

Not an answer.

It took everything in Reese not to yank the woman up by her food-stained T-shirt and march her outside to feed the dog.

Instead, he held on to his temper, turned his attention toward the woman.

"Mrs. Wright, when's the last time you saw Tanner?"

She shrugged, not bothering to look up from her tablet. "Sometime yesterday. Why?"

"Mrs. Wright, you understand your son's missing," Brantley stated firmly.

"He ain't missin'," Mr. Wright shouted from the living room. "He's out gettin' himself a piece of ass. It's all good."

A piece of ass. Wow.

"We told the police already, he's fine," Mrs. Wright chimed in. "Tanner does this all the time. Long as he ain't gettin' no girl pregnant, I don't much give a damn what he does."

Reese would've bet money these people had no idea what their son was up to. Ever.

"Tanner disappears for days at a time?" Brantley inquired.

"Yup. Ain't got no respect for his parents. Never around to help out with the chores or take care of that damn dog."

And it appeared no one else could be bothered with it, either, Reese thought. Based on the pile of dishes in the sink, they hadn't cleaned in … a while.

Brantley stepped over to the back window, his boots making a sucking sound on the peeling linoleum, as though he was sticking to it. He used a finger to pull down one of the slats, peered out. When he turned back, Reese ensured he saw the fury that had ignited. Based on the glare he got in return, he suspected the man was as irate as he was at the audacity of these people.

"Mrs. Wright," Brantley demanded. "Put the game down."

Her head snapped up, dull brown eyes narrowing on his face. "Who the fuck do you think you are?"

"My name's Brantley Walker," he bit back, gesturing to the badge clipped to his belt before setting his hand on the weapon holstered right beside it. "And I'm here to find your son."

Mrs. Wright popped another cigarette between her lips, spoke around it. "We didn't ask you to come here. We don't need your damn help." She paused to light the thing. "Tanner'll come back when he's good and damn ready."

Reese saw Brantley's shoulders tense, but before the man could launch into a tirade, Reese put a firm hand on his shoulder. They were getting nowhere here. Anything they said or did would only make matters worse.

"Were you aware your son isn't in school today?" Reese inquired.

"He goes when he wants to."

That was the opposite of what the school had told Detective Gallegos.

She stabbed the button on the screen. "Ain't my damn place to make sure he does what he's supposed to do."

Reese cleared his throat. Actually, that was exactly her job.

She coughed, a horrible hacking sound. "Boy's sixteen damn years old. He's old enough to take care of himself."

From the looks of it, that was what Tanner had been doing for some time.

"Mrs. Wright, we'd like to take a look at Tanner's bedroom. Then we'll be outta your hair," Reese informed her.

"Do whatever you gotta do," she said, puffing on her cigarette and exhaling a stream of smoke. "If you don't mind, we've got things to do."

Brantley snorted, but Reese helped him along, urging him back the way they'd come.

"Room's that way." Mr. Wright motioned without looking away from the television as they started for the hallway.

To get to Tanner's room, they had to step over a pile of clothes on the floor, which were stacked along a wall that had mold slowly growing in an outward arc. He could only imagine what the carpet looked like beneath.

When they reached the door, they steeled themselves before stepping inside.

"Holy shit. It's possible we're in a different house," Brantley said as they walked into Tanner's bedroom.

The room was the complete opposite of the rest of the house. There were no dirty dishes or clothes piled anywhere, the bed was made, dresser and nightstand dusted. There was a laptop computer sitting on a small desk in the corner, so Reese headed that way first.

Opening the computer, he tapped a button to bring it to life, found it was password protected.

"We need to get JJ on this," he said, pulling out his phone.

"How the hell does this kid stand it here?" Brantley muttered.

"Hey, JJ," Reese greeted when she answered.

"Any news yet?"

Reese refrained from telling her yes, they'd met the worst parents in existence. "Not yet, but I've got the kid's laptop here. It's locked, but I wanted to see if you could get into it from there."

"Probably. Give me a sec. Lemme see if I can get the Wi-Fi from your phone."

"I'm not on their Wi-Fi," he informed her.

She laughed. "I know that, silly. Doesn't mean I can't see what it is."

While she worked away, Reese pulled out the drawers in the desk. Even they were organized and neat. Pens, pencils, a couple of spiral notebooks. On the floor, there was a backpack, which held a textbook and a three-ring binder.

"Hey, Reese?"

He turned his attention back to the call. "Hmm?"

"Does Brantley have his keys with him?"

"Brantley. Keys."

Brantley frowned, pulled his keys out of his pocket.

"Yeah, he has them."

"On there, you'll find a USB drive. Plug it into the computer."

Reese took the keys from Brantley, found the small drive that was hooked to the key ring.

"What the hell is that?" Brantley asked when Reese plugged it in.

"Tell him it's just one of my many awesome toys," JJ told him.

Reese relayed the information, then watched the computer screen. A bar appeared, but the computer remained locked.

"I'm downloading all the information from the computer," JJ informed him.

"Is this legal?" he asked.

"Immunity and means, Tavoularis," she said easily. "That's the only answer you need. Leave it up until it shows one hundred percent, then you're good to go. When you can, plug it into your laptop. There's a program on there that'll shoot the data my way. Anything else?"

"Not right now, no."

"Later."

The call disconnected and Reese stared around the room, taking it all in. He briefly wondered if one of Tanner's parents might come in to see what they were doing, then shrugged off the thought. It was clear they had more important things to tend to than looking for their son.

And sure, it was possible Tanner was with a girl or even with a friend hanging out. Maybe he didn't want to come back. Reese certainly wouldn't blame him. But until they knew for sure, someone had to be out looking for this kid, and the more eyes, the better as far as he was concerned.

The computer finished downloading, so he ejected the drive and reconnected it to Brantley's key ring before passing it back.

"Looks like maybe the kid's hopeful," Brantley said, nodding to the contents inside one of the dresser drawers. "Box of condoms. Few missin'." Brantley looked up at him, closing the drawer. "At least he's safe."

Not because he'd learned right or wrong from the parents.

Brantley exhaled, hands on his hips as he stared around once more. "I think we're good here."

Yeah. The sooner they could get the hell out of there, the better.

The Wrights weren't any more interested to know they were leaving than they'd been when they arrived, so they slipped out without incident.

"Hold up a minute," Reese said when Brantley started for the SUV they'd parked at the curb.

He walked around the side of the house, through the chain-link metal gate, into the backyard. He knew from the placement of the windows the Wrights would've both been able to see him if they'd been inclined to look. He didn't give them a second thought as he walked over to the dog.

He moved slowly, talking softly. "Hey, there, buddy."

The closer he got, the more the dog shrank in on itself, cowering away from his touch.

Reese crouched down. "It's okay. I promise, I won't hurt you. Not now. Not ever."

When the dog's nose started to twitch, he held out his hand, let the dog sniff. He managed to get in a couple of pats, noticed the little guy's tail beginning to wag.

Oh, wait. Not a little guy like Mrs. Wright had said. This one was a girl.

His opinion of the mother dropped another notch although he hadn't thought it was possible.

"Whaddya say we get you outta here? Maybe get you a burger."

As though the dog could understand him, she took a step closer, allowed Reese to unhook the chain from the collar.

"Up you go," he said, lifting the dog into his arms to keep her from having to exert too much energy.

Poor thing was definitely underweight. Reese could feel her ribs protruding, her hip bones.

He tucked the dog in close to his side, rubbed her head to reassure her as he made his way back to the front yard. When he arrived at the rented Tahoe, he saw the back passenger door was open and Brantley was holding a bottle of water. "I had a feelin' you were gonna do that."

Thankfully, he didn't sound upset.

They made a few attempts to get the dog to drink, but she seemed more interested in getting into the SUV, her legs trembling so much she could hardly stand.

"So do we want burgers or chicken?" Brantley asked as they pulled away from the house.

"Burgers."

"You pick out a name for him yet?"

Reese's eyes snapped over to Brantley. "You wanna keep it?"

"That's not the plan?" Brantley countered with a grin.

Okay, maybe it was. It hadn't been. Not until he'd picked up the dog. Now he was invested.

"Hey, I'm game if you are."

There was that strange warmth in his chest once more. The one that constantly reminded him that he loved this man. More so with everything he learned about him.

SEBASTIAN BUCHANAN WATCHED JJ OUT OF THE corner of his eye while he continued to henpeck the keyboard in an attempt to draft the email he wanted to send to Gallegos as a follow-up to their phone conversation.

He knew JJ was watching him, could practically feel her anxiety.

Looked as though the hot little hacker had a pet peeve.

"What are you doin'? Please tell me that's not how you normally type," she demanded, turning in her chair to face him.

Baz took the opening, smiled, and paused what he was doing so he could do the same. "Do you have a problem with my keyboard etiquette?"

"You can't poke the keys like that. It'll take you a month to get anything done."

"I thought I was doin' quite fine," he said, peering over his shoulder at the words on the screen. Hey, Detective Ga—that was as far as he'd gotten before she interrupted.

"Baz."

God, he loved when she said his name. Especially when it was tinged with frustration and that sexy little edge she had going on.

He played innocent. "Yes?"

"Do you know how to type?"

If JJ would've thought about it for even a second, she would've remembered that he knew how to type, but where was the fun in that?

"If I said no?"

Her eyes narrowed to slits. "Would you be lyin'?"

He laughed, couldn't help it. Anyone else would've prompted him with something else. Something like, Would you like some help? Or maybe, I could teach you if you like. Not JJ. She was skeptical on a good day.

"Yes," he said, going for the truth.

"So you did it just to irritate me?"

"You're damn cute when you're irritated." He flashed her a grin.

"Well, you're…" Her lips pursed and she exhaled through her nose, making her nostrils flare.

She was even damn cute like that.

JJ spun back around to her computer. "Type your damn email, Detective."

Chuckling, he went back to work, utilizing his eleventh-grade typing class education to tap out a good sixty words per minute, finishing up, and shooting the message over to the detective.

He was about to ask JJ what he could help her with when his cell phone rang. Glancing down, he saw that it was his father, decided to take the call.

"Hey, Dad."

"This is a nice surprise," Wesley Buchanan said with a smile in his voice. "I figured I'd be bumped to voicemail."

"I have a few minutes. What's up?"

"Following up about your plans for Thanksgiving dinner. Aretha's working on the menu. Needs a final guest count."

Baz found it amusing that his father made Thanksgiving dinner sound like a plate dinner with the president. The funny thing was, the old man didn't see it that way at all, it just came across that way. Their Thanksgiving's were casual affairs, always had been, always would be.

"I'll be there," he assured him.

"Will you have a plus-one?"

"A plus-one? Hmm." Turning in his chair, Baz leaned back, studied JJ's profile. "It's possible I will."

"I like the sound of that. She must be someone special."

"Oh, she's special, all right." Too bad she didn't realize how special to him she was becoming.

JJ's gaze cut to him briefly. He knew she couldn't help herself, listening in because she was curious.

"Well, I'll let Aretha know."

"Is Mom comin'?"

"She is," Wesley said, sounding pleased. "The husband'll be out of town. Told her to join us."

Of course he had. Because that was exactly the sort of weird, nontraditional family he had.

"I look forward to it, Dad."

They ended the call with goodbyes, and no sooner had Baz set his phone on his desk than JJ asked, "I didn't realize you were datin' anyone."

"Is that curiosity I hear, JJ? Or are you merely makin' a statement?"

Her left eye twitched, something he noticed happened when she was irritated.

"I take that as a yes."

He gave a noncommittal sound, turning his attention back to his computer.

Baz wondered how long it would take before she interrogated him again.

And he looked forward to when she did.

Chapter Five

BRANTLEY HAD KNOWN THE MOMENT HE LOOKED out the back window of the house and saw that poor, pathetic animal that they would be getting a dog. Not necessarily because he'd felt the need to race to the rescue, but rather because Reese had seen it, too, and his entire demeanor had changed afterward.

Of course, he probably could've convinced Reese to get it the medical attention it needed and to find a home for it, but why bother? The look in Reese's eyes—fury mixed with a need to rescue—was one of the many things he loved about the man. He honestly couldn't say he would've been quite so calm had Reese not been there. While the Wrights showed blatant disregard for their kid, they were downright abusive to the dog.

And to think, it was highly possible their son was out there somewhere, tied up in some crazy fucker's garage, and they couldn't be bothered to look for him. Those two had no business having anything that required love and attention. Or food and water for that matter.

Since it was lunchtime and they needed to get their plan nailed down, the first order of business was to find food for the three of them, so Brantley pulled into a shopping center that was equipped with both a pet store and a couple of fast-food joints.

"You want the pet store or the food?"

"Pet store."

He'd known Reese would say that.

"While I'm in there, if you get a chance, send JJ the information on that thumb drive."

"And how do you propose I do that?" he asked, steering through the parking lot.

"She said to plug it into the laptop."

Seemed easy enough provided that really was all he had to do.

He pulled up to the front of the building. "I'll drop you off. Me and the runt'll run through the drive thru and come back for you. Cool?"

Reese nodded, then hopped out of the SUV.

"Dude, you might not feel lucky right now, but I think your life's about to change drastically," he told the mutt as he steered through the lot one more time. "McDonald's or Whataburger?"

The dog didn't answer, but it wasn't necessary. It was a no-brainer. Whataburger was the winner.

He probably went a little overboard ordering three extra burgers, plain and dry, but he was hoping the dog would give the meat a chance. After he paid, they waited patiently for the food to be prepared. While he did, he pulled out Reese's laptop, shoved the thumb drive in the slot, watched as it downloaded the information. When it showed complete, he shot a text to JJ, told her to start going through it.

His phone rang a second later, JJ's name coming up on the screen.

"Yeah?"

"Turn on your hotspot," she instructed.

"My what?"

JJ chuckled. "On your phone. So the laptop'll connect to the internet."

Thankfully, she walked him through the process with only minimal razzing. Once it was done, he put the laptop away and turned his attention back to the window while he waited for his food. Once it was passed over, he noticed the dog's little black nose perked right up, his knobby head lifting as though he could possibly see into the orange and white bags sitting in the passenger seat.

"While Reese is loadin' you down with presents—because I'm tellin' you that's exactly what he's doin'—why don't we get started on the grub," he suggested, backing into a parking spot near the pet store so he could keep an eye on the door

He made quick work of shredding some of the hamburger meat, giving it a chance to cool before reaching back between the seats and setting it on the floor.

"The rental company's gonna hate me," he rambled. "It's all yours, buddy. Eat up. We've got a long day ahead of us."

Rather than dig into his own meal, Brantley waited, snatching fries here and there, watching the sliding doors for Reese to return. When he finally did—carrying three large plastic bags full of God only knew what—Brantley smiled to himself.

"Told you. And to think, Christmas ain't for another month and a half," he mumbled. "Yep. You aren't gonna know what hit you. I know I damn sure didn't."

Reese didn't get in; instead, he opened the back passenger door, set his loot on the seat, and began rummaging through the bags. The dog was sitting between the bucket seats, watching him with both curiosity and a hint of fear.

"I got more water," Brantley told him, passing back another bottle.

"Perfect." Reese produced a small collapsible blue bowl, poured water in.

"He chowed down while you were gone." Brantley glanced back between the seats at the white paper on the floor, grinned when he saw it was empty. "Ate every bite."

After setting the water bowl in front of the dog, Reese went to work removing the collar around his neck, then popping on a new one. This one was chocolate brown. The leash he dragged out of the bag matched. No frills, thank God. He only prayed Reese hadn't bought the dog a sweater. He might have to put his foot down then. The dog deserved some dignity.

"Why don't you get up here and eat," Brantley suggested. "He'll probably need to make a bathroom run in a bit. The least we can do is give him some time."

Reese nodded, but before he joined Brantley in the front seats, he pulled out a blanket, laid it over the rubber floor mat, then put a dog bed on the other side.

Brantley couldn't help it, he laughed. "You coulda told me you love dogs."

A smile formed on Reese's mouth as he closed the back door and then got into the front passenger seat.

Brantley passed over Reese's food bag before tearing into his own.

"There's an extra burger," he told Reese around a mouthful of fries, "but I didn't want him to overdo it."

While Reese ate, he continuously peered behind them.

"I need to call Kennedy," Reese said. "I'm hopin' she can fit her in when we get back to Coyote Ridge."

Yes, Kennedy Walker—his cousin Sawyer's wife—was the town veterinarian. And it didn't surprise him one bit that Reese was already thinking ahead, figuring out what was necessary to take care of the dog. Though he probably wouldn't admit it, Reese was the nurturing sort. He was the first to take care of people. Brantley knew firsthand because it had been that caring side that had brought Reese to his bed in the first place. Albeit completely platonic thanks to the migraine Brantley had suffered.

"You think they'll even notice?" Reese asked, peering back at the dog while he took a bite of his burger.

"Doubtful. If they do, I'm sure they won't sweat it for a second. Not like they'll go lookin' for him. You come up with a name yet?"

"Tesha," Reese said quickly. "It's an Indian name for survivor."

"You know this how?"

"Smartphone." He grinned. "Internet."

Brantley considered it then recalled what Reese just said. "I like it. But you said you hoped Kennedy could get her in." He peered at her in the rearview mirror. "Sorry, little lady. Didn't mean to offend."

After they ate, Reese took Tesha for a quick walk to do her doggy business, but it appeared she was gun-shy. Rather than wait, Brantley decided to make a trip over to the high school so he could talk to the principal, see what information they could get on Tanner Wright. It wouldn't surprise him one bit if they knew more about the kid than his own parents. They were the ones who had contacted the detective, after all.

"You hang here with Tesha," he told Reese as he parked in a visitor's spot. "I'll be back in a bit."

The school he entered was nothing like the small-town high school he'd attended. This one was more like a college with its enormous campus and numerous outbuildings. He managed to make his way inside, past some metal detectors, which automatically went off and required him to flash his badge and his credentials, then into the office, where he found an older woman sitting behind a computer, glasses balancing precariously on the tip of her nose while her fingers were tapping away on the keys.

"Can I help you?" She looked up. Only her eyes.

"I'd like to speak to the principal," he said, holding up his badge.

That got her attention. The glasses were removed, set on the desk. "Are you with HPD?"

"No."

Before he could announce that he was with the governor's task force, she nodded as though it didn't matter. A badge apparently got your needs met. He wasn't sure if that was a good thing or bad.

She hit a button on her phone, then spoke softly. A few minutes later, an older woman stepped out of an office, her eyes narrowed on him from behind a pair of thin-rim glasses. Hers were sitting properly on her face.

"I'm Principal Rasher," she announced, offering a hand. "How can I help you?"

Producing his badge once more, Brantley introduced himself, told her the reason for his visit. As soon as he mentioned Tanner's name, her attention shifted.

"We've been worried," she said softly. "Please. Let's go into my office."

"I take it Tanner's not one to miss school?"

"Never." Her eyes scanned his face as though she was gauging what to say. She clearly decided he was on the up-and-up, because she said, "We can't get his parents to attend a single parent-teacher conference, but he's here every day. Perfect attendance last year, and so far this year, in fact."

"Seems like a big school. You on a first-name basis with all your students?"

Principal Rasher eased down into her chair. "I wish. But Tanner is one of those we keep an eye on. Not because he causes any trouble, mind you. He's a good kid."

Brantley took a seat across from her.

"A-B honor roll, perfect attendance."

"What got him on your radar?"

"Financial concerns." She clasped her hands on top of the desk, sat up straight. "Tanner never has school supplies or lunch money. He's been wearing the same tattered clothing for the past two years. We've got other students like him and we do our best to provide as much as we can."

Brantley remembered how Tanner's mother had been playing on her tablet, his father perched in front of the TV with an Xbox controller in his hand. If either of them had a job, or even bothered to look for one, he'd be shocked.

"Does he have any friends? Anyone I could talk to?" he suggested.

She nodded. "He's got a few friends he hangs out with regularly, but you should speak with Reggie. Reggie Dunbar. They're inseparable when they're not in class. He's the only person I know Tanner to really talk to."

"Would you mind callin' Reggie in? I'm hopin' he might know something."

Her eyes narrowed. "Who are you with again?"

"OTB," he said, trying the name on for size. "My task force assists law enforcement on missing persons cases. Detective Gallegos called us in to consult."

Her eyes softened with recognition when he mentioned the detective. She nodded, then picked up her phone, relayed a message, he assumed to the woman in the main office, to pull Reggie out of class so they could speak to him.

When she offered Brantley something to drink, he politely declined and waited patiently for Tanner's friend to arrive. He hoped like hell they got a lead from the kid. It would make his day a hell of a lot better. If not, they'd be back at Tanner's house, knocking on his neighbor's doors.

He hoped that was a last resort.

"YOU KNOW IF YOU DO YOUR BUSINESS out here, we're gonna be the laughin' stock of the school," Reese told Tesha as they wandered the grassy area on the far side of the parking lot. "But hey, you do your thang; I'll worry about anyone who picks on us."

Yeah, Reese was aware he was talking to the dog as though they'd known each other for longer than a minute. Probably helped that Tesha was looking up at him with those big brown eyes. There was something in those eyes, something that reminded him a lot of when he looked into Brantley's eyes. Or his own in the mirror. The three of them had been through a lot, and most of what they'd endured they kept to themselves. It seemed safer that way, Reese knew. All the trauma was better left scarring the inside rather than an open, gaping wound on the outside.

"We're survivors, the three of us," he said softly. "Stronger together."

His attention shifted to the school and he wondered if Brantley was making any progress. He'd been inside for nearly an hour. Hopefully he'd learned something that might give them an idea of where Tanner might be. He prayed like hell the boy had simply run away from home, found someone who gave two shits about him. God knew his parents weren't winning any awards. Not unless there was one for chain smoking and beer chugging.

"I should probably feel bad that I stole you outta their yard," he told Tesha. "I don't. Not even a little. Fuck them. They can hardly take care of themselves."

Tesha bumped against his leg as they walked, as though she wanted to keep close.

"Yeah. We're gonna get you all cleaned up, checked out by the doc. You'll like her. Nice woman." He peered down. "Safe to say, you'll be spoiled. Just wait till JJ gets a look at you. You'll like her, too."

They continued to walk.

"However, I won't be cookin' your dinner every night. And those burgers you scarfed … only on special occasions."

Someone cleared their throat and Reese looked up to see Brantley standing a few feet away.

He felt his ears flame from embarrassment, but he shoved it down, cleared his throat, and said, "You find out anything?"

Brantley grinned, nodding. "Yeah. That you like talkin' to the dog."

Reese canted his head to the side. "About the kid."

"Right." Brantley fell into step with them as they made their way back to the Tahoe. "Chatted it up with Tanner's friend Reggie. Turns out, there really is a girl. The name she's got online is fake, which explains why Gallegos couldn't find her."

"She go to his school?"

"Nope. Private school. Little Catholic girl. Reggie said she hangs out in that online group for their school."

"You gotta watch out for those private-school girls," Reese said, feeling a bit lighter. "And?"

"I called JJ. I gave her what to look for and she confirmed it from what she found. And I called Gallegos, gave him the details. According to Reggie, Tanner's just fine."

"You know this for a fact."

"Based on the text messages the kid showed me, yeah. Tanner Wright's bein' rebellious while, at the same time, losin' his virginity."

Reese laughed.

"Never in my life did I meet a teenager who talked as much as Reggie. If I would've wanted to stick around all day, I could've gotten the full backstory on Tanner and Reggie both."

"Well, I'm glad he's safe and sound." Reese exhaled. "Think we should get eyes on the boy though. Before we close it."

"Agree."

"Wasted trip, though, huh?"

Brantley glanced down at Tesha. "I wouldn't say it was completely wasted."

To his surprise, Brantley opened the doors for them, waited until they'd both gotten in before he sauntered around to the driver's side.

Reese smiled as he relaxed against the seat. "You know Travis is gonna have a conniption when he finds out we've got a four-legged travel companion on his brand spankin' new jet."

"Not if he doesn't know about it," Brantley countered. "So let's keep it to ourselves, shall we?"

It took roughly three and a half hours for them to tie up all loose ends and get back to Coyote Ridge. Brantley hadn't been willing to leave until he had a chance to talk to Tanner personally. The kid admitted that yes, he was hanging out with his new girlfriend. Yes, he had told his parents, actually. No, they never listened but he wasn't surprised they lied to the police. They liked drama. Turned out, the girl's parents had taken a cruise, leaving their sixteen-year-old home alone, and she'd taken advantage of the freedom, inviting Tanner over.

Reese wished all missing persons cases went like that.

Once they were back at the house, while Brantley went to the barn to fill JJ and Baz in on what happened, Reese made a call to Kennedy, who kindly offered to see Tesha today if he could get her over there now.

Reese shot a quick text to Brantley, letting him know, then loaded Tesha into his truck and made the quick trip into town.

When they stepped into the waiting room, it was to find the place looked like a ghost town. Kennedy and her tech, Olivia, were sitting behind the reception desk drinking coffee and chatting. Both women stood up when he stepped inside.

"Well, well, well," Kennedy said with a wide grin. "Who do we have here?"

Although she wasn't an imposing woman, Tesha still backed away when Kennedy approached. That didn't seem to faze the vet one bit. She simply took a seat in one of the reception chairs, leaning down with her elbows on her knees.

"Hello, young lady," she said softly, letting her hand dangle, her fingers fluttering as though enticing the dog to come greet her. "How're you doin' today?"

Reese didn't force Tesha over, but he did encourage with a couple of words. "She's good. We can trust her."

He could feel Kennedy's eyes on him momentarily before they shifted back to the dog. "You said you found her in someone's backyard?"

"Tied to a stake," he said, unable to hide the anger in his tone. "Water and food bowls were bone-dry and just out of reach."

She didn't appear pleased with the news. "Around here?"

"No. Case we had in Houston. Found her when we were doin' an interview."

"How'd you get her?"

"I walked in the backyard, unchained her, and carried her out." He waited to see if she would chastise him. When she didn't, he added, "I … relocated her."

"I'll check to see if she's microchipped," she noted. "Doubtful since it costs money and this girl doesn't look like she's seen a dollar in her lifetime." She smiled sadly. "But you're in good hands, sweet girl."

Olivia came over, carrying a couple of treats. She passed them over to Kennedy, who used them to coax Tesha her way.

Reese watched as she introduced herself, never rushing. She seemed completely content to sit right there until the dog was comfortable with her. It took a good twenty minutes before Tesha's stick-thin tail began to wag.

"I can tell you, she needs a bath," Kennedy said easily. "Probably some shots, but we've got to run some tests first. I'll draw blood, give her a quick physical inspection. If you want, Olivia can give her a bath."

"I can handle that part," he assured her.

Kennedy nodded. "We can schedule follow-ups if needed." Her soft gray eyes shifted to Reese's face. "You plannin' to keep her?"

"Yep."

"Good. She's gonna need some TLC. And she'll require some work. Doubt she's housebroken if they had her chained in the yard."

"We're willin' to put in the work. I promise." He peered down at Tesha. "Can you tell her breed? She looks like some sort of German shepherd mix."

Kennedy gently held Tesha's jaw, pulling back her upper lip, then opening her mouth wide. "I think you've got yourself a Belgian Malinois."

"A what?"

"Very similar to a GSD in appearance and traits. They're from the herding family, too. A little smaller though. She's definitely underweight. Should probably be close to fifty pounds." Kennedy continued to touch Tesha's face, leaning in closer, petting her gently. "Like GSDs, they need a lot of exercise. She won't like to lounge around. Might consider giving her jobs to do. Training will be easier than with some. Incredibly smart breed. Based on her teeth, I'd say she's right at a year." She looked up at him. "Have you named her yet?"

"We're callin' her Tesha. It's an Indian name for survivor."

Kennedy's eyes lit up when she smiled, stood tall. "I like it. You ready to come with me, Tesha? I bet I can scrounge up another treat. Maybe two."

Those big brown eyes lifted to Kennedy and Reese saw so much hope there. It warmed his heart and reminded him once again that everything happened for a reason.

Chapter Six

"HE WAS STILL AT THE GIRL'S HOUSE?" JJ asked, her eyes wide. "Seriously?"

Brantley nodded, leaned back in his desk chair. "Can't say I blame him. If you'd seen the house…" Christ, he still couldn't believe the parents had been so nonchalant about the whole thing. "The place was a pigsty. Dirty dishes piled everywhere, clothes on the floor. It reeked of cigarettes and mold. Dog chained up in the backyard, half starved."

JJ sat up straight. "Please, God, tell me you didn't leave the dog."

Brantley chuckled. "Not a chance. Reese strolled right into the backyard and took her."

Her eyes widened as a slow smile formed. "Really?"

"Yep. He's got her at the vet right now."

"You're keepin' her?" she exclaimed.

"Looks that way." He couldn't say he was disappointed, either. Brantley was constantly thinking back on the dogs they'd had embedded in his SEAL team over the years. His memories were good ones, and a part of him had always thought he would one day have a dog or two of his own. Since he didn't see kids in his future, a couple of four-legged fur balls seemed appropriate.

"Next thing I know, you'll be gettin' married." JJ's green eyes narrowed. "You're not gettin' married yet, are you, B?"

"Not yet."

"Holy shit. You didn't bat an eyelash when I said it. Who are you and what have you done with Brantley Walker?"

"He's in love," Baz chimed in, looking up from his computer for the first time. "You can just throw everything you knew about him out the window."

Brantley peered over at the detective. "Yeah? You speakin' from experience, Buchanan?"

"Not me. Hell no. But I've watched my old man fall in love a few dozen times in my life."

"Really?" JJ seemed surprised. "Your dad?"

"On his sixth marriage. One more hopefully-ever-after."

"What about your mom?" Brantley asked, curious.

"She's on husband number three. Believe it or not, my folks're still good friends. Even go to dinner a couple of times a month. Probably the reason they keep runnin' off the significant others time and again."

Well, there you had it.

"How old are you?" JJ asked Baz.

Brantley watched him, wondering if the detective knew this would make or break any chances he had with JJ. If she found out he was younger than her—which he was—Baz would have no chance in hell of making a move. For whatever reason, Brantley's best friend since childhood had an issue with younger men. The five-year age gap between them would send her running for the hills.

"Old enough to know better," Baz said, smooth as silk.

Smart man.

"Tells me nothin'," JJ countered.

"Does it matter?" Baz shot back.

"Maybe it does."

The detective grinned. "I can promise you it doesn't."

JJ mumbled something that sounded like whatever, then turned her attention back to her computer.

Baz met his gaze across the room, and the smile he shot back told Brantley he could hold his own when it came to JJ.

"I haven't had much luck on this social media thing," Baz said, "but reached out to a couple of buddies in other departments to see if they could get the word out that we're lookin' into it. I had JJ create a couple of profiles we could use to interact with some of these groups. Maybe we can lure them out of hiding eventually."

"You have a problem takin' point on this case?" Brantley asked.

Baz's dark blond eyebrows popped up in surprise. "Me?"

"Yep. You. And we're at your disposal. Whatever you need."

"What we need is another investigator," JJ grumbled.

Because he was in a good mood, Brantley decided to broach the subject now that they'd gotten approval. "Who you got in mind?"

It was her turn to look surprised, her head popping up from behind her computer monitor. "Really?"

"Sure." Brantley nodded at the pile of boxes they'd been acquiring with the cold cases from various departments who were hoping for some help.

"How many are you gonna hire?" Baz asked.

Brantley shrugged. "As many as we need."

"I've got two suggestions," JJ said.

Now Brantley was curious, so he waited patiently.

"Trey and Cyrus."

Brantley barked a laugh. "You're serious?"

"As a heart attack."

"You know Cyrus is a computer nerd, right?"

"Yep. And he's got some skills even I don't. Which might come in handy. And Trey, he's smart, determined…" Her grin formed slowly. "And plain nice to look at."

Brantley saw the way Baz's gaze snapped over to JJ. "He qualifies because he's hot?"

JJ peered over. "You're hot and you're here."

Baz leaned back in his chair. "You think I'm hot?"

"Oh, cool it, Detective," she snapped back. "That wasn't me comin' on to you."

Sure sounded like it to Brantley, but he didn't say as much.

"So? What do you think?" JJ's question was directed at him.

"We need some sort of structure," Brantley told them. "Partners or teams."

"Agreed," Baz said, his tone shifting from jovial to serious. "We could split up into teams, distribute cases, work them in tandem. Rather than focusing on one at a time, we could be lookin' into two or three at a time."

Brantley stared at the detective. Up to this point, Brantley had been using the excuse that they were still ramping up, getting their feet wet, so to speak. But after getting a glimpse of the cases they needed to solve, he knew they had to hit the ground running. And having a few teams seemed like the smart route.

"I'll talk to Reese," he told them. "If he's on board, we'll reach out to them. See what their thoughts are."

"Regardless of who you bring on, we could use a couple more warm bodies. Those who can travel," Baz said.

"Or hold down the home front," JJ inserted, "so I can travel."

"You want to travel?" Brantley was learning all sorts of new things about her today.

"I would, yes." She motioned to her electronic tablet. "You know I can do my work anywhere, right?"

Yes, he knew. How she had convinced him to spring for the new iPad with the fancy keyboard, he wasn't sure, but she had. Evidently, the laptop hadn't been good enough.

"Good to know," Baz said before ducking his head and getting back to work.

"Like I said," Brantley told JJ, "let me talk to Reese. We'll get back to you."

She nodded and smiled like he'd committed to hiring them already.

Then again, he had to admit, it wasn't a half-bad idea.

THE BAD NEWS, ACCORDING TO KENNEDY: TESHA had something she referred to as intestinal parasites.

When she had told him, Reese winced, although he had no idea what that meant.

Thankfully she had followed it up with the good news: they could treat them with medicine. Then she had gone on to tell him she was running other tests, including one for heartworms, which she said would take a couple of days but she would get back to him. Luckily there wasn't a plethora of issues. She'd been spayed already, which Kennedy had hoped meant she'd been adopted from a reputable place and they'd given her some shots, so now she was up to date. No microchip, but Kennedy had fixed that.

As he'd expected, Tesha was malnourished and dehydrated, but she said a regular diet would take care of that. She recommended some food, which he bought directly from her, and gave him instructions on when and how much to feed. Some flea and tick shampoo, nail clippers, and the meds she prescribed had also gone on the bill, but Reese didn't balk. He was invested.

Now, with Tesha in tow, Reese was heading back to Brantley's house … er … their house. He figured it would take some time to think of it that way. When he was there, it felt like home. Or it would once Brantley actually let him furnish it like he'd promised.

The thought of furniture reminded him they were set to have dinner with Brantley's parents on Saturday night. No sooner had he agreed when Brantley was on the phone with his mother, nailing down a time. Just the thought of meeting Iris and Frank Walker, Jr. for the first time was daunting. Of course, he was fairly certain he'd met them at some point, but it would've been in passing at one function or another that Curtis and Lorrie had held.

"We're gonna meet some folks this weekend," he told Tesha, who was curled up in the passenger seat. "Important folks."

The dog paid him no mind.

"Question is, what'll I cook?" He stared out the window, eyebrows furrowing. "What do they even like? Are they allergic to anything? Do they eat meat? Dairy?" His fingers tightened on the wheel. "Shit."

Reese could feel the panic coming on, but he choked it down. It was going to be fine. Brantley had assured him. He could figure it out tomorrow, get a menu in place. Plenty of time to get his head on straight, too.

By the time he was pulling into the driveway, Reese had settled himself by reciting algebra tables. It always worked.

"All right, you ready to get the full tour of your new house?"

He climbed out, waited for Tesha to follow only to learn the dog had no intention of getting out. At least not without being coaxed.

"You're gonna be fine," he assured the dog. "Why don't we go in, grab some dinner, then I'll give you a tour of HQ. Maybe I can convince Brantley to put in a dog door out there, give you free rein to come and go as you please."

Reese doubted it had anything to do with what he said, rather how he said it, but it finally worked. Tesha hopped down from the truck, then waited patiently for Reese to show her what to do next.

He gave the dog a moment to do her business, then led the way into the house, where the scent of food wafted his direction, reminding him it had been a long day and it'd been quite some time since they'd had lunch.

Brantley stepped out of the kitchen, smiled. "I hope you're hungry"—his head tilted down—"Tesha."

"So, what? You'll cook dinner for her but leave me to cook for the two of us?" Reese teased, relaxing as he'd come to do around Brantley.

"You're a better cook than I am," Brantley stated. "Can you really blame me?"

"True."

"Not even gonna argue," Brantley grumbled, leaning down to pat Tesha's boney head. "What's the news on our girl?"

Reese went on to relay what Kennedy had told him.

"What you're tellin' me is she's gonna be fine. Eventually."

"Let's hope."

"Well, for now, we'll get you some dinner. Maybe a bath."

Reese laughed. "You're gonna bathe the dog?"

"I didn't say that. But I'm not above ordering you to do so."

"Right." Reese headed for the refrigerator, grabbed a beer. "I saw Baz's truck outside. He still here?"

Brantley nodded, stirred what looked like pasta and vegetables on the stove. "I made him the lead on this online group case."

"That was smart."

Brantley cut his gaze over. "You sure?"

Reese tipped his beer bottle to his lips. "Why wouldn't I be?"

"No reason. I just didn't mention it to you before I did it, that's all."

"And you don't have to." Reese moved around the island, took a seat on a stool. Tesha came to sit at his feet. "You're the boss."

"I like to think of us as a team."

"Well, someone's gotta make the decisions. God knows you can't leave it to the rest of us. Nothin'll ever get done."

"Speakin' of decisions." Brantley opened the cabinet, pulled out two plates. "JJ's eager for us to hire more people."

"And?"

Those stormy blue eyes cut over to him again. "And I'd like your input."

"I haven't given it much thought. It just got approved. Did you have someone in mind?"

Brantley slid one of the plates over to him, then leaned back against the counter, holding the other as he began to eat.

"JJ mentioned Trey."

"Your brother?"

"You know another one?"

Reese grinned, holding his fork midway to his mouth. "Maybe I do, smart-ass."

That got a chuckle from Brantley. "Yes, my brother."

Was Trey qualified? Now that Reese thought about it, he had no idea what any of Brantley's siblings did. He'd never bothered to ask, so he did so now.

Brantley grinned. "You wanna know what they all do?"

"You act like I haven't picked up a few details about them," Reese told him.

"What have you learned?"

"Their names, for one," he answered before taking a pull on his beer. "Bryn, Sadie, Tori, Griffin, Cal, and Trey. And yes, I know I bungled the order. So yeah, I think I can handle their occupations."

"All right, but listen carefully. There'll be a test at the end."

"Bring it, Navy boy."

With a grin, Brantley said, "I'll start with Sadie, she's the oldest. She's married to Devon and she's a stay-at-home mom to two girls, Ashley and Meghan. Then Tori, who's married to Killian. They've got one son, Eric. Tori just recently got a part-time job at the bookstore in town. Something to get her out of the house. And the last of the girls is Bryn. She's full-time in school to get her teaching degree. She decided rather late in life that she wanted to do something different."

Yeah, Reese knew there was no way he could keep up with all this.

"Next in line is Trey. He's in security, though he's never really found anything that suited him. Usually works the night shift at high-end hotels and whatnot. I came next. Then Griffin. He holds the prestigious title of Coyote Ridge bank president. He's got a master's in finance." Brantley took a swallow of his beer. "And last but not least is Cal. He's a mechanical engineer, recently engaged to April."

Reese shook his head, forked food into his mouth, and attempted to line it all up in his head.

"Did you catch all that?"

He swallowed, took a drink, then met Brantley's gaze. "Oldest is Sadie. Stay-at-home mom. Then Tori. Part-time at the bookstore. Bryn, late bloomer, teacher. Next Trey. Security. Then you." He paused to think, then grinned. "Griffin, bank president. Youngest is Cal, mechanical engineer."

"Very good."

"I don't know why but I thought they were all married," Reese said.

"Nope. Only Sadie, Tori, and soon to be Cal. Trey and Bryn are each divorced. And Griff's never been married. What about your brother and sister? I know you said Z's married and works for that security company. What about Jensyn?"

"She's single. Married to her job."

"Which is?"

"Psychiatrist."

"Ouch."

Something nudged Reese's leg. He looked down, saw Tesha staring up at him.

"You hungry? Or need to go out?"

Those sad eyes implored him but gave Reese no clue as to what she needed.

"I'll get her food. You take her out, just in case," Brantley said. "I'll even do the dishes."

Reese peered up at him. "And for that, I'll make it up to you later."

"You bet your ass you will. But after you give her a bath."

Smiling, Reese led Tesha out into the backyard.

BAZ FINISHED HIS DAY ON A HIGH note. He had remained at HQ until he completed his call with the Seattle detective who had handled the initial case of the missing five-year-old boy, learning more than he'd hoped to from the discussion. So much, he used what he'd learned as an excuse to call JJ as he was leaving the office.

"Mind if I stop by?" he asked.

"For what?"

Her snippy response made him smile. This woman didn't trust easily, that much he'd learned already.

"I wanted to discuss the case with you."

"We don't have a case, Detective. If you don't recall, the kid in Houston was found."

He chuckled as he steered his truck toward the diner on Main Street. "I do recall," he said patiently. "We're still workin' on the nationwide social media scam though, right?"

JJ sighed. "It can't wait until tomorrow?"

"Nope."

"Fine. But you have to—"

"Bring dinner. I know. Got it covered. Be there in twenty."

Baz disconnected the call, headed into the diner. He placed a to-go order, selecting what he knew to be JJ's favorites, and waited at an empty table near the front while they prepared it. When the Styrofoam packages nestled in a white plastic bag were delivered to him, he jotted his name on the credit card receipt, added a hefty tip because karma was a real thing, then headed out the door.

Rather than assume JJ had drinks on hand, he dashed into the Gas n' Go, grabbed an orange Crush for her—another of her favorites—a Powerade for himself, and a single red rose from the scrawny selection near the register. He paid, hopped in his truck, and headed over to JJ's.

Before he could even raise his hand to knock, the door swung open, JJ's irritated yet still ridiculously beautiful face appearing.

"You're late," she grumbled, her gaze swinging to the rose he held in his hand.

Baz smiled to himself when he saw the instant shift of her expression. He was doing his damnedest to keep this woman off her game because he'd caught on to what she was up to. There was no doubt in Baz's mind that JJ liked him. The problem was, she didn't want to like him. Which meant he had to work doubly hard to stay on her good side.

"Didn't realize I had a time limit." He stepped into the house, offered her a quick kiss on the cheek—another surprising gesture on his part—then made his way to the kitchen.

He had only been here once, and that had been the night he'd dropped her off after they'd hung out at Moonshiners. He hadn't come inside, but the space wasn't overly large, so it was easy to navigate.

While he unloaded their food on the L-shaped counter that separated the galley kitchen from the small breakfast nook, he instructed her to get plates and silverware, then he moved their meals from the Styrofoam to plastic. He'd expected her to give him paper plates and plastic silverware, so this was a bonus.

"Sit," he ordered, motioning toward the table.

He heard her soft grumble, but she did as instructed while he rummaged through the cabinets to find glasses. Or rather, cups, as hers were plastic. He filled them with ice, poured in their drinks, then sauntered to the table to join her.

"I'm on to your game, Detective," she said sternly, her fork in hand.

"I assure you, darlin', there's no game."

And it was true. There was something about JJ that had drawn him to her the instant he'd laid eyes on her. Not only was she obscenely beautiful, even when she was grimacing, but her smile was radiant. It had the ability to warm the darkest recesses of his heart. To top it off, she was smart, funny, and easy to talk to. Not to mention quirky and easily excitable. He considered all those things a plus, and a damn good reason for him to ignore his usual MO of quick and dirty and shift to the courting stage.

Even if she wasn't yet aware that was the direction they were headed.

"There's always a game," she countered. "I just haven't quite figured out what yours is."

"But you said you were on to my game." He forked food in his mouth, gave her a winning grin. "Can't have it both ways." Once he finished chewing, he continued. "How about we play a little game."

"Strip poker's outta the question," she quipped.

"No strip poker. We'll save that for the third date."

"This isn't a date."

Baz wasn't going to argue. She would not see it his way no matter how hard he tried, and for now, he wasn't interested in arguing with her. He continued to eat, waited for her curiosity to win out.

He didn't have to wait long.

"What's the game?"

"Why don't you tell me what you think you know about me, then I'll do the same for you."

JJ's eyes lit up. Yeah, he'd already figured that out, too. JJ liked challenges.

"All right." She ate a couple of bites, took a drink. "You grew up with both your mom and dad, although they weren't living in the same house. They loved you to the moon and back, enjoyed alternating weekends."

He had to admit, she was pretty good at this.

"Go on."

"So I'm warm?"

"Right on the money. So far."

"Okay." JJ ate a little more, seemed to be considering her next words. "The stepparents weren't fun for you, though. They were too busy tryin' to win the affections of your parents. Mother's husbands were jerks, always lookin' to get you outta the way. The stepmommies weren't much better."

"False."

Her green eyes narrowed. "How so?"

"The stepmoms loved me. My mother traveled a lot for work, so I lived with my father most of the time. They divorced when I was four, so I was still young when they started rotating through. And if my dad has any specific preference in women, it's that they like kids. I spent more time with the stepmoms. Those who wanted to stay in my dad's good graces had to treat me like a prince. I knew how to win them over, get what I wanted."

"I just bet you did."

"You're right about the stepfathers though. Until my mom's current husband, I didn't really get along with them. I was more of a nuisance for them than anything. This one didn't come along until I was grown, so there's not much animosity there. I don't know him all that well. What else you got?"

Her gaze cut to him as she continued to eat. "You are a good detective, but you have an issue with partners."

"Yeah?" Baz paused, took a sip of his drink. "My superiors always said I had a problem with authority."

JJ shook her head slowly, wiped her mouth with a napkin. "No. I don't think it's that. I think you like to work alone. It's not so much you have a problem with people tellin' you what to do, but you're good at runnin' solo and you don't require much direction. Am I wrong?"

The way she asked told him she wanted him to prove it if he didn't agree with her. "You're not entirely wrong, no. I don't mind a partner, though."

She grunted, took another bite.

Baz decided to elaborate. "For example, you. I enjoy working alongside you, gettin' bossed around by you."

"I'm not bossy," she countered.

"Oh, you most certainly are." He leaned in, met her gaze. "It's one of the many things I find so hot about you."

Her soft gasp said he'd hit exactly the mark he'd been aiming for.

The rest of their dinner conversation went along the same lines. JJ would presume to know him; she would get it right about fifty percent of the time. Baz allowed her to steer them so she didn't have to talk about herself, something he could tell was a touchy subject for her. Considering he intended to be with her for the long haul, there would be plenty of time in the future.

"You didn't come here to talk about the case, did you?"

"We can if you'd like. I learned a few things tonight," he informed her as he carried the dishes to the sink.

"Baz?"

For the first time since he walked in the door, she didn't refer to him as Detective, he noticed.

He set the plate in the dish drainer, turned to face her.

"What is this?" she asked.

"What is what?"

"This. You. Me."

"What do you want it to be?"

"You know I don't have time for a relationship," she stated firmly.

"That's your automatic response." Stepping forward, he closed the gap between them. "Relationships don't take any extra time if they're the right ones." He leaned down, ran his finger along her jawline. "I'm not gonna press this, JJ. I like you. You know that. And you like me. If you wanna play hard to get, I'll chase. I don't have a problem with that."

Those stunning green eyes bounced over his face as though she was trying to read every expression to determine if he was telling the truth or not.

"But know this…" He tilted her chin back. "I will catch you, Jessica James. Of that you can be certain."

He expected a rebuttal, but it appeared he'd stunned her silent.

Being an opportunistic man, he leaned in, pressed his lips to hers.

He hadn't expected it to ignite, but it did. Like a match to jet fuel, it exploded into heat and light when JJ's arms wrapped around his neck, her tongue darting out to greet his. For a second, he was caught off guard. Enough that he didn't let the kiss consume them. The last thing he wanted was for this to go somewhere she wasn't ready for.

As much as it pained him, he pulled back and smiled.

"I will catch you," he repeated, softer this time. "No matter how long it takes."

Chapter Seven

Friday, November 13, 2020

"WE NEVER DID GET BACK AROUND TO talking about Trey last night," Reese prompted when Brantley walked into the kitchen the following morning.

Rubbing a hand down his face, Brantley attempted to wake up his groggy brain to remember what they'd been talking about.

Oh, right. Hiring Trey.

"Coffee first," he grumbled.

"You act like a man who didn't get any sleep last night," Reese said, a teasing tone in his voice.

Brantley shot a look at Tesha. "I prefer not to share a bed with a dog."

Reese peered down at the dog. "I tried my damnedest."

Brantley knew he had. To the point they'd both been up half the night attempting to get Tesha to snooze on the brand-new dog bed they'd put on the floor. Of course, Tesha would have none of it, insisting she be snuggled up between them. As much as Brantley liked that dog, he was not willing to go that route.

"If we had a couch, I could've relocated," Reese said, holding up a plate.

"Nope. Nuh-uh." Brantley shook his head. "I ain't givin' up my bed partner. Nor am I lookin' for a third. She'll have to figure it out." Following the heavenly scent of bacon, Brantley took a seat on a stool, picked up the fork. "Is this your guilt breakfast?"

Two eggs over medium, four pieces of bacon, and hash browns. On a good day, Brantley couldn't get the man to let him eat microwave bacon. Then again, it was microwave bacon. Who really wanted to eat it?

"It's my way of gettin' your day started off better."

Brantley took a sip of coffee, looked up into those beautiful brown eyes. "I can think of a better way for you to do that. And it involves you naked. In the shower."

"I'm game. But eat first."

He took a bite, then another, taking advantage of Reese's guilt. It took no time at all to finish off his food and get a second mug of coffee. He gulped it down, ignoring the burn in his throat as he got to his feet, marched around to the sink. After dumping both plate and mug into it, Brantley clasped his hand around Reese's wrist and dragged him toward the bathroom.

"We do have to talk about Trey. And the dog," Reese reminded him.

"And we will. After."

"After what?"

Rather than answer, Brantley stopped at the nightstand, retrieved the lube, then made a beeline for the bathroom. He managed to get the shower turned on before he pounced on Reese.

"Do you know how fuckin' bad I want you right now?" He yanked Reese's shorts to his knees.

"I've got a fairly good idea," Reese said on a long, strangled moan when Brantley closed his fist around his hardening cock. "Fuck yes."

"Not enough," Brantley mumbled. "I'm not gettin' nearly enough of you."

"How much more, oh, God, yes"—Reese thrust his hips, driving his cock into Brantley's fist—"do you want?"

Brantley paused his stroking long enough to yank his own shorts down his legs, kicking them aside. "Ideally? Three, four times a day."

Reese's eyes widened.

"A minimum of two," he conceded before crushing his mouth to Reese's.

Air was scarce, which made talking impossible as they maneuvered into the shower. Somehow Reese got him up against the wall. When Brantley attempted to flip their positions, Reese held firm.

"My turn."

Brantley moaned when Reese nipped his lower lip, his big hand cupping his throat, pinning him in place. He liked this side of Reese, the aggressive man who knew what he wanted and had no qualms taking it.

More moans and groans followed as Reese manhandled him into position, turning him around, planting his hands flat on the wall, forcing him to bend forward. Brantley did so without argument or complaint, his body desperate for Reese. Didn't matter who was the top, he just needed this man. And that was something he'd never experienced with his prior sexual partners. Brantley had bottomed a time or two, but he'd never cared much for it. And it had nothing to do with the act, more so with the submission that went along with it. With Reese … he found he craved it.

Reese's hands glided over his back.

"Reese? Baby? Fuck me."

"Don't wanna hurt you," Reese rasped, his fingers beginning to dig into Brantley's muscles, a sign he was holding back.

"You won't," he assured him. "Just. Fuck. Me."

When Reese impaled him a second later, Brantley grunted, keeping his palms flat as he rocked back against the intrusion. Reese filled him completely, his long fingers gripping his hips.

"Hold on," Reese said, the words sounding like a warning.

Evidently that was how they were meant, because the next thing Brantley knew, Reese was fucking him with so much fervor he feared they would end up through the shower wall and into the bedroom.

"Fuck… so … fucking … tight…"

Brantley shifted his feet wider in an attempt to accept the punishing thrusts while he dropped one hand to his pulsing cock. No way would he last like this. He loved the times Reese lost himself, forgetting all about gentle and fucking him like nothing else in the world mattered.

He jerked himself roughly, using the momentum of his body to drive himself into his fist while Reese continued to fuck him like a man starved for him.

"Brantley... Oh, fuck..."

"Come for me," Brantley bit out, the tingling that signaled his release too powerful to stave off any longer. "Fucking come for me, baby."

Reese drove into him one final time, his fingertips digging into his hips as they both let themselves get catapulted up and over into that glorious abyss.

Forty-five minutes later, Brantley was behind his desk in the barn, listening to JJ clack on her keyboard as though it had offended her. She'd also been mumbling to herself since he walked in the door, and the conversation sounded as angry as the typing.

"Not enough coffee this mornin'?"

Her head lifted slowly, eyes coming to rest on him. The expression on her face was one of embarrassment, as though she hadn't realized he was there.

"When did you get here?" It was a curious inquiry, telling him she hadn't.

"Long enough to know you're havin' a crappy mornin'."

Her gaze cut to Baz's desk.

"Problem with the new guy?"

JJ shot him a glare, then turned away.

Smiling to himself, Brantley shifted his focus back to his computer, recalled the conversation he was supposed to have with Reese about Trey. He knew better than to take JJ's suggestion to hire Cyrus as a potential opportunity. He wasn't willing to put Reese in that predicament. He knew there was some animosity on Reese's part thanks in no small part to Brantley's history with the guy.

Turning in his chair, he glanced up at the enormous whiteboard, noticed it had been cleaned recently, the glass front glimmering in the overhead lights.

Cases.

There should be cases on that board.

His attention shifted to the rest of the blank wall.

"I want more whiteboards in here," he decided.

JJ looked up again. "For?"

"I want them used to outline the cases we're workin' on."

"Right now, we're not workin' on any," she answered. "Except what Baz is diggin' into."

"That's the problem. There should be at least three active cold cases runnin' at all times."

"Three?" JJ looked at him like he'd lost his damn mind. "How are we supposed to handle three with only four of us workin'? Even if you hire two more, at best, we might be able to handle two, although not if you want us to actually resolve the damn things."

The door opened behind him, so Brantley peered over. Reese and Baz strolled in together, each carrying a cup of coffee, while Tesha trotted along at their feet.

"We're hirin'," he announced.

"I already told you," JJ said with a huff. "Bring on Trey and Cyrus."

"No to Cyrus." He wasn't willing to deal with the drama there. "But we'll talk about Trey. If everyone's in agreement, I'll talk to him. And I was thinkin' about the structure. Three team leaders. Baz, you're one. I want two more and each to have a team of two. And JJ, I want you to hire someone to assist you here in the barn. A data cruncher. Maybe two."

"Are those one and the same?" JJ asked. "The data cruncher and someone to assist me?"

"Depends on who you find. Up to you."

JJ nodded.

"Wow. Someone's brain kicked into high gear this mornin'," Baz said with a grin. "You want an ad in the paper?"

"No." Brantley peered back at the whiteboard. "But I expect those boards to never be empty. We should always be workin' on a case. They ain't gonna solve themselves."

"I've got a list of things to do," JJ stated. "I'll give you an update at the end of the day."

"Sounds to me like this is gettin' real," Baz noted, his expression sobered. "I'm honored to be a part of it."

Brantley met his gaze. "Likewise. Now let's get to it."

REESE WOULDN'T SAY HE WAS NECESSARILY SURPRISED by Brantley's abrupt decision to get things moving.

The truth was, he'd been expecting it. It had felt to him like Brantley was wading through deep water, attempting to get a feel for what was going on around him, fearful of stepping off the ledge or onto something that might blow back at him. Likely, in part, due to the PTSD he suffered after the explosion that had ended his career as a SEAL and very nearly ended his existence.

"Let's talk," Brantley suggested, motioning toward the door.

Reese led the way, stepping out into the brisk fall morning, holding the door for Brantley and Tesha. "Could probably close in a portion of all that square footage for a conference room," he suggested.

Brantley glanced behind him before joining Reese outside. "Good idea. You wanna hire someone or tackle it ourselves?"

Reese remembered how they'd built the staircase leading up to the loft. It had been during a dark point in their relationship, but they'd managed to get through it. And even when they didn't see eye to eye on the personal front, they'd worked well together.

"I'm up for it, but we'll need to handle it after hours. If you want us workin' cases, we have to do our part."

"Good point. I'm sure we can get it done in a few weeks."

Reese didn't bother to mention Brantley hated things to be in a state of chaos. How the man intended to work in a construction zone was beyond him.

"You really ready to kick things into high gear?" Reese asked when they reached the back porch that extended off the house.

Brantley took a seat in one of the chairs. "You and I both know we've been wingin' it so far. From the moment we decided to dig in and find Kate to tackling Lauren Tyler's disappearance. Those were spur-of-the-moment and we jumped on them without thinkin'. We found Lauren and Corinne three weeks ago, Reese. What the hell are we waitin' for? Now that we have actual cases to look into, we're stallin'. Why?"

"I don't think we're stallin'. I think we're gettin' settled. Baz has been gettin' the word out and apparently so has the governor. Hell, we took a case yesterday."

"The kid wasn't missing," Brantley ground out.

"No, but we still had to work it like he was."

"A few hours outta a day."

Okay, clearly something was bothering Brantley, and Reese didn't think it was the fact they'd closed a case in only a few hours. "What's this really about, Brantley?"

Brantley peered over at him, then shifted forward and pulled his cell phone out of his pocket.

He tapped the screen, passed the phone over. "Listen to it."

Confused, Reese held the phone to his ear.

"Brantley, it's me. I know you've got other shit that's more important, but…" The man sounded tired, distraught. "I need your help on this. You might not understand it, but if I'm expected to move on, that bitch has to be found."

Reese lowered the phone when the voicemail ended. "That was Travis."

Brantley nodded. "I get a voicemail like that every two or three days. Have since we brought Kate home."

"Is that what he came to talk about on Monday?"

The slow exhale made Reese fear the answer.

"In a way."

"What does that mean?"

"He threatened me."

"What?" That did not sound like Travis.

"He threatened to lure JJ over to the resort. Said money can buy pretty much anything."

Okay. That made him feel a tad better. Not a physical threat, at least.

"He can't let it go," Reese mused. "That's understandable."

"You're right. He can't." Brantley glanced out at the barn. "I know Travis, and I know he's obsessing over this. And I can't blame him at all. Hell, he's probably worried that bitch'll reappear and his daughter might vanish again."

Reese understood that. And since it was a very real possibility, they should all be worried about it.

"I have to help him get closure on this. Sooner rather than later."

"What do you need me to do?"

"What I need is someone to fuckin' find her," Brantley snarled.

"You know JJ's been workin' on it. She set up alerts, keeps a record of everything she's doin'."

Brantley's expression said he hadn't known that.

"I'm sure Travis has alerts set up, too."

"Probably. And that's the issue." Brantley met his gaze. "We can't let Travis go off the rails on this, Reese. My cousin … if he gets her in his sights, there's no doubt in my mind he'll take her out."

Reese didn't disagree. He knew Travis, had for a long damn time. He'd seen the man riled up a time or two, but he'd never seen him harboring the sort of rage plaguing him now. And that was saying something because Travis had recruited Reese to deal with one of Travis's cousin's ex-wife a few years back. Thankfully she'd heeded the warning. Otherwise, it might've been a death sentence instead of an ultimatum Reese had delivered. And if it had, Travis's hands would've never gotten dirty.

"I need to dedicate some time to helpin' him," Brantley said. "And JJ's right. We need more people if we're gonna get anything accomplished. Lookin' into one case every month or so … not feasible. And it won't justify the cost of this task force."

Reese leaned forward, touched Brantley's arm. "I agree, Juliet Prince needs to be brought to justice. You find her, you turn her in. That's your plan, right?"

Brantley's gaze bounced over his face. "That's my plan."

"But it's not Travis's?" Reese knew Travis too well, knew the man had crossed that line in the name of protecting his family and he wouldn't hesitate to do it again.

"Honestly, I don't know what his plan is, but I have to help him."

"Okay." Reese knew he couldn't argue. He understood Travis's need for closure on this. The man couldn't be expected to be looking over his shoulder for the rest of his life, waiting for the woman who had kidnapped his daughter to wreak havoc on his life again.

Brantley breathed out. "I'm gonna meet up with him next week. See what he has in mind and see if we can map out a plan."

"And I'll oversee what's goin' on here." Reese leaned back. "What about Trey? You goin' to talk to him?"

"What do you think?"

"About hirin' him?" Reese was surprised Brantley even had to ask. "The guy's got more experience with this than I do and you took a chance on me. I'm no detective, Brantley. Never have been, but I like to think I've got good instincts. I can hold my own. The same goes for you. If you think Trey's a good fit, I don't have any arguments."

As for Cyrus... Reese was just glad Brantley had vetoed JJ's suggestion before they'd been forced to discuss it.

"I'll give him a call," Brantley noted. "But I want you to interview him. See how well the two of you mesh."

"When do you plan to have all this done?" Reese asked. "The full team in place?"

"By the end of the year."

At least they had a little time.

Of course, that could change at any minute.

WHEN BRANTLEY AND REESE LEFT, JJ SHOT up out of her chair and headed for the kitchen. She needed coffee, but more importantly, she needed some distance from Baz.

Her thoughts drifted back to last night, to the dinner they had together, the conversation.

The kiss.

I will catch you. No matter how long it takes.

His words still played in her head, over and over. She had no idea why those words carried so much weight, but they did. No one had ever chased her before. No one had held out long enough to give a damn. Not even Dante.

Her heart fluttered at the memory of Baz speaking those words, so low, so sincere. Her blood began to heat the same way it had when he'd pressed his mouth to hers. It hadn't been much different than the first and only kiss they'd shared a few weeks ago at Moonshiners when they'd all gone to celebrate the fact they'd closed their first case.

Last night's encounter started with Baz proving he was patient and unwilling to push, then with JJ all but jumping him. Baz had then taken over, slowing things down, making her head spin with the overwhelming intensity of his kiss.

And then he'd left.

JJ spent the entire night battling the anger and frustration that erupted when he hadn't taken things any further. It made her a damn hypocrite, she knew. She'd all but declared she had no desire to sleep with him, and now it seemed to be the only thing she could think about.

"Need some help?"

Jolted out of her thoughts, JJ jumped at the sound of Baz's voice.

She spun around to glare at him. "I'm fine."

"You don't look fine," he said smoothly, stepping closer, those teal-blue eyes glowing with mischief. "I mean, you look good, but you look … preoccupied. Somethin' on your mind?"

JJ hated the way her heartbeat took off at a gallop, her breaths became labored. It was all due to how close he was, how hot he made her. How freaking good he smelled. It pissed her off that he could play her so easily and then turn and walk away as though she didn't matter.

The backs of his fingers brushed her cheek before pushing a lock of hair behind her ear. "Talk to me, JJ."

Her attention shifted to his mouth. That oh-so-sensual mouth.

"JJ?"

When he closed the distance between them, she backed up, found herself up against the wall, trapped between it and his big, hard body. All that delicious maleness made her head spin.

"Stop lookin' at me like that," he warned, his voice similar to last night, dark and soothing, and laced with promise.

"Like what?" she managed, her words coming out in a gravelly rasp.

"Like you want me for dessert."

So what if she did? It wasn't like she would indulge. JJ was on a diet. No men, no matter how charming or sexy or…

She sucked in air when his head lowered, his breath fanning her lips.

"Tell me to stop, JJ," he growled.

She wanted to. Oh, how she wanted to.

Lie.

It was a lie she continued to tell herself to keep some distance, because she knew Baz would hurt her the same way all the men in her past had. She wasn't special enough for anyone to put her first and she'd learned that time and time again.

"Push me away, JJ. Right now."

Her brain warred with her body, but before she made a fool out of herself, the door opened. Their connection was instantly severed as Baz took a step back.

Brantley and Reese had come to her rescue and they didn't even know it.

In an attempt to get her hormones under control, JJ grabbed the empty coffeepot and went through the process of starting another. By the time it was dripping, she felt better. Enough to join the others in the main room only to find the three men wielding tape measures and jotting down numbers.

"What's goin' on?" she asked, suddenly fearful they were about to undertake something beyond their scope of skills.

"We're gonna build a conference room. A place for a bit of privacy if it's needed."

Her mind instantly went into the gutter. They were talking about professional privacy, not…

"Okay." JJ considered the change, glanced around. "And what do you propose we do about all the desks you want added to this space?"

Brantley looked her way. "Desks?"

She grabbed the sheet of paper off his desk, waved it. "Remember this? We designed the new layout. You've got all these warm bodies you wanna hire. They're gonna need a place to sit."

His gaze shifted to the second floor.

"Oh, no. If anyone gets to work up there, it's me."

"Done," Brantley said quickly.

"What?"

"Make it your new office. You've earned it."

JJ wasn't sure what to say to that. "Seriously?"

"Yep. We'll move your stuff once you get it all taken apart."

She'd honestly been joking, but now that he offered her the space, no way would she turn it down. There was a window up there. A freaking window.

It was enough of a distraction, JJ nearly forgot all about that kiss.

Key word being nearly.

Chapter Eight

SATURDAY AFTERNOON FOUND BRANTLEY, REESE AND TESHA making a run to the hardware store to place an order for the materials they would need to build the conference room and to make a couple of adjustments to JJ's new space in the loft. When Reese had suggested they take Tesha along, he'd been skeptical but to his surprise, she'd done far better than expected. It seemed she didn't mind the leash as long as Reese was at the helm, and she took commands relatively well. With some additional training, Brantley figured Tesha had the makings of a canine partner.

Thanks to everything going on with the task force and the construction project they were undertaking, Brantley nearly forgot about his parents coming for dinner until Reese brought it up.

"I'm still on the fence about what to make," Reese said, a hint of real fear in his voice as they studied the main floor of the barn, considered their options for rearranging and accommodating more people.

"No need," Brantley told him. "I've placed an order at the diner and my parents are pickin' it up on the way over."

"I could go get it," Reese offered, the words coming out just a little too fast. "You know, so they don't have to. Play my part."

Brantley reached for him, pulling Reese in and then backing him against the desk. "Are you nervous, Tavoularis?"

"Not nervous," Reese said, those panicked brown eyes meeting his as a pained smile formed. "Terrified."

Despite the fact he was trying to play it off, Brantley knew there was a lot of truth to Reese's statement. It was kinda cute.

"There's nothin' to be scared of. They're gonna love you." Brantley kissed him, pulled back. "Almost as much as I do."

Reese cocked his head. "Almost?"

"Well, considerin' I get to share a bed with you, I'm not sure anyone can love you as much as I do."

"No?"

Brantley could hear the challenge in Reese's voice. "Would you like me to demonstrate just how much?"

"Yes."

He was pleasantly surprised by the agreement, so he leaned in and pressed his lips to Reese's. The kiss started out as a leisurely exploration but turned molten within seconds. While Brantley plundered Reese's mouth with his tongue, his fingers worked free the button on Reese's jeans, tugging the zipper. No better time than now for a distraction.

Reese assisted at that point, freeing himself so Brantley could palm his cock, stroking slowly, all that smooth, velvety flesh gliding through his fist.

"I could do this all damn day," Brantley breathed against Reese's skin as he slid his mouth over his neck. "Touchin' you, strokin' you."

Reese's head fell back on his shoulders, soft groans escaping as he braced himself on the desk.

"Do you need my mouth on you, baby?" he whispered. "You want to slide your cock deep in my throat?"

He took Reese's strangled moan as an affirmative.

Brantley went to his knees without hesitation, took that heated flesh into his mouth, and drew on him with enough suction to have Reese's hips thrusting forward.

"Oh, fuck, yes. Brantley … oh, fuck."

With a litany of profane encouragement as the backdrop, Brantley proceeded to work Reese right up to that precarious edge, held him suspended there for long minutes, easing back when he was too close, working more vigorously when he would begin to relax somewhat. And when he sent Reese over, it was with his name tumbling from those beautiful lips.

True to form, Brantley's parents showed up at eighteen thirty—half an hour early. Evidently his father knew how to sweet talk the diner into letting him have the meal earlier than planned.

Thankfully, Brantley had given Reese a heads-up, not wanting the man to be taken off guard when Iris and Frank Walker pulled into the drive sooner than expected. Not that it mattered. The instant their footsteps sounded on the front porch, Reese began to pace the kitchen, making circles around the island. His shoulders lifted and lowered, his chest rising and falling as though he was prepping himself for a big game.

"Relax. They're gonna love you," Brantley told him, then pressed a quick kiss on his lips and went to help his father bring in the food.

When he looked back, Reese was still doing his pregame routine, once again pacing the floor while Tesha stared up at him in confusion. But she didn't sit there for long. Her ears perked up as she turned her attention to the front door.

"Mom. Dad," Brantley greeted, opening the screen door. Lowering his voice, he tacked on, "He's nervous, so be gentle."

His mother's eyes glittered and a sweet smile formed. "He has nothin' to be nervous about."

No, he didn't, but Brantley knew Reese wouldn't believe him.

Brantley took one of the paper sacks from his father, held the door until both parents were inside, then led the way to the kitchen.

"Still no dining room table, I see," his father noted as they moved past the empty dining room.

"Soon," he assured the old man. "Reese insists on furnishing this place."

"At least one of you knows how to make a house a home," Iris said, stopping just inside the kitchen to wait for Brantley.

He moved past his mother, smiled over at the handsome man with the terrified expression.

"Mom, Dad, this is Reese Tavoularis. Reese, meet Iris and Frank Jr."

His father barked a laugh, stepping forward to set his sack on the table before moving toward Reese and holding out a hand. "We've met a couple of times. At Curtis's," Frank said easily, pumping Reese's hand twice. "And please, just call me Frank."

"It's nice to meet you," Reese said, his voice cracking slightly. "Again."

When Iris stepped up to him, she batted away his hand and went right for the hug. Brantley realized he probably should've warned Reese she was a hugger.

"Look at how handsome you are," Iris mused, cupping Reese's face in her small hands before glancing back at Brantley. "You did good."

That earned them a strangled laugh from Reese.

"And who do we have here?" Frank asked, peering down at Tesha, who was sitting obediently at Reese's feet, obviously not knowing what to think about their guests.

"This is Tesha," Brantley told them. "We adopted her a few days ago."

"Aren't you a sweet girl?" Iris said, bending down to offer her hand to Tesha.

They all watched as Tesha took a hesitant step forward, craning her neck for a sniff. She must've deemed Iris trustworthy, because she took another step closer, then another until Iris was able to give her bony head a scratch.

"She's a little underweight," Iris said when she stood tall again.

"It's a long story," Brantley explained. "But she's in a much better place now. The weight will come in time."

Iris nodded, understanding glittering in her eyes. "I'm glad to hear it."

"We thought we'd eat on the back patio," Brantley informed them. "Since it's a nice evening."

"That would be lovely. Why don't you and your father properly dish the food. We will not be eating out of Styrofoam. Reese and I will carry out the drinks."

"Be nice, Mom," Brantley warned, although he said it more to help Reese along than anything. One would've thought he was going before a firing squad, not meeting his future in-laws for the first time.

That thought had Brantley pausing as he lifted one of the Styrofoam containers out of the sack. That was … not where he'd thought he would be going so early in this relationship. But oddly enough, and for the first time in his entire life, the idea of marriage didn't scare the hell out of him. Of course, he'd never considered it before, wasn't even sure it was on his life's to-do list. There was no denying Reese Tavoularis had thrown him for a loop from the moment he met the man, so it made sense he was thinking long-term, right? If you've got something good, grab it with both hands and hold on tight.

"Somethin' wrong, boy?" his father asked in that grumbling tone that the Walker men were well known for.

Brantley shook himself back to the present. "Not at all, Pop. Somethin' wrong with you?"

Frank laughed that easy laugh Brantley was used to hearing from him. "Can't say there is, no."

They dished up the food onto plates his mother would approve of, then carried them outside, where his mother and Reese were already sitting. The instant Brantley stepped outside, Reese was on his feet, assisting by taking a plate, setting it in front of Iris. Once they had everything situated, Brantley took a seat beside Reese, reaching over and patting his thigh as reassurance.

"I heard a rumor you helped out my nephews a few years back," Iris said casually once everyone had started to eat.

Reese paused, his fork suspended in midair. "I'm sorry, ma'am. Your nephews?"

"Wolfe and Lynx Caine," she noted. "They live in Embers Ridge." She smiled kindly. "It's where I grew up. With my two brothers."

"Oh, yes, ma'am," he said, still stumbling over his words a bit. "I still talk to them every now and again."

"Good boys, those two," she tacked on. "A little rowdy, but good nonetheless."

"And your momma?" Frank inquired. "How's she doin'?"

Once again, Reese appeared tongue-tied.

"Keep in mind, my folks are part of the fabric of this town," Brantley said, hoping to ease some of Reese's obvious discomfort. "They know anyone and everyone who's ever lived here."

"Your folks are good people," Frank continued. "I was sure sorry to hear about your father."

"I … uh … yes, sir," Reese muttered, staring wide-eyed at Frank.

Iris reached over, patted Reese's hand. "Relax, child. We don't bite. I promise."

Brantley leaned toward Reese, lowered his voice. "Not like I do."

The choked laugh he got was the turning point.

Thank goodness.

REESE WASN'T SURE HE'D EVER BEEN MORE uncomfortable in his entire life. It sort of reminded him of the first time he had launched his ass out of an airplane. He'd been terrified but determined not to show it and intent on completing the task. Similar to how he felt now.

He had attempted to psych himself up for this dinner, but no amount of muttering had helped. Plus, even if it had, all that would've gone right out the window the minute Iris and Frank Jr. walked in the door. Why Reese was intimidated, he didn't know but he was. Intimidated and insecure, two traits he wasn't all that familiar with.

Then again, meeting the parents wasn't something he did on the regular.

Or ever.

"My mother's doin' well," he heard himself say, though he wasn't sure where the words were coming from because he was pretty sure his brain had gone offline in a desperate attempt at self-preservation.

"And your brother and sister?"

"Good. Both of 'em are up in Dallas."

"Not sure if you know this or not, but your sister dated our youngest in high school," Iris said.

Reese stopped chewing, stared at Brantley's mother. "Really?"

"One for the record books, that relationship." She smiled sweetly. "All of three days."

Brantley and Frank laughed.

"Evidently, Cal was smitten with her back in high school although he was a senior and she a sweet-faced freshman."

How the woman could remember that far back, with so many kids, so many memories, he didn't know.

"So what made you decide to stay down here instead of bein' close to your momma?" Iris inquired.

Reese turned his attention to her, respectfully. "I think I needed something familiar when I got out of the air force."

"Understandable." Her kind eyes remained on his face. "Will they be comin' down here for the holidays? They're more than welcome to join us for Thanksgiving. The more the merrier."

Reese felt his face warming from embarrassment. He wasn't used to this much attention. "No, but they've asked me … uh … us. They've asked us to come up there for Christmas."

"Which we'll be doin'," Brantley said. "Figured we'd have breakfast with y'all, head up there after."

"That's a fantastic plan." Iris glanced back at Reese. "Brantley brags endlessly about how good a cook you are. Perhaps you'd be interested in helpin' me prepare."

Please, God, no. "I'd be honored."

Her face lit up like he'd promised her the moon.

"How long were you in the air force?" Frank asked.

"Eight years," he said, his discomfort level rising.

"What is it that you did?"

"Dad, let's move on from the subject," Brantley said softly.

"No, it's okay." Reese couldn't spend the rest of his life avoiding the topic. "I was a PJ, then trained in special reconnaissance."

"Pararescue," Frank said with awe. "Thank you for your service, young man."

Reese nodded, never sure how to respond when someone said that to him.

He felt Brantley staring, knew he probably had some questions since they'd yet to share much about their time in the military. Sure, Reese knew Brantley was a Navy SEAL, an elite special operator, but Reese had never offered the details of his stint in the air force. Or his reason for leaving. In fact, he'd never shared that with anyone.

"How's the task force going?" Iris asked, as though she sensed the need for a subject change.

"Good," Brantley answered. "We're expandin' the team so we can make a dent in all the cold cases we've acquired. They keep comin' in, so I figure we need to get a jump on them. As it is, with only four of us, we're not doin' nearly enough."

"You know, your father was quite the sleuth in his day," Iris said to Brantley.

"Oh, hush now, Iris."

Curious, Reese said, "May I ask what it is you did?"

"Lawyer," Frank said simply.

"Assistant district attorney," Iris corrected, the words spoken with such admiration.

"Really?"

"Oh, yes." Iris beamed. "And my Frank ... oh, he was somethin'. It's how we met, actually. I had gone down to the courthouse for something"—she waved her hand as though that wasn't important—"and there I saw the most handsome man walkin' down the hall toward me. Not having a shy bone in my body, I stopped him under the guise of asking for directions."

Reese saw the color coming into Frank's cheeks. For some reason, it made him feel better to know someone else could blush so easily.

"It was love at first sight," she said dreamily.

Reese thought back to the first night he'd seen Brantley. At Moonshiners. But it hadn't been until the group had relocated to IHOP that he'd found himself inexplicably riveted by the man. Looking back, it had been a life-altering moment.

And here he was, meeting Brantley's parents.

"Well, I picked up a peach cobbler," Iris said with a smile. "Why don't we finish eating. After, you boys can show us around that fancy barn we've heard so much about. Then we can share some coffee and dessert."

Reese met her gaze for the first time and smiled a genuine smile.

Two hours later, all the nerves that had coiled him up so tight had finally dissipated, leaving Reese with a good feeling as they walked Iris and Frank out to their truck. When they were heading down the driveway on their way back to town, Reese exhaled heavily.

"You survived," Brantley said, stepping up behind him. "How do you feel?"

"Relieved that it's over."

"You didn't like my folks?"

"Now that dinner's over," he clarified, horrified that Brantley would think that. "The first meeting. I'm glad it's out of the way."

"Me, too." Brantley's breath fanned the back of his neck. "And I'm glad we're alone."

Those few words were enough to shift the remaining anxiety into something else entirely.

Chapter Nine

MONDAY MORNING ROLLED AROUND AND BRANTLEY KICKED it off with a five-mile run to clear his head and get his priorities for the week in order. He had a list of things to do, all documented on his notes app to ensure he didn't forget. The first of which was to meet Trey for breakfast to discuss the job opportunity he hoped his brother was open to.

When he got back to the house, he was sweaty and rejuvenated, ready to kick off the day.

"I'm back," he called out when he noticed the coffee was made and there was a bagel and cream cheese sitting out on the island. "Where are you?"

"Upstairs," Reese hollered back. "Come up here."

After grabbing a hand towel from the stash in the guest bath, Brantley made his way upstairs. "Where, exactly?"

"Back bedroom."

There were two back bedrooms, one on each side of the game room, so Brantley rolled his eyes and started in the direction Reese's voice had sounded. Tesha peeked her head out as Brantley approached, her tail instantly wagging in greeting.

"He's up to somethin', ain't he?" he asked the dog.

Tesha's big brown eyes gave away nothing.

Brantley paused to lean against the doorjamb when he saw Reese wearing only a pair of shorts and wielding a tape measure. The muscles in Reese's back flexed and moved, stirring that all-too-familiar hunger within him. The man turned him on simply by breathing.

"What are you doin' up here?"

"I had an idea."

"Does it involve you strippin' off those shorts? Because that's somethin' I could get behind."

"Easy, tiger." Reese turned back to him, grinned. "It involves some remodeling."

"More remodelin'?"

"Yes." Reese motioned to the windows. "I think we should add a deck off these rooms."

"A deck? And why would we do that? We have a perfectly good one down below."

"To be honest, I have no idea why. I just think it's a good idea."

"And when do you propose we'll use it?" He motioned around the room. "We don't even use the upstairs."

"But we will."

"For?"

"Offices."

"What?"

"Hear me out," Reese said, clearly detecting his confusion. "You want to hire on a truckload of people, and while the barn is big enough to house plenty, I figure maybe it'll be nice if we had a couple of offices here."

"And we can give up our desks to whoever needs them," Brantley chimed in. "That's not a bad idea. It'll keep me from tryin' to find a way to add more floor space to the barn."

"There's plenty over there. And with JJ in the loft, she's the only one who really needs a permanent desk. Well, her and whoever she hires to help her out. Everyone else should be traveling a good majority of the time. The cases we've acquired are across Texas, and we both know the groundwork can't be done from here."

"Good point. But why the deck?"

Reese's grin was sheepish. "Like I said, I don't know. Just sounded good."

"Well, if you want a deck, we'll build a deck."

That smile drifted away as Reese's expression sobered. "I'm not tryin' to redecorate your house, Brantley. I don't—"

"Our house," he said, pushing off the wall and moving toward Reese. "It's not just mine anymore. If you want to redecorate or add on, go for it. Might require us to use some elbow grease to cover the cost." Brantley hooked the towel around Reese's neck, pulled him in close enough their noses nearly touched. "Plus, I like the idea of some privacy when we're workin' from here. Means I can take advantage of you whenever I want."

"And vice versa," Reese groaned as he shoved Brantley back.

He hit the wall with a thud but felt nothing but intoxicating pleasure when Reese's mouth crushed down on his.

"Too bad you're runnin' off to breakfast," Reese mumbled against his mouth. "Otherwise, I'd just bend you over right here."

Brantley groaned, considered calling his brother and telling him he'd be late.

"What do you say we meet up for a construction meeting later," he suggested instead. "Discuss what needs to be done up here to make it happen."

"I'm game." Reese kissed him once more, then ducked out of the towel and stepped back. "Just think about me while you're gone."

Oh, he would. Hell, Brantley spent ninety-eight percent of his day thinking about Reese. The other two percent he was thinking about what he was going to eat and wondering if they could fit in a quickie before or after.

Forty-five minutes later, after a quick shower and a kiss from Reese, Brantley was pulling into the diner. His brother's truck was already parked and Trey nowhere in sight, which meant he was likely downing his first cup of coffee.

Brantley parked in one of only two empty spaces, then sauntered inside. Sure enough, Trey was in a booth chatting it up with a couple of guys at a table across the way. That was one thing about Trey. The man had never met a stranger.

Easing into the booth across from his brother, he waited until the conversation ended, then smiled in greeting. "Thanks for meetin' me."

"I figured since you were offerin' to buy me breakfast, it wasn't like I could turn it down."

"How're things with you?"

Trey leaned back, relaxed. "Can't complain."

"How's Cyrus?"

That happy-go-lucky smirk slipped away as Trey glanced down at the table, reaching for the generic white mug.

That look could've meant any number of things, but Brantley suspected he knew. He'd known Cyrus long enough to understand the guy was very much like Brantley had been before Reese. Not willing to settle down and always keeping an eye out for the next big adventure. Whether it was a man or a job, Cyrus was always prepared to jump on the train out if the routine became too much for him. And that was the very reason he and Cyrus had worked so well for so long. They'd been looking for the exact same thing: nothing.

"Talk to me," Brantley urged after motioning the waitress to bring him coffee.

Steel-blue eyes lifted, not a hint of emotion reflected in them. "Nothin' to talk about. He got his thrill, now he's moved on."

Well, hell.

A smirk formed on Trey's face. "Don't worry about me, little brother. I'm a big boy. I'm resilient."

Yes, he certainly was. The man had made it through one bad relationship already, divorce and all.

"So why'd you bring me here?"

"Coffee and food," Brantley said. "Then we'll chat."

"You're such a hard-ass." This time Trey's smile was genuine.

They ordered breakfast, chatted about the mundane: changes taking place at the barn, who was bringing what pie to Thanksgiving dinner, the last movies they'd seen. Brantley filled him in on Reese meeting the folks for the first time.

"I assume he's havin' Thanksgiving with his family?"

"Nope. He'll be hangin' with us."

"Is that right?" There was a mischievous gleam in his brother's eyes.

"Fair warnin', Reese isn't nearly as easygoin' as he seems. You fuck with him, you can expect him to come at you hard."

"Yeah? You know this from experience?"

"He's no pushover."

Trey took a sip of his coffee, kept his gaze pinned on Brantley. He knew Trey would attempt to do something, and he considered warning Reese but figured it would be more interesting to watch it play out.

"All right, so why'm I here? I know you didn't invite me so we could chat like a couple of gossipy girls."

"I want to offer you a job," he said, getting right to the point. "On the task force."

Trey looked shocked as he slowly set his cup on the table. "Seriously?"

"Yeah. Seriously."

That surprised expression turned to skepticism. "You talk to your boss about this yet? Get his approval?"

"Don't need to."

Brantley knew what his brother was worried about. In Trey's younger years, he'd had a few brushes with the law, nothing too harsh, but those incidents had left Trey with a bad taste in his mouth when it came to cops. It was the very reason he'd abandoned his goal of going to the police academy.

"Yeah, well, you might wanna do that before you go and get my hopes up."

Leaning in, Brantley lowered his voice. "I'm the boss. The governor has no say in who I do or do not hire. You want in, you're in."

"Why me?"

Brantley leaned back, grinned. "Is this where you want me to kiss your ass and shower you with praise, big brother?"

Trey rolled his eyes, leaning back when the waitress delivered their food.

"You need someone to sweep the floor? Keep an eye on the place overnight?"

To be fair, Brantley hadn't expected this to be easy. Anyone who knew Trey well understood he was a complicated person beneath all that good-boy joviality he portrayed. He'd been betrayed and hurt by those who weren't his family and he didn't trust easily.

"You'd come on board as a team leader," Brantley explained, keeping all emotion out of his tone. "For now, I'm establishing three teams, each with its own leader who'll build their team, run it, and report to me. In turn, I'll be reportin' to the governor, keepin' him apprised of our progress. Our objective is to tackle the cold cases we've got, see if we can bring some closure to the families. It'll involve frequent travel across the state, but I'll do what I can to distribute the workload so everyone has equal time to work in and around the area."

The good news was, Trey was listening.

"Right now, Baz is my only team leader. He doesn't have a team yet, but he's workin' on it."

"What about you and Reese?"

"We'll be workin' cases, too. Mostly current ones. When we do have an active case, it might require one or more teams to come in and assist."

"How many would be on my team?"

"I suggest you hire two. One you'll partner with out in the field, the other to assist from here. JJ will be manning the office and she's hirin' a couple of people to assist on the cyber front. She and her team will be available to all who need her."

Trey continued to stare, so Brantley kept going, "You'll be required to maintain your license to carry. You'll need to be armed at all times. There are a couple of additional trainin' courses we've got to take, as well. All of us. Those are comin'. There is no dress code, but you do have to wear clothes."

That earned him a smile.

"The need to expand this team was a sudden one," Brantley admitted. "And the first person I wanted to bring on board was you, Trey."

"Insurance and benefits?"

"Through the state, yes."

Trey's eyebrows lifted as though he was impressed.

"I'd like you to meet with Reese so you can get an idea of what his vision for the team is as well. It's the real deal," Brantley assured him. "And it's time we hit the ground runnin'. What do you say?"

His brother's eyes leveled on his face. "I need to think about it."

"No, you don't. Either you're in or you're not," Brantley countered because he knew Trey. Given too much time to think on it, he would take the safe route. "It's that simple. You want it or you don't. I know you. If you dwell on it for too long, you'll only get pissed at yourself or angry about your past and you'll use that as an excuse. I want you to join my team. Tell me you will, Trey."

His brother's jaw clenched, his eyes glittering. Brantley knew it was because he'd hit home with Trey.

"Fine," Trey snapped, then exhaled heavily, his tone softening. "Fine. I'll do it."

The relief that flooded him was surprising in its intensity. Brantley didn't know why it was so important to him that Trey come on board, but it was. Something told him it was necessary.

"I THINK IT'S SAFE TO SAY WE might have to fence the yard," Reese muttered when he continued to call Tesha, who had wandered around to the front of the house.

Thinking about a fence—which he honestly hoped wasn't necessary—only reminded him of the other projects they'd discussed. A conference room, deck, new offices, furniture.

Reese sighed.

Perhaps now was not the time to think about remodeling anything. He wasn't sure where they were going to get the money for repairs, let alone updates.

"There you are," he greeted Tesha when she reappeared.

Seeing him, the dog trotted over, tail wagging. It had only been a few days, but Reese was sure Tesha was going to fit in just fine. She was already relaxing, eating better, sleeping better, and they'd started with a few basic training steps. Reese had even caught her stealing one of Brantley's socks. He took that mischief as a good sign.

As well as something to keep an eye on.

"Good girl. Whaddya say we hang out in the barn for a while?"

As he walked toward the office, Tesha now in tow, Reese's cell phone rang. He dug it out of his pocket, saw it was Brantley, and tapped the screen.

"Hey, how'd it go?"

"Trey's on board. I told him to head over there, get with you. Interview him like we discussed. I wanna know where he'll fit in the best. For now, I want him as a team leader, but it might require a little ramping up to get there. Then I figured you could introduce him to Baz, show him around, tell him our ideas for expansion."

"When can he start?"

"He said immediately. Evidently, one of the other guards where he works wants to come on full-time, but they didn't have a position for him. Now they will."

"Perfect. Where're you headed now?"

"To talk to Travis. See what he has."

That trickle of unease slid down Reese's spine the same way it had when Brantley first mentioned Travis's frequent phone calls and his roundabout threat regarding JJ. He knew the man was like a dog with a bone when it came to resolving issues. He wouldn't stop until it was gone or buried. In this case, he hoped to hell it was putting the woman behind bars. Not in the ground.

"Keep me in the loop," he told Brantley.

"Will do."

Reese was opening the door when the call ended.

"I was wonderin' if maybe you'd have time to interview someone for me," Baz stated as soon as he stepped inside.

"Sure. When?"

"This afternoon."

"That was fast." Really fast. "A friend of yours?"

"No, actually. More of an acquaintance. We worked a case together a few years back."

"Local?"

"Yeah. Charlie's been with Taylor PD for a while now."

"Charlie?"

Baz's gaze swung over to JJ briefly, then back to him. "Charlotte Miller. Goes by Charlie."

Reese noticed the way JJ's head snapped up, her eyes narrowing on Baz. Although it was obvious something was on the tip of her tongue, she held it back.

"You want her for your partner? Or backup here at the office?"

"She'd make a great partner."

He could feel the tension beginning to rise, but he ignored it. No way was he going to get in the middle of anything going on between Baz and JJ.

"If you think she'd be a good fit, I'm happy to talk to her. I plan to be here for the rest of the day," Reese told him. "Just set up a time."

Because that tension wasn't dissipating, he opted to avoid asking JJ how she was doing. Instead, he took a seat at his desk and began searching online for office furniture to get an idea of what they were looking at price-wise. Not only did they have to add to the barn, his idea for converting the two extra bedrooms in the house would require some furniture, too.

"Do you want to interview my peeps, too?" JJ called out a short time later.

Reese looked up. "Only if you need me to."

"Maybe. A couple of guys I've hung out with before," she noted, her green eyes swinging over to Baz as though to rub it in.

Ah, hell. That was what this was? Jealousy?

Shit.

"If you need me to meet with them, I'm there," Reese told her. "But, please, both of you, if you're gonna take time out of my day, be serious about your choices."

He couldn't miss the glare Baz shot her way and decided the last place he wanted to be was in the middle of … whatever the hell was going on with them.

"Come on, Tesha," he said to the dog sleeping near his feet. "Let's head over to the house. Need to get some measurements."

With that, he snuck out the door.

Before it closed behind him, he heard JJ say, "A woman, Baz? Really?"

No, he definitely didn't want to be in the middle of that.

"YOU GOT A PROBLEM WITH ME WANTIN' to hire a woman?" Baz shot back, pleased that JJ would be bothered enough to confront him on his selection.

"As your partner?"

"I didn't say my partner," he clarified. "I said she'd make a good partner."

"Like there's a difference."

He leaned back in his chair, clasped his fingers behind his head, and stared at her. She really was a beautiful woman, especially when there was that sparkle in her eyes. Today she wore her auburn hair back in a sleek ponytail. Between that and the dark liner on her eyes, the light green seemed almost iridescent. That or it was her ire that had them sparkling.

"Technically, there is a difference," he informed her. "I was gonna make a suggestion to—"

JJ waved him off. "Do whatever you want, Detective. With whoever you want. It's not like I give a damn who you spend your time with."

And now he was back to being Detective.

Something inside him snapped, had him surging to his feet. In three steps, he was at her desk, spinning her chair around so she faced him. Baz bent over, planting his hands on the arms of her chair and putting his face in hers.

"First of all, don't feed me this shit about you not givin' a damn," he said, his voice low. "You can pretend all day long that there isn't somethin' here, but I'm not buyin' it. I feel somethin' for you, JJ. What, I don't know yet, but I'd damn sure like to explore it and find out."

Her mouth opened, then closed. She'd clearly cut off her retort.

Baz shifted his hands so he could make the chair lean back, allowing him to look down on her.

"This ... whatever this is, JJ, is worth explorin'. Don't pretend otherwise."

"It's not if you have a female partner," she whispered back.

Baz released her chair, stood tall, then forced himself to walk away. Part of him was relieved that JJ was actually showing a reaction at all considering this back-and-forth they'd been doing since he started working here. No, it hadn't been long, but with the tension growing between them, it felt like an eternity.

As he strolled away from her, he recalled his conversation with Reese. He had mentioned JJ's ex had taken up with his secretary while they were together.

Son of a bitch.

He exhaled slowly, calmed himself so he could be rational.

And to think, he'd entertained the idea of talking to Brantley about keeping him here in the office with JJ. He could manage the caseload for the teams, work through what he could, reach out to the original detectives to get a feel for what you couldn't learn by reading notes and divvy them to the teams based on who had the time or the most experience with that particular situation. He seriously doubted Brantley or Reese would have time to do that. From what he could tell, they were anticipating handling the new cases.

And right now, Baz was the only one with real experience when it came to missing persons. Trial by fire notwithstanding.

"She's gay, JJ," he finally said when he turned back to face her.

"What?"

"Charlie. She's a lesbian."

"So you didn't sleep with her?"

He laughed, but it sounded a bit hysterical. "Just what do you think of me, JJ? That I'm some sort of player? The hit-it-and-quit-it type?"

"I don't know what you are," she snapped back. "I don't know you, Baz."

"But the time you've been with me? Is that how I come off to you?"

She had the decency to look embarrassed. "No. That's not how you come off."

He took a step toward her, then decided he would extend the olive branch.

"I like you," he admitted. "A lot. No, a helluva lot. And like I told you, I'm in no rush. I'm willin' to be your friend until you deem me worthy of datin'. If that day never comes, I won't consider it a waste of my time. I just want to spend time with you, JJ." He held up a hand before she could argue. "No, not only here in the office, either."

She was staring at him as though he'd grown another head but she didn't say anything.

"Okay." He blew out a breath. "You think about that for a little while."

He headed for the small kitchen area, reached for the coffeepot. Before he could get his hand on it, there was a firm grip on his other arm and the tug had him pivoting.

Baz didn't have time to say a word when JJ kissed him.

All thoughts about taking things slow went right out the window when her soft, cool hands cupped his face.

Instinct and overwhelming need had him plastering her to the wall, his mouth pressing more firmly to hers while JJ's fingers slid around his neck, twined in the hair at his nape. His hands went to her hips, sliding upward, nudging her T-shirt high enough so he could feel smooth, warm skin.

Her soft moans nearly undid him, and they were a vivid reminder that they were in the office, not somewhere private.

"I like you, too," JJ said on a rush of air when their lips separated. "And I don't give a shit about slow."

Yes, she did. He already knew that about her.

Baz met those beautiful green eyes, saw more emotion than he expected.

"Don't hurt me, Baz," she whispered.

"It'll never be my intention," he promised, knowing full well no one could guarantee it wouldn't happen.

He cupped her face, pressed his lips to hers once more, slowly, lingering for a few seconds before pulling back and stepping away from the temptation that was Jessica James.

Chapter Ten

BRANTLEY HAD NEVER BEEN INSIDE ALLURING INDULGENCE Resort, never had the desire to, really. It was a place the locals talked about in hushed tones and out-of-towners came to visit with enthusiasm. For Brantley, it was the extremely lucrative business his cousin Travis owned and operated. Several of Travis's brothers managed bits and pieces, some of their wives in on the action as well. What they did inside these walls, he didn't really care. Provided it didn't impede on his well-being, Brantley made a point not to pass judgment.

The instant he stepped through the doors, there was no doubt in his mind what went on here.

Sure, it looked like any other five-star or multi-diamond—whatever the scale—hotel with its grand ceilings, uber-expensive floor coverings, crystal chandeliers, and well-dressed employees. The space was wide open, a mountain-high wall of crystal-clear windows allowing the brilliant Texas sun to flow in as though breathing life into the building.

But it wasn't the fancy decor that gave off the sensual vibe. That seemed to be something ingrained into the very essence of the building. Everything was sleek and smooth. Sexy, if you would. Even the music that softly played from somewhere up above.

"Mr. Walker, Mr. Walker will see you now," the woman who had greeted him upon his arrival said.

He stared at her, wondering if she realized how ridiculous that sounded.

She didn't show any signs of it being awkward. "If you'll follow me."

Brantley did as he was told, taking stock of his surroundings as he walked. Rather than go down the grand, curving staircase, they circled around to a hallway. At that point, the grandeur diminished, replaced by what one would expect to see in an office building. A high-end office, maybe, but an office, nonetheless. The walls were a softly muted gray tone, the tile on the floors white with gray veins running through them, a few random paintings decorating the walls, upgraded light fixtures above. No halogen or ceiling tiles in this place, no, sir.

There were white wood doors everywhere, most of them closed, a few open with people working inside. No one he recognized but why would he?

The woman stopped, motioned for him to go through one of those open doors.

Brantley held back the I'm impressed whistle when he stepped into the masculine space that was Travis Walker's office. It reminded him of the conversation areas in the main part of the hotel with the sleek, modern elements. If someone would've asked him who this office belonged to, Travis would've been the last name on his list.

"You made it," Travis said, looking up from his computer. "Shut the door, would you?"

There was an edge to Travis's voice, one he'd gotten used to hearing in the voicemails he'd been leaving as of late. As though with every passing day, Travis's rubber band was stretching, growing tauter and thinner by the second.

He closed the door, then stepped deeper into the space, watching Travis closely.

"I thought Gage worked with you," he said simply to make conversation.

"He does." Travis waved a hand. "Off doin' somethin' else. Have a seat."

With the only other option standing, Brantley took a load off, planting himself in the comfortable leather bucket chair across from Travis, waiting for his cousin to finish typing. A few minutes passed and then Travis closed his laptop, took a deep breath, and became the cool, calm man Brantley knew him to be.

"I suppose you didn't bring me in to give me shit about takin' the jet."

"Not at all. I'm glad to know the boy wasn't lost," Travis said, referring to the kid in Houston.

"Not lost. Ran away, more like. And I'll say I can't blame him. Parents were somethin' else."

"I heard Reese adopted a dog. Tesha, I believe?"

Being that Kennedy was Travis's sister-in-law and their entire branch of the Walker tree had dinner every Sunday, it made sense he'd been brought up to speed. That or Travis had every residence and business in Coyote Ridge bugged so he could keep up to speed on what was going on. To be honest, he wouldn't put it past the guy.

"He did."

"How's that workin' for you?"

Brantley considered it, remembered how the dog had basically taken over their bed since the day she came home.

"I like her," he admitted. Truth was, he was getting used to having her around.

Before Travis could make another inquiry, Brantley got right to the point. "Why am I here, Travis?"

Once again, that cool facade slipped. "I … I need to apologize."

"For?"

"My behavior last time I saw you."

Brantley knew he was referring to the threat to lure JJ away from the task force.

"I can't begin to imagine the stress you're under, Travis. I don't have kids, so I can't put myself in your shoes. But I can imagine, so I get it." He held Travis's gaze. "But one thing you should know about me: I don't take kindly to threats. Not ever."

117

He could see the steel in Travis's eyes, knew the man wanted to argue, to establish his dominance in this realm. Problem was, Brantley wasn't one to be pushed around. He'd worked too hard to get to where he was in life, and it damn sure hadn't been by backing down.

Travis nodded curtly. "Understood." Those steel-blue eyes notorious to the Walker family implored him. "I know I'm obsessed with findin' her, but I've got my reasons."

Brantley figured he knew some of them, but he suspected Travis needed to get some of this off his chest. As it was, he looked as though he'd been bottling it up for a decade.

"Such as?"

"Well, for starters, I won't feel that any of my children, or even my wife, are safe as long as that bitch is out there."

And they wouldn't be. It was obvious Juliet Prince had a few screws loose and she'd set her sights on Travis as being the one who tore apart her world. It had been in this very hotel when her husband had found the woman he decided to trade her in for. In the process, the husband had fought for full custody of their daughter and won, leaving Juliet flailing after losing everything she had, including her only child.

"Kate has nightmares," Travis said softly. "Every night she wakes up screamin', terrified she's back in that house, abandoned."

Brantley remembered how the little girl had been cuffed to that bed, left all alone. Seeing her like that had sent a surge of rage through him, so he understood. They still had no idea how long Kate had been there like that or how long she would've remained that way if Brantley and his team hadn't pinned down her location.

"I have nightmares," Travis admitted, the words barely above a whisper. "I wake up in a cold sweat, Brantley. This is my fault."

"The hell it is," he snapped, leaning forward and planting his elbows on his thighs. "You're not responsible for Juliet's life unraveling."

"Maybe not, but it sure feels like it."

The man was defeated. Brantley could see it in his eyes, in the lines around them.

"What does the FBI know?" he asked.

"Not a fuckin' thing. She simply vanished into thin air."

Relaxing again, Brantley decided to tell Travis about the changes he was making to the task force, the effort he was putting in so they would have more time and resources.

"With more people, we can split up the work, get some of those cases underway. As for Juliet Prince, I can assign—"

"You," Travis interrupted. "I don't want anyone else, Brantley. You and Reese. I want you to find her, and I want…"

It was there in those shimmering eyes that he saw the truth of what Travis wanted. Not only did he want Juliet Prince found, he wanted her dealt with.

"I can't do that, Travis," he whispered. "You can't do that. We will bring her to justice. And we'll see to it that she's dealt with accordingly. But I can't…" Eliminate her.

Their gazes held for long seconds. Travis was the one to fold first, leaning back and taking a deep breath.

"I need you to find her," he said, calmer now. "And when you do, I want to be the one to go with you to retrieve her."

Brantley knew he couldn't commit to that. Not until he knew Travis wasn't going to go off and do something incredibly stupid. The last thing anyone needed was for Travis to end up in prison for killing a woman who wasn't worth the brain power it took to think about her.

"I'll pay you, Brantley," Travis blurted. "A million dollars."

He was serious.

"I don't want your money," Brantley said, keeping his voice level. "You're family, Travis. I won't take your money. But we will find her. I can't promise it'll be me, though. I've got a brilliant team and I'll utilize them the best way possible. We won't stop lookin' until we find her. That'll have to be enough."

He didn't look happy, but there was a little less strain around his mouth. "It's more than I have now."

"That's not true. We never stopped lookin' for her. JJ's got alerts set up in the event she's seen. She runs facial recognition software all the time. We haven't left you high and dry."

Brantley wanted to find the woman, too. Could they dedicate more time, more resources to finding her? Yeah. And he would.

"I need to know my kids are safe," Travis said, a plea in his tone, something Brantley had never heard from him before.

"I understand." Brantley stood. "We'll keep at it. I'll juggle the remodeling I've got underway and make this a priority."

Travis got to his feet. "What remodeling?"

He explained about adding a conference room to the barn and Reese's idea to convert two of the bedrooms into offices and add the deck to the back of the house.

"I'll take care of it," Travis stated, walking around his desk.

"What?" Brantley shook his head, laughed. "No, that's not what I meant."

"I know." Travis's face was stony. "I owe you, Brantley. I owe you and Reese for bringin' my baby girl home. I can never repay you completely. So let me do this."

Because he knew Travis was a man who didn't want anything for free, Brantley agreed. He would take Travis's assistance because it was a surefire way of ensuring things got done.

AFTER MEETING WITH TREY, SHOWING HIM AROUND, Reese ended up working from the kitchen island for much of the afternoon to avoid JJ and Baz. Then, with JJ keeping an eye on Tesha, he rode with Baz to meet Charlotte Miller, a.k.a. Charlie, at the Coyote Ridge bakery at fourteen hundred to discuss the opportunity with the team.

After only fifteen minutes, Reese understood why Baz was so fond of the woman, and it had nothing to do with her appearance, although she was attractive with her flawless dark skin and shiny black hair. The makeup she wore accentuated her full mouth and light brown eyes, the hairstyle professional. But it wasn't her beauty that made him like her for the role. It had everything to do with her demeanor. Charlie was the no-nonsense type who didn't beat around the bush yet managed to have a conversation without intimidating someone into submission.

"I live and work in a small town," she explained. "As you can understand, there's not a lot of room for advancement in a PD the size of ours."

Reese had a feeling she was understating her difficulty advancing. More than likely, it was the fact that she was a black woman in a predominantly white male force. Women, regardless of their skin color, had difficulty enough advancing despite their education and ability.

"Have you considered movin' to Austin? Or even San Antonio?" Reese asked, merely curious about why she would remain there if she was looking to move up in the department.

"No. I don't care to hire on with a big department. Red tape's a pain in the ass and the bigger the department, the more they weave."

Made sense.

"You have a problem with travel? Our task force is charged with assisting all branches of law enforcement in the state," Reese explained. "And based on previous cases, we've been known to cross state lines."

"I thought it was relatively new," she said, her inquisitive gaze shifting to Baz, then back to him.

"We are. Officially, we've closed three cases. One just last week. Unofficially, four if you count the one that spurred the decision for the task force in the first place."

"And we've got a storage area full of case files from departments all across the state," Baz told her. "All needin' our attention."

"Are you taking point on these cases?" she asked. "Or are we workin' for the individual departments in that regard?"

"We're our own entity," Reese explained. "We work independent of all law enforcement agencies. As you've probably experienced, it's in our best interest to work with the departments, not against them. We're not lookin' to step on toes, but we are lookin' to get the job done."

"I admire that."

"Brantley Walker, the man in charge," he continued, "has decided to restructure from the jump. He's clearly got a plan in mind and hirin' is necessary to implement it."

"Three teams with three people on each team," Charlie said. "Baz told me."

"Four teams if you count me and Brantley. As of now, there are two team leaders in place. Baz has one team, Trey Walker the other. We're lookin' for a third."

Baz had mentioned on the way over that he thought Charlie might make a good team leader based on his experience working with her. If she was interested, of course. Reese decided he would refrain from making that offer until he could get a better understanding of her background, her motivations.

When she didn't ask a question, he kept going. "If you're interested, I'd like you to take a tour of the facility, meet JJ, our IT guru. You can talk to Brantley. He's the man in charge of everything, including pay and benefits."

The door opened, the bells overhead jangling. It drew Reese's attention and he looked up to see Autumn Jameson walking in. A smile appeared when she looked his way.

"Hey," she said, stepping up to the table, her eyes scanning Baz, then Charlie, then moving back to him.

Because his parents had forced manners upon him growing up, Reese stood, greeted her in kind. Despite the interruption, those same manners wouldn't allow him to brush her off, so he offered up introductions.

"Autumn Jameson, I'd like you to meet Sebastian Buchanan and Charlotte Miller."

She greeted them with a nod. "Please, don't let me interrupt. I just wanted to say hi."

"Excuse us for a second," Reese told Baz and Charlie, then gestured Autumn away from the table.

Autumn spoke first. "How's it goin'?"

"Good. And you?"

"Really good, actually."

"How's Walker Demo treatin' you?"

Autumn's expression warmed. "It's keepin' me on my toes. Kaden and Keegan are a handful. More so Keegan, I guess." She smiled. "But he can't throw anything my way I can't handle. I'm enjoyin' it."

"And the apartment?"

"Well, let's just say, I took your advice and opted to get a bed instead of sleepin' on a couch. It's not as big as I'm used to, but bein' that it's just me, I don't need a lot of space."

He noticed she was glancing back at the table, at Charlie and Baz, so he decided to quell her curiosity. "Baz is one of our team members. We're here talkin' to Charlie about an opportunity with the task force."

Autumn's brown eyes sparked. "Is she single?"

"It's not a requirement of the job, so…" His words died off when he saw the glimmer in Autumn's eyes. "Oh. You mean … you're askin' personally."

Her smile was slow and wide. "I didn't mean to put you on the spot."

"It's not … I … uh… Shit." Reese forced a smile. "Honestly, I don't know if she is, or if she's…" gay.

"No worries. I've never been shy."

Reese studied her briefly. "I'm sorry. I had no idea."

"What? That I'm a lesbian?" She laughed. "How would you? It's not like I wear a sign."

His ears began to heat from embarrassment.

"It's fine, Reese," Autumn said quickly, giving his arm a squeeze. "I'll let you get back to it. It was good to see you."

"Same. Take care." When he turned back to the table, Reese shook his head as though that would dislodge the weird conversation they'd just had.

As he approached the table, Baz and Charlie stood, their attention shifting to him.

"If the invitation still stands, I'd like to take that tour," she said with a smile.

Charlie followed them back to HQ. Once there, Baz gave her the tour, introduced her to JJ and Tesha. Leaving the chatting and touring to Baz, Reese helped JJ carry a few things upstairs. She'd held off until now so they could get the cable and phone lines run up there. Now she was moving piece by piece, a little at a time, but it looked as though she'd been focused on that for a couple of hours, which meant she didn't have much more to move aside from her computer tower, monitors, and her desk.

"Hey, Charlie, would you like some coffee?" JJ offered.

"I would love some," she said easily.

"While us girls take a break, would you two strappin' boys mind movin' my desk upstairs?"

Reese looked at Baz. "You up for it?"

"If you are."

No time like the present, he figured, although it would've been a hell of a lot easier if Brantley—

As though summoned by his thoughts, the door opened and Brantley strolled in.

—was there.

For whatever reason, the sight of him struck Reese hard. Seeing Brantley backlit by the sun, the door closing behind him. His hair was a little longer on top than it had been, he realized, his face a bit fuller. In seeing him, there was a warmth that filled his chest, and Reese found himself smiling. Not so much on the outside but on the inside.

"Just in time, boss man," Baz called out. "We could use your help gettin' JJ moved upstairs."

Brantley pushed up his sleeves and walked over.

It took only a few minutes and a couple of trips for them to haul the heavy load up the stairs. They didn't bother trying to put it in a particular place, knowing full well JJ would only insist on moving it again as she'd done numerous times since they had started working in the barn. Instead they wandered back downstairs. Reese plopped down on the black leather sofa, and Brantley dropped down beside him while Baz went over to talk to JJ and Charlie.

"How'd it go with Travis?" he asked, keeping his voice low.

"We've got to prioritize findin' Juliet Prince."

"I thought the FBI was handlin' it."

"And we both know they're doin' a shit job."

"Travis still not takin' it well?"

"Not at all." Brantley dropped his head back, sighed. "He's a mess, Reese."

"I figured he was lookin' into it. The guy knows more people than God. Seriously. He should be able to pull a few strings."

"It's personal for him. He wants to keep it between us. We can't keep it on the periphery. It needs to be a priority. We need to get him some closure so their lives can go back to normal."

Reese knew Brantley meant their new normal. He seriously doubted anything would ever be the same after what they'd been through. However, if they could locate Juliet and get her behind bars, perhaps Travis and his family could stop looking over their shoulder.

Speaking of new normal… "I forgot to tell you, I got a call from Corinne Greenwood yesterday."

Brantley's head turned toward him. "Yeah? How's she doin'?"

"Better. She's back at school, eager for the holidays so she can take some time off, and she said Lauren's comin' around."

"That's good news." Brantley exhaled, closed his eyes. "Damn good news."

Considering all that Lauren Tyler had been through—kidnapped as a teenager, held hostage and brainwashed for nearly a decade—for her to come around so quickly did seem to be a good sign. According to Corinne, there was still a long road ahead, but if all went well, maybe Lauren could have some sense of normalcy as well.

"What're you boys doin' sittin' down on the job?" JJ teased when she stepped out of the kitchenette. "These other desks ain't gonna move themselves."

Oh, so it was a complete rearrange. Reese should've known.

"Just waitin' for you, Your Highness," Brantley mumbled, eyes slowly opening. "Where'd you like it?"

Reese and JJ both laughed.

"Walked right into that one, didn't I?"

"Baz can help me with my desk first," she said, then turned to Charlie. "It was great to meet you. I look forward to workin' with you."

With JJ guiding the process, she led Baz back upstairs to get her desk where she wanted it while Reese introduced Brantley to Charlie.

Once they'd made each other's acquaintance, Reese opted to take Tesha outside, let the two of them chat for a few minutes while he tossed the ball around and put a smile on the dog's face.

New normal, he realized.

That was what this was for him, too.

"I LIKE HER," JJ HOLLERED TO BAZ when Charlie left. "You think she'll take the job?"

His voice carried up to the loft when he said, "I think she'll give it some serious consideration."

Since Charlie had spent a solid hour talking to Brantley, JJ figured he was right. There was a good chance she would be part of their team in the coming days, maybe weeks. That was the best they could hope for, she figured.

"You done up here?" he asked, appearing at the top of the stairs.

She honestly hadn't given much thought to being able to communicate with the rest of the team while she was tucked away up here. Good thing was, her voice carried and she wasn't opposed to shouting.

"Almost." She paused to look up at him. "Why?"

Looming over her from in front of her desk, he answered with, "I'm treatin' you to dinner."

JJ leaned back in her chair, considered him. "I thought you told your dad you were datin' someone."

"I am."

She felt like someone had stabbed her in the gut. "Then you should go and find her for dinner," she bit out, hating that she'd been stupid enough to fall for his charm.

"I did. You, JJ. That's who I was referrin' to."

Her? "We are not—"

"Yes, we are. And like I said before you started arguin' with me, I'm treatin' you to dinner."

How he could stand there and be so cool in the face of opposition, JJ didn't know. But Baz didn't seem at all fazed by her continued rejection. But worse than that, JJ was getting tired of resisting him. She'd already given in to her urges, kissing him when she shouldn't have, thinking about him when it was inappropriate. So what would it hurt to have dinner one more time? Give it a chance. If it failed tonight, she'd know that they had to step back from this mutual attraction and move on with their lives.

She relented with a sigh. "The diner again?"

"No."

Her eyebrows popped in curiosity. "Where?"

"My place."

Instantly she was shaking her head. "Not a good idea, Baz."

"Your place then."

She continued to stare up at him, wishing he would truly understand her confusion on this matter. She liked him. Not only because he was hot as sin with that unruly hair and those wicked blue eyes but because he was a true gentleman. It had been a really long time since she'd had someone she could open up to, feel comfortable with. For a little while, she'd had Brantley, but now that Brantley had Reese, those times were few and far between. Not his fault but hers. She didn't want to impose on their new relationship.

"How about someplace neutral," she suggested.

"I'm game." He crossed his beefy arms over his chest. "Suggestions?"

"How about breakfast for dinner. IHOP?"

His eyebrow rose slowly, his words dripping with incredulity. "You want me to take you to IHOP? On a date?"

Oh, if he only knew how much she had needed him to react that way. IHOP was not a date place and no one could ever convince her otherwise.

"I like pancakes," she admitted.

"Then I'll treat you to pancakes." His arms lowered as he walked around her desk, offered his hand. "But I'm cookin' them."

When she was on her feet, he tugged her arm, pulling her closer. JJ stared up at him, fearful about the direction this was going to go. No doubt about it, he was going to invite her to his place, or come to hers, this time she would relent, as would he, and they'd end up in bed together. One or both of them would realize the sex was phenomenal, but relationships couldn't be based on sex, then they'd decide to be friends with benefits. That would run its course until one day they ended up hating each other.

"Baz—"

He cupped her face in his big palm, the warmth of it sending a chill down her spine.

"I'll be the perfect gentleman, JJ. We're takin' this at your pace."

"That's what I'm worried about."

His smile was slow and wicked. "I've got enough restraint for both of us."

It sounded like a promise, and JJ really wanted to believe him. She wanted to see where this went, to let herself get lost in the moment, enjoy her time with him. It terrified her that she might actually like him for more than just his body, though.

"Slow down," he whispered. "We've got all the time in the world. Let's just enjoy dinner together. We'll figure out the rest later."

Because she couldn't come up with a decent argument, JJ found herself nodding.

Chapter Eleven

THURSDAY FOUND THEM DOING PRETTY MUCH THE same thing they'd been doing all week. Not looking into cases the way Brantley had hoped. No, they were knee deep in remodeling. An attempt to get organized so they could take on the world. Or so JJ said.

"Only a crazy person would take on a task of this magnitude a week before Thanksgiving," Reese grumbled as he hoisted up the header board so Brantley could fix it in place.

"What better time than the present? At least it's not a week before Christmas."

"By the time you're done adjustin' this, it might be."

Feeling ornery, Brantley stepped back, stared at the sexy man who was currently in a fine predicament, his hands raised above his head, his T-shirt rising high enough to reveal a sliver of smooth, bronzed skin.

"Don't even think about it," Reese warned. "Get this thing nailed in, would ya?"

Brantley smiled. "Fine."

A few well-placed nails got the board in place, the newly relocated door for Brantley's new office creating an opening in the wall the room shared with the game room. Thanks to Travis's interference with the design—the man couldn't simply do, he had to take over—their upstairs project had turned into a complete overhaul. They'd already completed the French doors in Reese's future office, and he was hoping to get these finished up by the end of the day so they could move on to getting the conference room in the barn underway.

Although Travis's crew was tackling the majority of the work, Brantley wasn't one to sit idly by when he could help. Having two more sets of hands only meant they'd be done that much faster.

"Why did you decide to tackle this now?" Reese asked, shaking out his arms and taking a step back.

"When Travis Walker offers to foot the bill, you don't delay." Brantley set the nail gun down after flipping on the safety. "Speakin' of… Any news from JJ on Juliet?"

Reese grabbed his bottle of water from the sawhorse. "No, but if I know JJ, she'll have it figured out before everyone sits down to turkey in a week."

Brantley honestly hoped so, but he had serious doubts. Wherever Juliet Prince was, she did not want to be found. Since she hadn't surfaced in the past two months, forgoing even her supervised visitations with her daughter, he knew she was intent on not getting caught. He remembered the look on JJ's face when he told her they were going to continue chasing down that woman until they found her and got her into police custody. It had been as though she'd been waiting for that moment, to get the go-ahead. He wasn't sure she'd worked on anything else since.

"I doubt it'll be that easy," he told Reese. "Unfortunately, it looks like she's gone to ground. Maybe even left the country. Otherwise, Travis would've found somethin' by now."

"Travis doesn't have the skills JJ does."

True. He didn't. And since Travis hadn't been cluing Gage in, there'd only been one set of eyes focused on the investigation. Now there were several.

"Why don't we take a break," Brantley suggested. "Go check on them, see if they need anything."

"Pizza," Reese said, turning toward the stairs. "They need pizza."

"Do they now?"

"Yes."

Before Reese took the first step down, Brantley grabbed his arm and pulled him back, slamming him up against the wall.

"You know what I need?" he whispered roughly, his hands already snaking beneath Reese's T-shirt.

A soft moan echoed back at him. "I've got a good guess."

In a shocking twist, Reese took over, spinning them around so that Brantley was the one pinned to the wall. That hard body he'd come to love so fucking much pressed into him, holding him in place while Reese's tongue forced its way into his mouth. The kiss was a blinding mix of heat and need, coalescing into a firestorm that had Brantley's blood pumping faster, his heart kicking in his chest.

"Anyone could come in," he warned when Reese's mouth trailed down his jaw, his teeth nipping his neck.

"They could."

Since Reese didn't seem at all worried, Brantley wasn't, either.

Then again, they were upstairs in the privacy of their house. Even Tesha was hanging out in the barn today. Chances of someone coming over to check on them were slim.

Brantley's stomach muscles tightened when Reese yanked free the button on his jeans, parted the denim, and slipped a hand inside.

"What're you doin'?" he grunted as Reese wrapped a firm hand around his cock.

"I'm gonna make you come," Reese said, nipping Brantley's chin. "With my mouth."

Oh, fuck. "What're you waitin' for then?"

With a wicked smirk and a glint in his eyes, Reese went to his knees, maintaining eye contact as he did.

Brantley steeled himself for the onslaught of pleasure but it didn't matter. He was never fully prepared for how good it felt to have Reese's mouth wrapped firmly around him. Keeping his palms pressed flat to the wall, Brantley watched his sexy man, enthralled by the sight, the sensations.

"Fuck, yes," he moaned softly. "Suck me, baby. Goddamn…"

Seeing Reese like that, so open to this thing between them, it still affected him in a way nothing else ever had. It was the greatest high to know this man had never been with another man before him, would never be with another if he had anything to say about it.

"Slow down," he pleaded. "Oh, hell … don't make me come yet."

Reese did as he asked, slowing his pace, but increasing the suction as he drew Brantley deep into his throat, cupping his balls, his fingertip lightly grazing his taint. Their eyes met and held while Reese sucked and licked, driving him right back up again.

"I'm gonna pay you back for this," he promised. "I'm gonna… Oh, fuck…" He punched his hips forward as he reached for Reese's head, holding him in place. "I'm gonna come. Down your throat, baby."

His hips rolled and gyrated as he fucked Reese's face, pushing in deep, hissing when teeth scraped sensitive skin, but never losing his pace. It went on for what felt like days but was likely only minutes, and the vibration from Reese's encouraging moan was the detonator. With one final thrust of his hips, he held himself still, muscles spasming as his cock jerked and spurted. He managed to keep his heavy lids open so he could watch Reese drink him down. When he was spent, Brantley slumped against the wall with a winded exhale, wondering if his legs would work long enough to carry him down the stairs.

Back on his feet, Reese kissed him slowly, leisurely, giving Brantley time to come back to himself.

"What brought that on?" he asked as he tucked himself away, righted his jeans.

"It was payback."

"For?"

"Last night."

Brantley grinned. "Oh, when I rimmed your asshole with my tongue?"

Reese exhaled sharply, his eyes glazing with heat and hunger. With Reese, it was the words as much as the actions, Brantley realized.

"You like when I do that?"

"Oh, yeah."

"Or you like when I tell you all the dirty, filthy things I want to do to you?"

"Both."

"Mmm." Brantley kissed him gently. "I'll have to remember that."

"WHEN DID THOSE GET HERE?" REESE ASKED when he joined Trey, JJ, and Baz in the barn a short time later.

"While you and your boy toy were playin' kissy face," JJ said without looking back as she surveyed the wall.

"Installin' doors," he corrected, moving over to the new whiteboards that now covered the length of one entire wall. There were five in total, the one in the center bigger than the others.

As he studied them, Tesha came over, nudged his hand with her head in an obvious request for attention. Reese squatted down beside her, scratched behind her ears and beneath her chin, continuing to stare at the whiteboards.

Reese had no idea what JJ's plan was with them, but he figured she had one. She and Brantley, anyway.

He noticed that above the glass whiteboards, a television screen had been mounted, probably seventy inches or so. The screensaver was on, the letters O T B bouncing like pinballs off the four edges.

"Any news on Charlie? Is she comin' on board?" Baz asked, joining them.

"She is," he confirmed. "She'll start mid-December. Brantley's workin' with the governor to ensure she keeps her tenure with the department and her pension."

"That's great news," JJ said with a clap.

"Plans for her?" Trey inquired, coming over.

"I think that's what Brantley wants to discuss."

JJ did turn now, peering over at the door. "Where is he?"

"He got a call. Said he'd be over in a minute."

"I've got another delivery comin' this afternoon. Desks," JJ announced, her attention shifting to Baz and Trey. "If you two would make sure you're around to help."

"Please tell me we're not puttin' them together," Trey said, a hint of true concern in his voice.

"Nope. I negotiated delivery and setup for free," she answered with pride. "But I will need you to help rearrange."

Reese glanced around, noticed how things had already been shifted.

It looked as though they were finally settling in. Now if they could get some of these cases underway and hopefully solved, he'd feel a hell of a lot better. As it was, it felt like they were wasting time, although he knew that wasn't so. Baz was continuing to give updates on the social media group he was trying to uncover while JJ was spending her time digging into Juliet Prince, although she'd had no luck up to this point.

The door opened, all eyes turning that way.

"What're y'all sittin' around for?" Brantley asked, his gaze scanning the room.

He had a box tucked under one arm, a neutral expression on his face.

"Waitin' on you," JJ said, but then held up a hand. "Before you turn into Mr. Bossy Pants, we've done our daily reports, shot them over to your email."

"A little early in the day, is it not?"

"It's so you can review the layout, see what else you might need so you can do your own report for the governor."

Brantley nodded as he perched on top of Trey's desk, set the box beside him. "I don't expect daily reports. But I do want weekly. On Friday, before you call it a day."

Reese took a seat on the couch, JJ stealing the other end, while Baz hopped up on his own desk, and Trey wheeled over his chair.

"Weekly reports," JJ noted, snagging her Apple Pencil and jotting notes on her iPad. "Got it. I was just tellin' them we've got desks comin' this afternoon."

"Laptops and computers'll be here tomorrow," Brantley added.

"What about the other iPads?" JJ asked.

"What about the people to fill 'em?" Trey asked.

"What about…" Baz grinned. "Sorry, I got nothin'."

Reese couldn't help but smile. He had to admit, he did like that this group meshed so well.

Brantley nodded toward JJ. "Ordered." He glanced over at Trey. "They'll be here soon enough. Hirin' takes time."

"What's in the box?" Baz asked.

Brantley reached over, picked it up, and held it out to JJ.

She jumped up as though it was Christmas. "What is it?"

Rather than answer, Brantley waited while she looked inside. Her eyes widened as did her grin. "Phones. Fancy ones."

"Your phone plan's now covered by the state. If you want to keep your current number, let JJ know. She can get them all set up."

"Does this mean Big Brother can now track me?" Trey asked.

"Oh, don't be naive," JJ countered, her tone relaying that she thought Trey was being ridiculous. "Big Brother's always been able to track you."

Reese didn't doubt that one bit.

"Also, I've been told that if an Amber Alert or a Silver Alert are issued in the state, we will immediately receive as much detailed information as was submitted. Those will be our priorities, of course. Doesn't mean we can up and go, but we do have a responsibility to help if it looks as though we're needed."

"What about comms?" JJ inquired, referring to the wireless communication devices they hoped to have for when they were out in the field. It wasn't always feasible to use a phone, Reese knew. Especially not with a weapon in hand.

Reese answered that one. "My brother's hookin' us up on that front. Sniper 1 Security's got a patent on some they'd like us to try out."

"Rockin' those contacts." JJ smirked. "Smart."

"Reese mentioned Charlie took the job," Baz said, speaking to Brantley.

"She did. And she's the reason I wanted to talk."

"Problem?"

"Opposite, actually," he continued. "Based on my conversations with her, and the info I received when callin' her references and past and current superiors, I think she'd do well as a team leader. However, I didn't want to make that decision without discussin' with y'all first. Anyone have an objection?"

No one spoke up.

"Does that mean you've found your three team leaders?" JJ questioned.

"Actually, Baz offered to be responsible for assignin' cases, rather than leadin' a team in the field. Since he's got the most experience, I think it's worth tryin'. He will also be responsible for followin' up if we don't get the responses we need, so use him for escalations and whatever else that might help." Brantley looked at Baz. "I want your plate full, so figure out what else you can take on to make that happen."

Baz nodded. "Of course."

"That leaves us with a team leader position open, as well as the rest of the teams. I reached out to local PDs and we've got a handful of people who've been referred to us. I'll email you their info. If you're interested in anyone, call them in for an interview. At least three people need to talk to them before a decision can be made. One of those must be me or Reese."

"Do we have a time frame on gettin' them hired?" Trey asked.

"Yes." Brantley hopped off the desk. "Yesterday."

"How did I know you were gonna say that?" JJ started toward the stairs leading up to her office. "Oh, and I've got three people scheduled for interviews. Two tomorrow, one on Monday. These are my peeps, but I'd appreciate someone helpin' me with interviews."

"Just holler," Reese told her. "One of us'll be there."

She gave him a curt nod, then bounded up the stairs, the box of cell phones in her hand.

"Until we're at full capacity, I want you to start goin' through the case files with Trey," Brantley told Baz. "Let's separate them out in a manner that makes sense. That way we can start lookin' into them as soon as we've got the teams in place."

"Got it."

"Oh, and last thing," Brantley called out. "Travis is sendin' in a crew this weekend to get the conference room completed. So make yourself scarce."

"A construction crew that works weekends? Impressive," Baz said with a grin.

"Travis is owed some favors," Brantley told him.

"Tell me y'all don't hang around on the weekends," Trey said, his gaze darting between the three of them.

"Only when it's necessary." A smirk slowly formed on Baz's face. "For some reason, I get the feelin' it's about to become necessary."

Yeah, Reese had to agree with him on that. The time for settling in was over. It looked as though they were gearing up to get to work.

Chapter Twelve

Friday, November 20, 2020

THE FOLLOWING MORNING, BRANTLEY WOKE GROGGY BUT thankfully without the migraine that had hit him with a vengeance last night. One of those that gave no warning and had been relentless in taking him down. He'd been expecting it. They were still coming once a week at minimum, sometimes more, and it had been about that long since the last.

He didn't remember much except for Reese taking care of him, urging him into bed, feeding him the pill that would help to alleviate the excruciating pain, or at least lessen the time it lasted. Brantley had shut down his brain and drifted off into nothingness.

The mornings after were always a gamble. The fear of another headache lingered, making him move slowly. It took only a few minutes for him to realize he was fine and the day wasn't quite underway since it was still dark out. Perhaps some exercise would help, get his adrenaline flowing, make him feel human once more.

Getting in a five-mile run was his intention, but that goal went right out the window when he stretched his arm and found Reese was still in bed. Only one part of his anatomy seemed content to get up at the moment, so he rolled toward the warm body and spooned Reese from behind, sliding his arm around him. He had another form of exercise in mind.

Reese's hand glided over his forearm, gripping his wrist gently as he pushed back against him. "Feel better?"

"Yes," he breathed against Reese's ear. "Thank you."

"My pleasure."

"What pleasure would you like me to give you in return?" he asked.

"Depends. Is the headache gone?"

"Long gone," he assured him, pressing a kiss to Reese's shoulder as he pulled him in close.

A soft moan escaped Reese, so Brantley trailed his lips over Reese's shoulders, licking and sucking until those moans grew louder, the tension in his body making his muscles flex. Sliding his hand down Reese's abs, he continued until he had his steel-hard shaft in his hand.

"Brantley…" Reese's hips rolled.

"Hmm?"

"Fuck … feels good."

"That's it, baby," he whispered, nipping Reese's earlobe. "Fuck my fist. Make yourself come."

Another groan, this one long and low. "I want inside you," Reese growled. "Let me come inside you."

Brantley didn't have time to respond before Reese moved, pinning Brantley to the bed as he laid out over him. His weight was sheer perfection as Brantley's hands roamed over the smooth, muscular contours of his back. Reese kissed him, a long, wet exploration that went from playful to urgent as their lower bodies ground together. Breaths became raspier, the air thick with the electricity that sparked whenever they were together.

Brantley threw out an arm, reached for the nightstand. He managed to get the drawer open, but the lamp nearly took a header. He fumbled until he found the bottle of lubricant they kept stashed there.

Reese never stopped grinding against him, their bodies growing warmer, sweat slicking their skin as the need became a driving hunger that had to be sated.

More fumbling one handed before Brantley broke the kiss. "A little help."

Reese glanced over as though he had no idea what they'd been doing. His eyes focused on the bottle, then he held out a hand, getting to his knees and shoving Brantley's legs wide as he slicked his cock. And then Reese was on him again, forcing his legs back as he probed Brantley's ass with the wide head of his cock.

"Fuck me," Brantley pleaded, their eyes locking. "Inside me, Reese. Don't hold back."

Pain, hot and bright, lit up his nerve endings when Reese drove deep inside him, but it dissipated quickly, replaced by an overwhelming pleasure. The sort that had the hair on his arms standing on end, his lungs seizing for fear he would come before Reese retreated.

When Reese's mouth descended again, Brantley met him, palming the back of his head while their tongues dueled and danced. His grunts were swallowed as Reese began fucking him, driving in deep, punching his hips so Brantley felt every glorious inch of him.

There was a determination to Reese's movements that Brantley hadn't seen before. As though his goal was not only to bring them both to orgasm but to get as close as possible while doing so. More so than merely their bodies.

Reese was the one who broke the kiss, his head tipping back as he thrust again and again.

Brantley stared up at him, admiring the long column of his throat, the whiskered shadow along his jaw, the tendons that stood out in stark relief as though Reese was holding on by a thread. God, he was beautiful.

When Reese repositioned, hooking his arms behind Brantley's knees, Brantley gripped his cock and stroked in rhythm to the pounding he received. He stared down his body, watched as Reese slammed his hips down, driving in deeper, harder, faster.

His cock swelled and pulsed in his fist as he rode that fine line between ecstasy and orgasm. His skin tingled when the electrical spark lit deep within him, drawing his balls up tight to his body.

"Fuck!" Reese roared, slamming into him one final time.

It was that powerful emotion he felt in Reese's stare that sent Brantley over.

Their gazes held strong as their lungs labored to return to normal.

Before he'd come back to himself completely, Tesha's head appeared. She was standing on her hind legs, front paws on the mattress and staring at them like they'd lost their minds.

"Has she been there the whole time?" Brantley whispered, as though Tesha might be offended by the question.

"Probably." Reese chuckled. "But I think she's learned her lesson."

"What's that? To stay back until we're done?"

"Exactly." Reese smiled down at him. "I love you."

Brantley felt Reese's words deep in his soul, and like always, it turned on the light that had been dark for so long.

"I love you, too."

Because Tesha hadn't interrupted them, Brantley decided a run was in order after all. After pulling on clothes, they leashed her, then took off along their normal route. They ran in silence, Brantley using the time to clear his mind so he could focus on the tasks he needed to complete for the day.

Once they made it back, showers were taken and breakfast consumed before Brantley, Reese and Tesha ventured over to the barn. They found Trey and Baz standing over a dozen or so stacks of files, staring down at them as though they would perform tricks.

"Problem?" Reese asked as he headed over to join them.

Brantley started that way, but his phone buzzed, so he stopped to take the call.

"Governor?" Brantley greeted as he stared over at the whiteboard where JJ was adding something to a long list of what appeared to be names.

"I've got a case for you," Governor Greenwood relayed, his voice calm with only a hint of worry weaved in. "In Dallas. Young woman went for a run this morning, didn't return."

"Sounds relatively straightforward. Why us? They overloaded?"

"No. But I want eyes on this. Fresh ones. This isn't the first woman to go missing in the area and the cases continue to go unsolved. The mayor's worried because the FBI hasn't uncovered anything, either. I want you on this from the start."

"Who's handling it?" he inquired.

"DPD. The chief of detectives is expecting your call."

Snagging a pen and paper from Trey's desk, Brantley jotted down the phone number the governor provided, then disconnected the call.

He didn't wait to answer the questions he knew the team had before placing the call, not surprised when the man answered on the first ring. The pleasantries were exchanged before Chief Max Denver launched right into his reasons for wanting Brantley and his team there.

"Walker, I appreciate your urgency with this matter. How long before you can get to White Rock Lake?"

"Depends," he answered, propping himself on the edge of Trey's desk. "How fast do you need us there?"

"If I had my way, you'd already be here."

"Understood. How long's the woman been missin'?"

"She went out for her daily run at six this morning. Her husband called it in a little after eight after he'd gone out looking for her."

"He doesn't believe she ventured off on her own?"

"No. Six kids at home, the youngest is four months. Full-time mom, bigwig dad, happy home."

Did anyone ever describe it as anything other than? Brantley wondered.

"Any sign of foul play?"

"I'll be honest with you, Walker," Chief Denver stated. "Right now, we've got nothing. The more eyes we can get, the better."

"Why's that?"

The chief sighed heavily. "This is the fourth woman who's gone missing from this area in the past year."

"Any recovered?"

"No. Not dead or alive."

Son of a bitch.

Brantley glanced at his team. "We'll be up there as soon as we can. Let me secure travel, and I'll let you know when you can expect us."

"Good. We've already got a detective assigned to the case. John Collins. I'll make sure he's expecting you."

The call disconnected and Brantley immediately turned his attention to JJ. "Call and get the jet ready for Dallas. We'll need two vehicles when we get there."

"On it, boss."

"Reese, Trey, Baz, pack a bag."

"Got one in the truck," Baz announced.

Brantley grinned. "Good, then we won't need to waste any time. JJ, would you mind keepin' an eye on Tesha until we're back?"

"Not at all."

"Food's in the house," Reese informed her. "She's got some meds, too. I'll write it up for you."

Just under two hours later, Brantley was getting behind the wheel of a black Escalade while Reese was keying information into the navigation system. In a similar SUV, Baz and Trey were behind them.

"Cadillac," Reese said with approval. "Travis is gonna spoil you if he's not careful."

"I'm just waitin' for him to hit us with a bill." Gas wasn't cheap. Not for the jet or the cars.

"Detective Collins gonna meet us at the crime scene?" Reese asked.

"No. He said he's bogged down with paperwork, so I told him we'd come to him at his office."

"Out of curiosity, why're we bein' pulled into this one? Have they even had time to look for her?"

"This one fits into a pattern they've seen recently. The governor and mayor are worried."

"More than one?"

"At least four. Although Collins seems to think there's no way they can be related."

"Shit."

"My sentiments exactly."

"Sounds like it might not be a missing persons case," Reese noted.

Brantley agreed. Since no bodies had been found and there were four missing, it was difficult not to think serial killer. Kidnappings generally had reasons, most of them sexual assaults or ransom. If they were still being categorized as missing and nothing more, there was certainly a problem.

"If it isn't, we'll adapt. We go where the governor tells us to go," he said simply.

"Not complainin'," Reese said. "Just curious. So there is a crime scene?"

"I'm still confused on that. They've got a general area." Brantley steered the SUV onto Mockingbird Lane. They would drive right past the lake on the way to the precinct.

"Is it secured?"

"One can only hope." Brantley hadn't yet worked with DPD, but he prayed like hell they had a handle on their cases.

"These other women ... what makes the mayor think they're related if the detective doesn't?"

"Location, I think. According to what JJ got from Collins's notes, the four women who've gone missin' were all joggers, and after they disappeared, their cell phones were found with their headphones sittin' neatly on top of them."

"This guy wants them to know he's the one takin' them."

"That's my assumption, too." Brantley glanced over. "Only problem is, they didn't find a cell phone for the recent victim. So it's a big possibility it's not related."

"Well, let's assume it is. Does Collins have any leads?"

"Nothin' concrete. Despite them rampin' up video surveillance in the area, they've yet to catch any of the women comin' or goin'. But most of the cameras are set up in the parkin' areas. Since these women have all lived close enough they could walk, we don't know where he comes into contact with them, but he's abducting them somewhere along their path."

"And no one's seen anything?"

Brantley wasn't surprised by Reese's doubt. "No."

"It's a popular jogging trail?"

"From what I understand, yes. But it winds around, and the cell phones've been found in areas that aren't visible from the busy streets that surround it."

The conversation waned until they made it to the police precinct only for them to learn that Detective Collins had stepped away but he would be returning any minute now.

"Fine time for him to take a lunch break," Reese muttered under his breath.

"We can always go introduce ourselves to the man's boss." Brantley certainly wasn't above escalating when the situation warranted it.

It took asking a few people, but they finally learned which direction to go but before they got to their destination, they were approached by a dark-haired man wearing a light blue pin-striped shirt that was a size too big, the cuffs rolled up to his elbows, his dark blue tie partially undone.

"You Brantley Walker?"

"I am," Brantley confirmed. "And you are?"

"John Collins," he said, offering a hand. "Right this way."

Brantley wasn't sure what to make of the man, but he decided to give Detective Collins the benefit of the doubt. They followed him to his desk where he dropped down into his chair and began rummaging through folders, stopping when he found one with Henderson scribbled on the front.

"Mind if I take a look at that?" Brantley asked, nodding at the case file. "Do you think these women are targeted specifically?"

He passed it over but didn't look Brantley in the eyes.

"We've found no link between them," the man said, leaning back in his chair. "They live in neighborhoods that border the lake but not the same neighborhood. We don't have much on Jody yet, but as far as the other three go, I haven't even been able to put them at so much as the same coffee shop."

While he spoke, Brantley assessed him. Figured Collins for somewhere in his mid- to late-forties. Dark hair, receding hairline, dark eyes that showed a good many lines, a few days' worth of stubble on his jaw, unkempt to say the least. It was possible the stress of the job had made him age faster. Based on the disarray on his desk and the wrinkled state of his clothing, Detective John Collins was buried beneath cases. Why would they choose to assign this case to him, Brantley wondered.

"Your notes said they're sticklers for routine," Baz stated, stepping forward to look at the other files. "Did they jog at the same time every day?"

"Yes." Collins picked up another file. "Shelly and Debbie ran in the early mornings, like Jody. Maria in the evenings, after dark."

"Shelly Masters , Debbie Struthers, and Maria Espinoza?" Baz asked, raising the files he was holding.

Detective Collins nodded.

"Any similarities between the women? Does he have a type?" Trey inquired.

"They couldn't be more different," Detective Collins said, tossing the file back on the desk. "Shelly's Caucasian, five foot three inches, blond hair, blue eyes. Maria's Hispanic, five foot seven inches, dark brown hair, dark brown eyes. Debbie's African American, five foot five with black hair and light brown eyes."

Brantley saw the way Detective Collins spoke of these women. He didn't need to look at a piece of paper to know their height, weight, or eye and hair color. More than likely, he had pored over these cases for so long, he saw them when he closed his eyes. The women he was determined to bring home to the families who missed them.

What Brantley found interesting was that he was using only their first names. Maybe he felt as though he knew them since he'd been working the cases for so long.

"Jody's five foot eight, red hair, and green eyes," the detective noted, a tad too casually.

Again, Baz clarified, lifting another folder. "Jody Henderson?"

So clearly Baz had noted the oddity as well.

"Maybe it's the drastic differences he's attracted to," Trey noted.

Collins shrugged.

"Do you think these are crimes of opportunity?"

"Looks that way," he answered with a heavy exhale.

"And these women…" Brantley paused until Detective Collins met his gaze. "You said their bodies haven't turned up anywhere."

"These particular women, that's correct. However, my old partner thought it was a serial who snagged them. That maybe these aren't his first victims." The man lifted a notepad, grabbed a stack of photographs, and tossed them over.

Brantley knew what he would see when he looked at them, but he did so anyway. He took his time, memorizing the horror that this bastard had inflicted upon these women because he knew it would help him. It would be what drove him to find Jody Henderson before anyone could do the same to her.

"How long before their bodies appeared?" Baz asked, taking the pictures when Brantley passed them over.

"Those girls? Three hundred forty-seven days from the date of their disappearance."

"That's rather specific," Trey noted. "Intentional, obviously."

"Does he keep them alive during that time?" Reese asked.

"Yes. Each woman was kept alive until a few days before they were found." His eyes darted to all the faces around him. "According to the ME, of course."

"Any chance we can speak to your old partner?" Brantley asked, wondering if someone else might be able to shed some light on these cases.

Collins shook his head. "Up and moved to Montana. Said he was done with all this. Left no forwarding address, either."

Interesting.

"How much time do we have?" Reese asked.

"Shelly's been missing for three hundred and thirty-nine days."

Shit. That meant they needed to work fast. There were four women missing, possibly taken by the same man, and if they didn't find them soon, they would be dead.

Detective Collins met each face again. "If these are related, we don't know why he targets them, what he does with them, or what that timeline signifies, which is why my boss insisted we bring someone in to help. The FBI's been actively workin' the case, determined it's a serial killer, but he said the more eyes, the better."

Brantley understood the urgency but he wasn't so sure Detective Collins did. The man seemed a tad aloof for something that required immediate attention. After all, if this asshole stuck to his usual pattern, they only had a few days to find these women.

"WHERE TO FIRST?" TREY ASKED AS THE four of them walked out of the Northeast Dallas police station.

"The lake," Brantley and Baz said at the same time.

Reese agreed. They needed to see it firsthand, look for any clues that might help them to locate this woman. If they were lucky, some of the crime scene techs would still be there, possibly able to give them something to go on.

"Why isn't Collins at the scene? Or talkin' with the family?" Reese wondered aloud.

"Technically not a crime scene," Brantley noted. "As for the family … he's probably already covered it. It did take us some time to get here."

Yeah, maybe. But why didn't the detective mention it?

"You think they're right?" Trey asked. "These are related?"

"Not enough to tell right now," Baz said. "But the plan is to figure it out, right, boss?"

Brantley stopped, turned to Reese. "What do you think?"

He figured the man had heard the wheels turning in his head. "I get that we've got four missing women—at least that we know about right now—but I can't help but think we need to focus our efforts on Jody Henderson. She's only been missin' a few hours and hers is the warmest case we've got."

Brantley nodded. "Your theory bein' that, if we find her, we'll find the others?"

He met Brantley's gaze, held it. "Yeah."

"Good plan. Let's see if we can find ourselves a crime scene."

"We'll follow you," Trey said, splitting off toward their SUV with Baz beside him.

"Do you agree? Think we should keep the scope on Jody?" he asked Brantley when they got into the SUV.

"I do. According to Collins, these are crimes of opportunity, but I don't think so. If I'm right, it means Jody came into contact with her kidnapper at some point, somewhere. We backtrack through her last few days, we might just get a hit on something."

Reese liked the way Brantley's mind worked. They were similar in their thought processes, although he got the feeling he was able to take a further step back than Brantley was. Brantley's intensity was the reason he needed a team of people, not just one person to assist. With all their heads together, they had a much better chance of resolving this.

He only hoped like hell they could do it in time.

Fifteen minutes later, they were at the lake, walking the winding hard-packed dirt trail that circumvented it.

"This is where they found one of the other cell phones," Brantley said when he stopped near a towering tree, its branches bare, the leaves that had once adorned it littering the ground.

"How do you know?" Trey asked.

"Picture had that mile marker in it."

Reese remembered seeing it. He was impressed Brantley had been able to pick it out considering they'd been following the path for a half hour while crime scene techs continued to search the area for clues. There were a handful of gawkers standing in the parking lot, staring out at the scene, wondering what had happened, piecing together the puzzle in their mind based on things they'd seen on television or maybe even firsthand. If only one of them could know which direction Jody went, or a description of who she was with. Unfortunately, according to the two officers stationed at the entrance to the trail, no one had seen anything.

"Tell me what you see," Brantley urged Reese.

He took a deep breath. "Jody's out gettin' her mornin' exercise. Has her headphones in, lost in her own head because it's not only about exercise but about the escape. Six kids at home, this is her time alone."

"Good point," Baz noted. "That means she's comfortable here, uses it as her personal track. Probably doesn't pay much attention to those around her because she's interested in the independence and freedom. The few people she does see, she recognizes them. They're regulars out here."

"Keep goin'," Brantley encouraged them.

Reese turned, studied the wide-open space around them. "He didn't take her here. He would've taken her somewhere more private, which means he lured her away, likely talked her toward a more private spot, then knocked her out or whatever bastards like him do."

"So we're goin' with the assumption she knew him?" Trey asked, hands on his hips as he cast a skeptical glance at their surroundings.

"If so, she only recently met him," Brantley mused. "Probably pleasantly surprised to see him here, doesn't mind takin' a minute out of her day to say hello."

"Keep in mind, she's married. Six kids," Baz inserted. "Who would she be pleasantly surprised to see? She's not in the market for dates. Her youngest is four months."

"Doesn't necessarily mean she's happily married," Trey remarked. "But we'll go with your assumption."

Reese was curious as to what had jaded Trey, but he refrained from asking. Not the time or the place. Nor was it any of his business.

"No, not a man she's interested in datin'," Reese agreed. "But he has somethin' to offer. We need to talk to the husband, her friends, find out if there's somewhere she frequents. Her usual routine. Or maybe a place she recently discovered."

"So, he knows her, but we don't know how," Trey said aloud. "She recognizes him, considers him friendly. He lures her somewhere private, renders her unable to get away, and then what? Where—"

"We've got something over here!"

Reese turned along with Brantley, peering over to where a tech was kneeling on the ground near a dense thicket of brush.

As they approached the tech stood, placed a numbered marker down and began taking pictures from various angles.

"The cell phone?" Reese asked, his voice low. "I thought you said—"

"There wasn't one," Brantley finished for him before stepping closer to the tech. "How long've y'all been lookin' out here?"

"We started about an hour after the call came in."

"And you didn't go over this area yet?"

The woman glanced up at him. "We did, yes. This wasn't here."

Reese glanced around again, mentally taking note of anyone in the area. He only saw others wearing department issued uniforms and coats.

"We'll get this processed," an officer said when he neared.

Brantley nodded, then stepped back to stand with Reese. Baz and Trey had moved closer.

"No way to deny it's related now," Baz said.

Reese turned away from the area. "If he leaves this here, how did he get her away from here?"

"Only way would be to knock her out," Baz mused. "Six o'clock in the mornin' on a popular jogging trail… Gonna be a few runners out."

Reese nodded. "Agree."

"Okay. She's unconscious," Brantley decided. "Deadweight. So he has to carry her. Can't let anyone see him."

The four of them pivoted, scanning the area.

"He had to have a vehicle," Reese said.

"Yep. Somethin' to transport her in." Brantley pulled out his phone, dialed. "Hey, JJ. I need you to do a search of traffic cams in this area. See if we can get plate numbers for anyone who came and left the lake or the surrounding areas between five thirty and roughly seven thirty. We can track them down, see if they saw anything."

Reese wondered if that would be more difficult than it seemed. From what he could see, the lake was surrounded by neighborhoods and they weren't too far away from downtown. Probably a lot of morning traffic, people heading off to work within that time frame.

Reese continued to look around while Brantley rattled off the information they had so far on Jody Henderson. Whether or not JJ would find something, Reese knew it was a good starting point. After all, it had been through cameras that JJ had ultimately identified the woman who took Kate from the capitol.

"Yeah, that's the plan," Brantley was saying. "I'm gonna have Baz and Trey go talk to him. Reese and I will start knockin' on doors around here. A few houses back up to this area. Maybe someone saw somethin'."

After directing Baz and Trey, Reese followed Brantley to the SUV. They drove around to the row of houses that backed to the lake. He figured it was a long shot, but it had to be done. Perhaps someone had noticed a man and woman chatting. Or maybe even two women. He could've used someone as a lure. Or maybe their suspect was female. Although he wasn't leaning that direction considering the amount of effort it required to move a body.

However, it was too early to rule anything out.

"HOW LONG WERE YOU ON THE FORCE?"

Baz peered over at his passenger. He didn't know Trey all that well, but he had to admit, what little he'd been around him, he liked the guy. Like Brantley, Trey seemed the sort to go with the flow. Not led by ego. Unlike Brantley, he seemed to lack that intensity. Where Brantley had storm clouds in his eyes because of the hell he'd lived through during his career in the Navy, Trey's were likely more personal. It was in the way he assessed people, as though he wasn't exactly sure who to trust.

"I got two years of college right out of high school, then went to the academy. Spent a few years workin' the streets, then fast-tracked it to detective because of a task force I'd been selected for."

"You think you'll end up missin' it?"

"Doubtful. I don't see much of a difference between this and that."

"You work any homicides before?"

"No." And he wasn't sure how he felt about that now.

Granted, at the moment, he wasn't thinking about Jody Henderson as deceased. He was leaning on the positive, hoping she was alive and well and they were going to find her in time for dinner tonight.

Of course, he knew that wasn't likely—finding her so quickly—but sometimes a positive outlook was the only thing that got him through the day.

"How long you been datin' JJ?"

Baz grinned. "Not long. And don't let her hear you say we're datin'."

Trey laughed. "Oh, I know. The only way JJ'll be okay with datin' is if she decides that's what it is."

"You sound like you know her well."

"She's been Brantley's best friend for as long as I can remember. He dated her brother back in high school."

"She mentioned that."

"She's a good one, JJ." There was approval in Trey's tone. "A little flighty, but good in her bones."

Baz could feel Trey's eyes shift toward him.

"Don't worry, I won't poach. Not my type."

"You mean, she's female," he said easily.

"Exactly."

"JJ mentioned you were seein' Cyrus."

"You know Cyrus?"

"Met him at the bar one night when I was with the team."

Trey's gaze shifted out the window. "That's done."

He didn't sound happy about that, but Baz opted to let it go because they were pulling up to Dale Henderson's house.

"If you don't mind, I'm gonna let you lead on this," Trey stated when they'd exited the SUV and met around at the front. "I've had my fair share of conversations with people, both civilians and cops, but I'll admit, it's never been at this level. Last thing I want is to overlook somethin'."

"I'll lead, but if you have a question, feel free to ask it at anytime. The more information we can get out of him, the better."

Baz headed up the walk, taking in the house. It was in an older neighborhood, but it was meticulously maintained. Fresh coat of paint on the trim and shutters, shrubbery lining the front pruned to near perfection, still carrying most of its leaves despite the fact they were in mid-November.

He walked down the narrow walkway and up the three steps to the front porch. After knocking on the glass storm door, which was locked, he noticed, Baz took a step back, waited.

The door opened to reveal a frantic older man whose blue eyes were puffy and lined in red, his dark hair, sprinkled with gray, stuck up haphazardly on his head.

"Mr. Henderson?"

"Yes," he replied through the glass separating them.

"My name's Sebastian Buchanan and this is my partner, Trey Walker. We're with the OTB Task Force, assisting the police with the investigation. Would you mind if we come in?"

"I need to see some identification," he said warily.

Although they both wore their shields on their belts, they pulled out their credentials, held them up to the glass so Mr. Henderson could review. He must've been content with what he saw, because he unlatched the storm door and gave it a nudge. Baz opened it outward, then stepped inside, Trey directly behind him.

For a house with six children, it was in remarkable condition. The living room was open and airy, the furniture functional. To the right, there was a dining room where a long table sat, a hutch behind it, the lights inside glittering off crystal and china.

"Please tell me you know something," Dale pleaded, leading the way over to the table.

"Where are your children, Mr. Henderson?" he asked, not wanting them to overhear anything they shouldn't.

"My oldest daughter has them upstairs in the playroom. They're doing their lessons for today. They're homeschooled. My wife…" His voice wavered. "She usually handles that."

When the man began to fidget, Baz suggested they sit.

"Please," he said quickly, "let's go in the kitchen. Just in case one of the kids comes down."

"Of course."

The kitchen was like the living and dining rooms, tidy and gleaming. It was obvious it had been redone in recent years, because the modern decor and stainless steel appliances did not match the age of the house. And more than likely, a few walls had come down to open it up.

"We know you've answered questions already, but we need to go over everything again with you," Baz told him when they'd taken their seats.

"That's the thing," Mr. Henderson looked a bit wild-eyed, "no one's asked me anything."

"Excuse me?" Trey leaned in. "No one?"

Mr. Henderson shook his head. "My wife went for her morning jog, and when she didn't come back, I called the police. A uniformed officer came out, like he was confirming I was telling the truth. Told me the detective handling the case would be getting in touch." His eyes darted between the two of them. "I just assumed that's why you're here."

Baz glanced at Trey, frowned. For some reason, he'd gotten the impression Collins had already come out and spoken with the man. Based on the details he had about the family, anyway.

"Well, let's go through what happened this morning," Baz suggested.

Mr. Henderson nodded, seemed to compose himself. "As usual, Jody gets up at five every morning. Even weekends. She says it's important to maintain a routine so the body doesn't get confused." There was a wistful smile on his face. "I don't argue with her. She seems to know what she's talking about. I mean, look at this place. She keeps it in pristine condition, takes care of six children all day…" He met Baz's gaze. "I'm sorry."

"No," he said easily. "It's fine."

"Anyway, Jody got up at five. I was a bit slower getting out of bed, but by the time she was tucking her headphones in her ears, I had ventured in here for coffee." His gaze swung over to the sink. "She gave me a kiss on the cheek, said she'd be back in an hour, and practically bounced out the door. She's a morning person," he explained. "Me, not so much."

"So she left at the same time she does every day?"

"Yes. She's meticulous about her schedule. She has to be out the door by five twenty so she'll be back by six twenty. I leave for work at seven and she likes to have the kids downstairs by then, so she starts breakfast as soon as she walks in the door." His gaze shifted to the back door. "Only today, she didn't walk in the door."

"Has she ever run an errand after? Maybe she needed something from the grocery store."

"Her car's here," he said as though Baz was an idiot. "She doesn't drive to the lake, says she enjoys the scenic route out of the neighborhood."

Baz considered how long it had taken to get here, figured she must have cut through somewhere. "Are there walking trails in this neighborhood?"

Mr. Henderson nodded. "All three neighborhoods connect by some trails that were put in about a decade ago. They lead directly to the lake. That's the route Jody takes every day."

"Does she have a runnin' partner? Maybe someone she goes with on occasion?" Trey suggested.

"No. Jody likes to be alone. I even offered to start jogging with her but she told me that was her time." His eyes glistened with unshed tears.

Baz still had a million questions, and unfortunately, he knew this wasn't going to get any easier.

Not for Mr. Henderson.
Or his missing wife.

Chapter Thirteen

"HOW'D YOU FARE?" BRANTLEY ASKED WHEN REESE returned to the SUV after they'd completed their door knocks.

"Nothin'. Two houses, no one answered, no cars in the driveway. One, the woman said she works the night shift, didn't get home until after seven. The last one, a little old couple invited me in for coffee cake. I politely declined, and they assured me they hadn't been outside yet today. No one has cameras directed that way, if they have them at all. You get anything?"

"Nope." Brantley relaxed against the seat, resting his hands on the steering wheel. "Trey messaged me, said they're still talkin' to the husband, tryin' to get a list of her friends."

"Gotta start somewhere. In the meantime, I think lunch is in order," Reese said with a heavy exhale. "Give us some time to talk, pool our thoughts, and hear what the husband had to say."

The mere mention of food had Brantley's stomach rumbling. "Let me know where we're goin', then text Trey and have 'em meet us there when they're done."

Brantley drove, his thoughts scattered. This was always the daunting part of the investigation. Where to begin when there was someone out there, possibly injured, scared, fighting for their life. The thought of taking time for lunch felt like abandonment on his part. He could still remember the time he spent during that op gone sideways. Alone in that room beneath the house in the middle of a hot zone. Right before the place caved in on him. He'd feared his team wouldn't come, wouldn't be able to reach him. They hadn't known where he was, if he was even alive, yet he'd held out hope that someone would make the effort. He never should've doubted because they wouldn't leave a man behind.

What was Jody Henderson thinking? That she prayed her husband went looking? That he called the police? Surely she knew he would. Based on the minimal information Trey had relayed, Dale Henderson was beside himself with fear.

"There's an all-you-can-eat buffet just down the road," Reese said from beside him.

Brantley glanced over. "Hmm?"

"Lunch."

Oh, right. Lunch. All you can eat.

"About two miles down on the left," Reese directed, then began tapping out a text on his phone.

While Reese was still texting, Brantley's cell phone rang. He hit the button on the steering wheel to take the call through the speakers.

"Hey, JJ," he greeted.

"Y'all find anything yet?"

Brantley hated to dash the hope in her voice, but he answered with a glum, "No."

"Well, I've been doin' some research on my end," she explained. "I pulled together the details of the women Detective Collins said were missing. Did a side-by-side comparison."

"We already know they look nothing alike," he told her.

"No, they don't. And that's not all that's different. In fact, the only similarity is the proximity to the lake that they lived. Same general area. Anyway, as you know, Jody Henderson's a stay-at-home mom."

"Yes."

"She's thirty-two, married, with six kids," she continued.

Beside him, Reese was writing down the information she was rattling off.

There was a soft chuckle. "I'll shoot it to you, Reese. You don't have to write it down."

Reese looked up, peered around the truck as though he expected to find a camera. It was enough to have Brantley grinning.

"Then you've got Maria Espinoza," JJ continued, "twenty years old, student, no spouse, still lives at home with her parents and two younger siblings. Shelly Masters, forty-three years old, registered nurse, divorced single mom to two little boys. And last but certainly not least, Debbie Struthers, twenty-nine, junior partner at a prestigious law firm, lives with one female roommate."

"What you're sayin' is they couldn't be more different."

"From that angle, no," JJ said. "Different race, height, weight, shape, marital status. They're a very diverse group of women."

"What do they have in common besides their relatively close addresses and their jogging patterns?" Brantley asked.

"Children."

Frowning, he glanced at Reese, then back out the window as he pulled into the parking lot of the restaurant.

Reese skimmed his finger down the notepad he was holding. "You just said two of them don't have children."

"They don't. But they live with people who do. Maria Espinoza has two younger siblings, and Debbie Struthers's roommate has a three-year-old daughter."

"You think he's somehow connected to these kids?"

"I think it's possible," JJ said. "But I haven't had a chance to dig into everything yet."

"Well, keep diggin'. We're gonna stop for lunch, meet up with Trey and Baz, see what they found out from the husband."

"Okay. Keep me in the loop."

"Hey, JJ?" Reese said before she could disconnect.

"Yeah?"

"How's Tesha?"

Brantley couldn't stop his smile. He loved how much Reese loved that dog.

Her voice softened. "She's doin' great. She's here with me right now. We went outside a little while ago. I'll send over a pic."

"Not necessary, but thanks."

"Anytime. Talk to y'all in a bit."

The picture came through a couple of minutes later and yes, it made Reese smile, which in turn made Brantley.

A good half hour later, Brantley was sitting at a table with Reese, Trey, and Baz, the four of them finishing up their second and third helpings of food.

How was it you could go to an all-you-can-eat and always attempt to eat until you puke? Well, everyone except for Reese. He was the one who mentioned the place and he never ventured anywhere except for the salad bar.

Reese was telling Trey and Baz about JJ's theory that the missing women were somehow tied to this man through the kids.

"According to the husband," Baz said, "that's a good possibility. He said Jody spends a tremendous amount of time carting the kids around to various functions. Dance class, violin and piano lessons, painting, karate. You name it, I think their kids are doin' it."

"What about the social scene?" Reese asked. "Do they take the kids any one specific place?"

Trey spoke up. "Like those trampoline places or bounce house things?"

Brantley stared at his brother.

"What? I've taken Meghan, Ashley, and Eric a couple of times," he admitted, referring to their nieces and nephews.

Reese was jotting the information down. "The only way we'll find out is to talk to the families of the other victims."

"I can tell you, Mr. Henderson won't be much help," Baz told him. "He seemed clueless as to where Jody took the kids. At least specifically. I got the feelin' he spends a lot of time at work and she takes care of everything else."

"Like the house," Trey inserted. "Holy shit. If it weren't for the fact she was into workin' out, I would've thought she was a Stepford wife."

"One thing that bothered me," Baz noted, "was the fact Mr. Henderson said no one but an officer had been by to talk to him."

Brantley frowned. "Not Collins?"

"He said he called the police and they sent an officer out, but they told him they'd be in touch. We were the first to make face-to-face since."

Reese leaned back. "Maybe Collins is overloaded, had the uniform go out in his place."

"Maybe." Baz appeared disturbed ty the idea. "But his top priority should be the hot case. It's true what they say about the first forty-eight hours. That's critical time to piece together clues."

"Well, that's why we're here. I say we split up the families of the other victims," Brantley suggested, "go pay them a visit, see if they might be able to provide some puzzle pieces. Then we'll split up Jody's list of friends, reach out to them, see if they can shed any light."

"Sounds like a plan," Trey and Baz said at the same time.

Reese merely offered a nod of his head.

And now they had their next step.

"YOU KNOW, TESHA, IT'D PROBABLY BE GOOD to have some warm bodies in this place," JJ told the dog as she stared at her computer screen. "Seems a little too quiet without them here, doesn't it?"

She probably should've felt strange to be talking to a dog, but considering there was no one else to talk to, or to overhear, she didn't much care. Plus, Tesha was a damn good listener. Especially after she'd ventured over to the house, retrieved one of three dog beds Brantley and Reese had stashed in different rooms, and relocated it to her new loft office. Three. Seriously. They'd had Tesha a week and she was already spoiled.

However, she did seem content with the bed. Ever since they returned, she'd been snoozing away beside her. Every so often, Tesha would open an eye, peek up at her as though to ensure she was still there.

"Too bad I had to reschedule the interviews," she told him. "But it's probably smart to have someone around when I invite a stranger here, huh?"

JJ stared at her computer screen, at the images of the four women who'd gone missing. They were all attractive, albeit a little plain, but there wasn't a single thing about them that was similar. So what did they have in common? Besides the fact they all liked to jog and there were children that resided in their orbit. How would this person—because yes, it could still be a woman as far as she was concerned—come in contact with them and know they all utilized the same jogging path? That was the key, she knew. Something about the jogging path. Or the location as a whole.

As she stared, her cell phone rang, startling both her and the dog.

"Shit," she mumbled to Tesha. "Sorry, honey. I'll turn the ringer down. Hello."

"Hey," she greeted Baz.

The deep, resonant voice on the other end somehow managed to soothe her nerves. It was almost instant, too, something she wasn't used to.

"Hey. Sorry, I don't have anything else on—"

"I'm callin' to check on you, JJ. Not about the case."

"Oh." She smiled, relaxed in her comfy chair. "I'm fine. Me and Tesha are just hangin' out. I hear you've partnered up with Trey."

"Yep."

"What do you think? He gonna cut it?"

"Yeah. Takes him some time to warm up, but I think he'll be fine once he's been doin' this for a while. But he's honest about it. That's the key."

"He's a good guy," she told Baz. "Solid."

He chuckled, the soft rumble making her belly clench. "That's the same thing he said about you."

"Really?" They had talked about her? "I love Trey."

"Hey, now."

She giggled. "He's gay, remember? I'm not his type."

"Today," he stated. "Who knows what tomorrow might bring?"

"You know it's not a choice, right?"

"Have you met Reese?"

JJ laughed. "He's an anomaly."

"I was hopin' to take you out tonight."

His comment caught her off guard, but it brought another smile to her face. Perhaps it was because he was so far away that she realized how much she missed him being around.

"Rain check."

"I'm gonna hold you to that."

He would, she knew.

Her body suddenly warmed as she remembered the kiss they'd shared, the way his work-rough hands had slipped beneath her T-shirt, sliding sensually over her skin.

"JJ? You okay?"

Shit. She was breathing heavily.

"Good," she said, coughing to clear her throat. "Great."

"How 'bout I call you tonight? We can talk more."

"I'd like that."

And she realized she really, really would.

Provided she could keep the call PG. God only knew what she was capable of when it came to Sebastian Buchanan.

Ugh.

"WHERE'RE WE HEADED?" BRANTLEY ASKED ONCE THEY'D made it back to the SUV after lunch.

"I got an answer from Debbie Struthers's mother," Reese told him. "I think she was surprised to get my call. Said she's been waiting tirelessly since her daughter went missing on March eighteenth."

"She hasn't heard from anyone?"

"According to her, no. She's left messages for the detective and he's left a couple in return, but they've never actually spoken."

Brantley glanced over at him. "Are you tellin' me she hasn't spoken to Detective Collins face-to-face?"

"That's what she said."

"Hmm." Brantley steered the truck out onto the road. "I think that's somethin' we have to look into."

"Agree. Maybe we can stop by and chat with the detective after."

Brantley nodded.

They rode in silence for a few minutes, Brantley following the directions provided by the navigation system. While Debbie Struthers lived in a house near the lake, her mother resided roughly thirty minutes north of her daughter.

The neighborhood they pulled into wasn't anything fancy. In fact, it looked a bit run down, the houses older, the cars, too. It gave the impression it was a street occupied mostly by renters rather than owners.

"This is it," he said, pointing to a single-story tan brick house with dark brown trim and an inset porch.

There were bushes lining the front of the house, covering all the windows. The grass had seen better days, withering but not only from the cold spells they'd had lately. The sidewalk was cracked and broken, as was the walkway leading up to the house.

At the door, Brantley took the lead, ringing the doorbell and taking a step back.

It didn't take long for the door to be answered by a woman who was quite a bit younger than Brantley had expected. Debbie Struthers showed to be twenty-nine years old, and he figured her mother was barely over fifty. She was a tiny woman with dark skin and dark hair that she wore brushed into a bun at the back of her head. Her eyes were a little wide, her lips a little small, and she looked none too happy to see them.

Brantley held up his credentials and Reese followed suit, then they were let into the house, the door closing behind them.

It was a dark space, no light in the wide hallway.

The place was relatively clean. Not spotless and not cluttered but there were a couple of dishes sitting on various surfaces, some books stacked in the corner, the fireplace screen crooked where it sat on the hearth.

"We can talk in here," Mrs. Struthers said.

Reese followed them into a dining room on the right. There was a table in the center of the space, two windows high up on the far wall, a door that appeared to lead into the kitchen on the left.

He was about to sit when he noticed a huge corkboard mounted on the other wall. Pinned to it were various pictures, the missing poster that had likely been distributed when Debbie first went missing.

"I've done quite a bit of work," Mrs. Struthers noted. "Figured since the police won't do anything, someone had to."

Reese noticed the hostility in her tone, couldn't really blame her.

"Do you mind?" he asked, motioning toward the board.

"Not at all."

While Brantley and Mrs. Struthers sat down at the table, Reese took stock of what was on the board. There were pictures of the lake and the surrounding areas, one of what looked to be the crime scene photo showing Debbie's cell phone and headphones.

"Mrs. Struthers, could you tell me when the last time you spoke to Detective John Collins was?"

"Please call me Alicia," she said softly, then sighed. "It would've been probably a week after Debbie went missing. I called him. He must've been having an off day because he actually answered the phone."

"Have you spoken to him in person? At the station, maybe?"

Reese glanced over to see her reaction.

Mrs. Struthers was frowning. "I tried. Three times. I was always told he was out and it would be best to reach him by telephone."

Reese did not like the sound of that. Granted, he wasn't a police officer, but he couldn't imagine the detectives were never available to speak one on one with the families of the victims they were working for. He would have to ask Baz about that.

While Brantley began asking questions pertaining to the day Debbie disappeared, Reese turned back to the board on the wall. He noticed what looked to be red yarn was strung from one pin to another in a couple of places. If he was correct, Mrs. Struthers was noting that those two things connected somehow. As much as he admired all the work she had done, there really wasn't much to go on.

He was about to turn around and take a seat when he noticed a piece of paper peeking out from beneath another one. He lifted the top one to read what it was.

Police report. Dated March fourth of this year.

"Ma'am?" Reese glanced back at her, tapped a finger on the paper. "Can you tell me what this is?"

"It's the police report my daughter filed."

"It says it was filed two weeks before her disappearance."

Mrs. Struthers nodded but she appeared disappointed. "Can't find that it's relevant, but I figured it was worth noting."

Reese read the complaint and he wasn't so sure that was an accurate assessment.

"Would you mind if I took a picture of this?" he asked.

"Go right ahead."

Since she gave him the go-ahead, he took a picture of the page, then several pictures of the entire board.

He hoped like hell it would give them some sort of clue they could follow.

After spending the afternoon talking to the distraught families of the other victims and three of the four friends of Jody Henderson's from their list, Reese was glad to be at a hotel. He needed time to process what he'd learned, but more importantly, he needed a minute to come back to himself. He'd spent all that time putting himself in the shoes of those women and their loved ones, experiencing the hell they'd been going through for so long.

"You okay?" Brantley asked, stepping out of the bathroom, a towel wrapped around his hips, steam billowing out from behind him.

"I will be." Reese peered up. "Does it feel wrong to be sittin' here? While those women are missin'?"

"Of course it does." Brantley walked around, leaned against the dresser, crossing his arms over his chest. "But what other choice do we have? Stayin' up all night won't get us anywhere. We need to start fresh in the mornin'."

Yeah, he knew that. He did.

Brantley dropped his arms, planted his palms on the dresser. The move had the muscles in his chest flexing, his abs contracting. There were drops of water trickling down over the planes and angles, mesmerizing Reese momentarily. Funny how he was so easily distracted by this man.

"I told Trey and Baz I'd meet them down in the bar for a drink. You wanna join us?"

Reese forced his gaze to Brantley's face. "What?"

"Bar? Drink?"

"Yeah, sure. In a little while. I'll shower, meet you down there."

Reese could see the concern in Brantley's eyes, but he simply nodded, then reached for his bag, retrieving clothes. While Brantley got dressed, Reese went into the bathroom, turned on the shower.

He let the hot water beat down on him while he focused on breathing, clearing his mind. It didn't take long before he felt more like himself. The moment he stepped into the empty room, he realized he really did want to go down and have a drink with Brantley. Hell, he just wanted to be where Brantley was. Especially at a time like this.

The heater kicked on, rattling the metal grate that covered it, and the sound was so loud in the otherwise silent room it made him flinch. He was instantly taken back to a different place, a similar sound that had ground through his brain for months on end. A generator, not a heater. Endless noise. It had run constantly, powering the tents that had surrounded the concrete cell buried partially below ground that he'd been forced to live in. It'd been no more than six by six, and he'd spent months waiting and hoping, praying like hell he wasn't forgotten.

His brain kicked him back to the present, to the hotel room. Reese took deep, cleansing breaths, forcing the memories away, willing his heart to stop the drumbeat in his chest.

Shaking off the memory, praying a nightmare didn't follow tonight, Reese snagged clothes from his bag.

After dressing, he grabbed his cell phone and wallet, tucked them into his pockets.

He'd just stepped on the elevator when his phone buzzed. He checked it and a smile instantly came to his lips.

The picture was of Tesha, sitting obediently on the floor, staring up at the camera as though it was a treat. A text message followed: I don't think she knows what to do without you here. She keeps searching the house like you're playing a game.

Reese didn't realize how attached he'd gotten to Tesha until that moment.

His phone buzzed again: I was thinking we should get her certified in search and rescue. Then you'll have your very own four-legged partner.

The elevator doors opened and he stepped out. He was obviously grinning like a lunatic, because Brantley looked over, his brows furrowing.

They met halfway between the elevators and the bar.

"You look different than when I left you," Brantley said in greeting.

He held up the picture to show him.

"I should've known. And here I thought I was the love of your life."

"It's a tie."

A sharp bark of laughter escaped Brantley. "I'll take it. But like I said before, only because I'm the one who sleeps with you every night. You want a beer? Somethin' stronger?"

"Beer's fine." He had no intentions of getting drunk. And for some reason, Tesha had managed to soothe those rough edges he'd had after this hellish day.

While Brantley went up to the bar, Reese took a seat at the table Baz and Trey occupied. There were only six or eight more tables in the entire space and all were empty except for one other. Not a lot of business at this particular establishment, but he figured that was because it wasn't a five-star hotel, nor was it in a hot spot for nightlife.

"You can't be serious," Trey was saying to Baz. "Married six times? What the fuck is wrong with him? I learned my lesson after the first."

"Didn't end well, huh?"

Trey shook his head, glanced over at Reese briefly before turning his attention back to Baz. "Let's just say he wasn't quite ready to settle down."

"How long were you married?" Reese inquired, curious.

"The longest two and a half years of my life."

"Ouch." Baz took a sip of his beer. "How long ago?"

"Not long enough."

"So you kicked Cyrus to the curb, huh?"

"More him bootin' me, but the outcome's all the same."

Reese wanted to ask what had happened but held his tongue. It wasn't his business.

"Cyrus prefers the single life," Trey noted. "More specifically, he's more interested in a different man every week."

Brantley returned, passing over more beers before taking a seat beside Reese.

"Ain't that right?" Trey asked Brantley.

"What?"

"Cyrus is better off single."

"Sounds to me like you're bitter," Brantley countered.

Trey gave him the finger. "He's takin' a job in California."

"He's not the sort to settle down, but I figured you knew that. It was your reason for hookin' up with him in the first place. No strings," Brantley said without heat. "You can do better than Cyrus."

"Trust me, I intend to. A hundred times over," Trey grumbled, leaning back and taking a long pull on his beer.

The conversation shifted to work, about the plans for tomorrow, thoughts about the detective on the case, and was it possible they'd be home for Thanksgiving. After two beers, Reese was relaxed enough he was ready for sleep, so he excused himself up to the room with Brantley not far behind.

When Brantley crawled into bed beside him, Reese turned his way, found him in the dark. Their mouths melded together, tongues exploring as the temperature in the room soared. And when Brantley urged him onto his stomach, Reese went willingly, eager to feel him, to be one with him.

"I love bein' inside you," Brantley breathed against his neck. "Let me have you, Reese."

"Always."

After some preparation, Brantley twined their fingers and pinned him to the mattress, pushing in deep, filling him slowly. Reese relaxed, accepting Brantley inside him, loving how perfect he felt with this man. Complete. Whole. Something he'd never known before. Not until Brantley.

They moved together for long minutes as the pleasure soared to a crescendo.

Brantley nipped his shoulder, his voice nothing more than a rough whisper. "I'm gonna come, Reese. Oh, fuck." He grunted and groaned, then rocked into him one final time.

When Brantley pulled out, Reese rolled to his back, gripped his cock in his fist, and jerked roughly. Brantley's hand slid up his thigh, his finger brushing his balls, and Reese lost it. He came with Brantley's name on his lips.

Chapter Fourteen

Monday, November 23, 2020

BY THE END OF THE DAY MONDAY, Brantley was feeling the pressure and no closer to finding Jody Henderson, or any of the others, despite the effort they'd put in for the past three days.

Brantley and his team had talked to people who knew the victims or came into contact with them due to their routine, going over the case files, which were surprisingly detailed without having much information at all. He was even able to have a sit-down with the FBI's special agent in charge of the case but hadn't learned much of anything from her. He got the feeling the feds didn't play well in the sandbox, and since Brantley's team was above and beyond law enforcement, at least in the great state of Texas, they seemed overly irritated that he was pushing so hard for a resolution.

Which was why Brantley decided to forgo the FBI and the police department and run his case independent of both. He took what data he could, had JJ weed through it to pull out the pertinent details, then they started knocking on doors. Residences, businesses. They visited every place these women had frequented, never finding any that overlapped between them.

Thanks to a preliminary deadline set based on what Detective Collins had told them, they were running out of time.

Because they'd exhausted their efforts where visiting friends, families, and co-workers were concerned, Brantley decided to send Trey and Baz back to Coyote Ridge. No sense paying a hotel expense when they could sleep in their own beds. Rather than use the jet, they set out mid-afternoon, adding a couple hundred miles to the odometer of the rental car. A text from Baz had confirmed they'd just made it back and he was heading to HQ to look in on JJ, see if she needed anything.

Brantley wasn't an idiot. He knew Baz had far more interest in his best friend than merely her well-being. Then again, because of that interest, Baz was likely more concerned about her. There was no denying he was glad to know JJ had someone looking out for her. Someone who was not that douchebag Dante Greenwood. Considering that idiot couldn't look out for his own damn self, he was of no use to JJ. Baz, on the other hand, was proving to be worth his salt.

Now, as Brantley sat on the hotel bed, leaning against the headboard, legs out in front of him, he added a few things to his to-do list for JJ, hoping with Baz and Trey there to help her, she could dig a little deeper into these women's pasts. At some point, they had crossed paths with the same man. The question was when and where. Once they figured that out, they would be that much closer to finding them.

"I was thinkin' we could take a couple of hours to relax. Meet up with Z and RT for dinner."

Brantley looked up, processed Reese's words. "Your brother?"

"Yeah. He happens to be in town right now. I thought it'd be good to introduce you."

"You remember I went to high school with him, right?"

"Right." Reese appeared hesitant, as though Brantley's statement had been a refusal to go to dinner.

Brantley dropped his feet to the floor, stood. "I'm happy to have dinner with your brother. What about your sister? And your mom? You wanna see them while we're in town?"

"Thought about it," Reese said, grabbing his boots to pull them on. "But they're in Tahoe. Girls' trip. Skiing and gambling, my mother said."

"Well, that's too bad. For us. For them, it sounds like a good time."

"My mom's not a big gambler and she hates the cold. If I had to guess, they're holed up in a cabin, sitting in front of a fire, and enjoying a break from the real world."

"To each his own. I'll have to wait until Christmas to meet them." He grabbed his wallet, tucked it into his pocket. "So where're we goin' for dinner?"

"Their place."

"Oh, yeah?" Brantley grinned. "They trust me enough to invite me into their house, huh?"

"They're armed to the teeth," Reese said easily. "They aren't worried about much."

That was something Brantley had in common with them.

Because he knew the area better than Brantley and seemed to have an idea of where they were going, Brantley let Reese drive. While he did, Brantley exchanged a few text messages with JJ, asked how Tesha was doing so he could relay the information to Reese. He knew his man was worried about the dog and part of him wished they'd brought Tesha along for the trip. He got the feeling Tesha would be a good partner for Reese.

"You're not the least bit nervous, are you?"

Glancing over, he studied Reese's profile. "Should I be?"

"I was a basket case when it came to meetin' your parents."

Brantley turned his attention back to the window. "I mean, if you want, I could stutter when I talk to Z."

"I did not stutter," Reese said on a rush of air, his forehead creased with worry when he looked over. "Did I?"

"No. Well ... not much, anyway." He laughed, couldn't help it. "Kidding. You did fantastic."

Reese's sigh of relief made Brantley's heart swell. He didn't want Reese to be nervous around his family, but he couldn't deny that it was the little things that he'd fallen for. Reese's vulnerability was part of it. Mainly because he knew it was a rare characteristic, one that only came out when Reese truly cared about something.

Brantley rested his arm on the center console, turned his palm up, and wiggled his fingers.

Reese glanced down, over to Brantley's face, then back to the road. And when their fingers twined, he wondered if Reese felt as secure in their relationship as he did.

AS WAS ALWAYS THE CASE, AT LEAST since he'd been an adult, Reese was thrilled to see his brother. More so these days because it was such a rare occurrence. Back during their father's last days, they'd spent quite a bit of time in one another's presence, talking about the past, laughing about their childhood antics. Despite the depressing nature of the encounter, Reese looked back fondly at the memories. No doubt about it, he'd always looked up to his big brother.

"Well, I'll be damned, Walker," Z greeted when he stepped out onto the front porch. "I think you mighta grown since high school."

Brantley laughed, held out a hand. "I could say the same to you. What are you? Seven feet tall?"

"A few inches shy." Z turned to Reese. "Hey, little brother."

A hug ensued because that was what Z did. At least with those he was close to. Reese figured by the end of the evening, Z would be hugging Brantley goodbye. He considered how Brantley would react. Go with the flow, that was what he would do, because he was smooth like that. Nothing seemed to faze him with the exception of nightmares and migraines, both of which were reoccurring at a rapid pace.

"Well, come on in. RT's in the kitchen."

"Cookin'?" Brantley asked, just as at ease with Z as he seemed to be with everyone else.

Reese certainly envied his ability to interact with anyone and everyone.

"Hell no," Z answered with a chuckle. "We ordered out. But I'm sure he's dishin' it up in order to pass it off as home cooked. Never really understood that myself. What if it tastes like shit and you passed it off as your own? Screwed the pooch, right?"

Reese grinned. It was good to see Z so laid-back, so … happy.

RT looked up when they stepped into the kitchen, smiled. "Hey."

Ryan Trexler looked the same as he had every other time Reese had seen him. Blond hair, ice-blue eyes, and a build that leaned more toward a swimmer than a gym rat, RT was a handsome man, something Reese had always thought. Granted, it had never been from an interested perspective and it still wasn't. Try as he might, Reese hadn't met a man who'd caught his eye. Not the way Brantley had.

"Brantley, meet my husband slash boss, Ryan Trexler. RT for short. Babe, meet Brantley Walker. My little brother's main squeeze."

Reese felt his face heat but heard the relaxed chuckle from Brantley. He'd known going in that this would be uncomfortable, but he had vowed to get through it for Brantley's sake. Last thing either of them needed was for Reese to let his nerves get the best of him. This was a judgment-free meal and he would do well to remember that.

"It's good to meet you," Brantley said, shaking RT's hand. "Heard a lot of good things."

"About him?" Z asked, turning to Reese. "You talk about my man?"

The teasing in his tone was meant to put Reese at ease and it worked. "If there was anything good about you, I'da talked more about you, but…" He shrugged a shoulder.

Z laughed. "Go sit down."

"I was referrin' to Sniper 1 Security," Brantley clarified as the two of them sat at the table while Z and RT set down full plates at all four spots. "Heard a lot of good things."

"We aim for good press," RT replied with a grin. "Family business and all."

Z pointed at Brantley, then to the refrigerator and back again. "Somethin' to drink? Beer? Wine? Water?"

"I'll take a beer," Brantley said easily.

When Z looked Reese's way, he nodded in agreement.

"I was wonderin'," Z said, his expression thoughtful, "does it make the Tavoularis men the submissive sort since we seem to fall for our bosses?"

Again, Reese's face flamed, but he managed a response. "In my defense, Brantley wasn't originally my boss."

"I'm still not," Brantley said, glancing over. "I consider us equals. He's my partner. Hell, he's probably more competent than I am when it comes to runnin' a team."

"Says the decorated Navy SEAL," Reese countered. "Master chief if I recall correctly."

He got a wink from Brantley and he suspected it was meant as warning he would get payback later.

"Thank you for your service," Z said, his tone serious.

"Yes, thank you," RT added when he joined them at the table. "So, tell me what this task force entails."

The four of them started to eat, the conversation moving steadily as they did. Brantley filled them in on how the task force came about, their first cases.

"Talk about trial by fire," RT stated. "First case involved your family?"

"My cousin, yeah." Brantley took a bite, chewed. "It was instinct. I didn't think about what needed to be done, I just did it. Reese was right there with me."

Reese could feel Z's eyes on him, knew his brother was watching. They'd never discussed what had happened to him during his time in the air force, but he knew his brother believed something had happened.

Thankfully, the topic shifted to their current case, and RT and Z were riveted.

"Four women." Z seemed to mull over the information. "In a year, you said?"

"Yep." Brantley took a swig of his beer. "All abducted at the lake, all during their daily run."

"The only connection we've made," Reese explained, "is that each woman lived in a household with a child. Sister's kid, roommate's, their own. But our investigation's given us no clue that they actually met this person because of a child."

"Grocery store?" Z mentioned.

"Nope. According to their family members, they shopped at different places."

"Gas station?" RT said.

"Same. Not that we could find."

"Bank? Dry cleaners? Gym?" Z took a swallow of beer. "Liquor store? Coffee shop? Ice cream? Donuts?" He grinned. "Sorry. Just thinkin' about the places I frequent."

Reese shook his head with amusement, as did RT.

"Police department?" RT glanced between the two of them.

Brantley was the one to respond. "You mean for an issue?"

"Yeah. Traffic violation, court date, complaint."

Reese glanced at Brantley and a surge of hope flared inside him. "The complaint Debbie Struthers filed."

"Oh, damn. Didn't think about that," Brantley answered, evidently thinking about it now. "We'll look into that."

"You said the detective mentioned his ex-partner thought it was a serial? That these women aren't the guy's first?" RT said, glancing between the two of them

"That's what he said," Brantley confirmed, "but the old partner's not around for us to talk to."

"You track him down?"

"Not yet. But I think it's a trail we'll have to follow."

Reese glanced at Brantley. "That's interesting."

All eyes turned to him.

"What's that?" Brantley asked.

"Baz and Trey mentioned the victim's husband said no one had come to take his official statement. No one other than the initial uniform. But that doesn't jibe with the detective's notes. He had a lot of information for someone who hadn't paid a visit to the family yet."

"What're you thinkin'?" RT inquired. "That the detective might be involved?"

"I don't want to think that," he said quickly, "but there's been an itch between my shoulder blades since I met the guy."

"Go with that," Z stated firmly. "In this line of work, the gut's rarely wrong."

Brantley was staring at him. No, studying him seemed a more accurate description.

When Brantley looked away, he was reaching for his phone, pushing his chair back. "If you'll excuse me, I need to make a call."

"I like him," Z said when Brantley left the room.

RT laughed. "You say that like Reese needs your approval."

"He does." Z shot him a beaming grin. "He's my kid brother."

Reese laughed, relaxing. "I like him, too."

It still felt awkward to say it aloud, but it was getting easier. Reese found the more he ignored his own nerves, the doubt that crept in at the most unexpected moments, and focused on the fact he truly loved Brantley, the more he didn't feel the need to hide. Not entirely, anyway.

Admittedly, he'd been nervous to see Z. Mostly because he feared what he would see in his brother's eyes. Did he doubt Reese could truly fall for a man when he'd never been interested in men before? He should've known it wouldn't matter to Z. Hell, he'd always been Reese's rock, the one looking out for him, the one he could talk to. There were a few years between them, but since he went into the air force, Z had been the one he kept in touch with most. More so than even his mother. Reese wasn't sure why that was, either.

Footsteps sounded behind him, then Brantley reappeared, taking a seat.

"Sorry about that. I called JJ, told her to dig up whatever she could on the detective and to look into the possibility of police reports."

"I could be way off base on that," Reese said defensively. The last thing he wanted to do was point the finger at an innocent man. Much less a police officer.

"It's an avenue worth pursuin'. If it doesn't pan out, at least we can say we covered all the bases."

"If there's anything we can do to help out, just holler," RT said. "We've got some resources you may not."

"I appreciate that," Brantley told him.

"How about dessert?" Z offered. "RT made Jack Daniels pecan pie."

"I never turn down dessert," Brantley said, winking at Reese again.

By the time they made it back to the hotel, Reese could tell Brantley'd gotten his second wind. Probably didn't help that JJ was blowing up his phone with information. So much so, Brantley had called to let her know they'd do a FaceTime call to get it all sorted.

Now that they were in their room, Brantley had set up his laptop on the desk, and JJ's face was plastered on the screen, her eyes flashing with fire. Every so often, Reese would see Baz move behind her.

"I think you're on to somethin' here, Reese. Not sure what gave you the heebie-jeebies with this guy, but you hit the mark."

Heebie-jeebies? Reese wasn't even sure what that was.

"What'd you find out, JJ?" Brantley asked, watching the screen intently.

"From a psychological perspective, guy's got all the necessary triggers for a serial killer."

"Since when are you a psychologist?" Brantley asked.

"Oh, you know, I study up in my spare time." She grinned. "I'm not. And that was me bein' facetious. I mean, a lot of us had a shitty childhood. Doesn't mean we're gonna resort to routinely killin' people."

Reese admired Brantley's patience. It was obvious he was on a hair's trigger, but he wasn't rushing her. Too much.

"Anyway," JJ continued. "Johnathan Jacob Collins, forty-five years old, grew up in and around Dallas. Spent his childhood in Pleasant Grove. His mother and father separated when he was four, divorced by the time he was five. He lived with his mother until he was twelve, when he went to stay with his grandparents. I think CPS might've been called in a couple of times, but it looks like someone tried to redact the details."

"CPS?" Brantley asked. "Child protective services?"

"One and the same," JJ confirmed. "Neither Mom nor Dad held jobs or stayed in one place for long, so I figure it's not a leap that they didn't bother to take care of their child. Volatile relationship from what I've read. Quite a few run-ins with the law for drugs. Mostly marijuana."

Reese didn't like where this was going.

"When his grandparents died, John couch-hopped until he graduated from high school." Her eyes lifted to the screen. "At least that's what his juvie file says. And aside from this, there isn't much documented on him."

"Juvie? He's got a record?"

"Sealed, so I don't have exactly what's on it, but from the gist of what I've found, the guy roughed up his girlfriend a time or two. They chalked it up to teenage hormones. According to some notes, he's got one younger brother, Jake, I think it was, who lives with him. Looks like John took care of him growin' up. Notes show the brother's got some mental issues."

"You said he couch-hopped durin' high school," Brantley noted. "What'd he do with the brother?"

"Actually, there's nothin' I can find referrin' to the brother. Maybe he lived with another family member? Says his mom had a brother."

"Had? Where is he now?"

"Dead. Hit-and-run accident about two miles from the house he lived in. The house was left to John because there was no other family." She peered back down, Reese assumed to read from something. "After high school, John got just enough college credit to get him into the police academy. Worked patrol in the same area he grew up until he made detective."

"When did that happen?" Reese asked.

JJ's light green eyes sparkled. "Three years ago."

"And you said he's forty-five?"

"Yep. But get this," she said, her tone growing more excited. "I did some diggin' in and around the area he patrolled, and during the time he was on the street, there were eight women who went missin'. Age and race vary drastically, like the women we're lookin' for now. Eight women over the course of thirteen years."

"Probably spaced just enough not to connect the dots," Brantley mumbled.

"Where has he lived since he became a detective?" Reese asked, seeing a strange pattern forming.

JJ tapped the keys, her eyes swinging to the top of the screen. "It says…" Her eyes widened as she looked back at them. "In the same neighborhood as Jody Henderson."

"Not a coincidence," Brantley stated.

"And during the time he's been a detective? How many women have gone missin' in his area?" Reese asked.

"Eight."

"Holy fuck," Brantley breathed. "He's poachin' women in the neighborhood where he lives and works."

Yes, it certainly looked that way to Reese.

Chapter Fifteen

"I WANT MORE ON THE BROTHER," BRANTLEY demanded, processing all the information JJ had relayed. "Plus, I need you to track down anyone Collins previously partnered with. And send me the link to your notes. We need to read through them again."

"Sure thing, boss. I'll call you back in a bit."

Brantley disconnected the video call, got up to pace the floor.

"We need to talk to the officers who answered these calls, the ones who went to the houses. I want to know why they were sent instead of a detective."

Reese sat on the edge of the bed. "What I want to know is, how did Collins get assigned to all of these cases? Was it by chance? Rotation? From what the families said, they called in to report the women missing. Considering how overworked Collins says he is, how did he end up with Jody Henderson's case?"

"Wait." Brantley stopped moving. "You said the families reported them missing?"

"Correct. All four of their families confirmed that."

"So who found the cell phones and headphones at the lake?"

Reese's eyebrow lifted as he stood. "Good question."

Brantley resumed pacing when Reese took a seat at the small desk and began typing something on the computer.

"Jody Henderson's husband said he went lookin' for her," Brantley said, recalling what Trey had told him. "Did he find the cell phone?"

"Collins doesn't have any notes regarding who found them, but he does reference that they have them in evidence."

"That doesn't make any damn sense. Either he's a shitty detective"—he turned to look at Reese—"or he's coverin' somethin' up."

"Or both," Reese muttered.

"I want to see them." Brantley wasn't sure what they would tell him, but he needed to see those damn cell phones for himself.

"Right now?"

"Why the hell not?"

They were in the SUV heading back to the Northeast substation ten minutes later. While Brantley drove, his mind churned through the information. He was vaguely aware of Reese talking on the phone with JJ.

How the hell did they have cell phones and headphones when the families were the ones to report the women missing? Who knew to go look there? They knew in Jody Henderson's case that she had been jogging, because her husband informed them of that. Had the other women's families said the same? Was an overall grid search done? That could've been how they found the phones, only Brantley didn't recall seeing any information regarding a search.

"We need to ask Mr. Henderson specifically where on the trail that he looked for her. The crime scene tech said the phone hadn't been there during their initial search. I wanna know if Mr. Henderson looked in the same place."

He realized he was talking to himself when he glanced over to see Reese was still on the phone.

Then he got an idea.

Brantley tapped Reese on the shoulder.

"Yeah?"

"Tell JJ to send us a picture of the detective."

Reese relayed that information, then glanced back at him. "Why?"

"Because we're goin' to talk to Mr. Henderson ourselves. I want to know if he's seen Detective Collins before."

He wasn't sure why he had a hunch the detective and the officer who went out to the house were one and the same, but he did. The question was, why would he do that? Why pretend to be an officer versus the detective assigned to the case? Yeah, it sounded a little crazy when he thought about it that way, but now that the thought was planted in his brain, he couldn't seem to shake it.

"I need directions," he told Reese. "Now."

Reese ended the call with JJ and used his phone to pull up the map. The automated voice began telling him where to go, so he followed dutifully until they'd made it to the Henderson residence. He parked on the street, glanced up at the house. It was lit up like the surface of the sun, so he had to assume they were still awake. It was nineteen thirty, so he hoped it was still early enough for a house call. With so many kids, he had no idea when they went to bed.

Brantley glanced around as they made their way to the porch, smiling when he remembered reading Baz's notes and the reference to the shrubbery being neatly cut. The guy didn't miss a detail.

On the porch, Brantley knocked on the door, then rang the doorbell for good measure, silently apologizing if he was waking a sleeping baby. He stepped back to stand beside Reese, hearing footsteps and chatter coming from inside. When the door opened, a young girl appeared. Probably somewhere around ten or so, Brantley figured.

"Is your dad home?" Brantley asked.

She looked over her shoulder, shouted, "Dad!"

"Ella Mae, you know better than to answer the door," a male voice said firmly.

A second later, an older man appeared behind the glass storm door. "Yes?"

"Are you Dale Henderson?"

"Yes."

"My name's Brantley Walker. This is my partner, Reese Tavoularis. We're members of the OTB Task Force. You previously spoke to members of my team, Sebastian Buchanan and Trey Walker."

His shoulders relaxed.

"Sir, if you don't mind, we've got a couple of questions to ask."

He looked over his shoulder, forehead creasing.

"If it's easier, you can step out here with us," Reese told him. "This won't take but a minute or two."

Mr. Henderson nodded, then stepped outside, pulling the front door closed behind him.

"We're lookin' into your wife's case," Brantley explained. "And I need some clarification on a couple of things. Mr. Henderson, you said you were the one who contacted the police to report your wife missing. Is that correct?"

"Yes. After I went looking for her. Why?"

"When you went looking, did you go to the lake?"

He nodded. "I woke my oldest daughter, had her stay with the kids, then took the car to the lake. I got out and walked the path. At first, anyway. I started to get anxious because there weren't many people out, so I started to jog. Followed the trail all the way to where it disappears back into my neighborhood."

"Did you find anything of hers along the way?"

Mr. Henderson looked confused. "Like what?"

Brantley took that to mean he hadn't noticed a cell phone.

"Was it daylight when you went to look for her?"

"It was still mostly dark on my way from the parking lot, but on the way back, the sun had started to rise."

"But you didn't find a cell phone or her headphones."

Mr. Henderson's eyes widened, his confusion turned to terror. "No. Why? Do you have… Do you know what happened to my wife?"

Reese was the one to speak up. "Mr. Henderson, right now, we're simply gathering information while we follow every lead we get. We do know that a cell phone and headphones were discovered on the trail the morning your wife went missing. We can't confirm these belong to your wife because we haven't seen the report yet. However, we are headin' over to look at them. We just needed to know if you saw anything, maybe reported it but the details were missed."

He shook his head adamantly, his hands shaking. "No. I... I... No, I didn't find anything."

One thing Brantley knew for sure, Dale Henderson did not have anything to do with his wife's disappearance. Or if he did, he deserved a fucking Oscar for that performance.

Brantley's cell phone buzzed at the same time Reese's did. Since Reese had his in his hand, Brantley let him show the picture to Mr. Henderson.

"Do you recognize this man?"

Mr. Henderson took the phone, brought it closer to his face and squinted. "Yeah. That's the officer who came to speak to me Friday morning."

"Do you recognize him from anywhere else?"

"No. Why? Do you think he has something to do with my wife's disappearance?"

Unfortunately, it was starting to look that way, but Brantley kept the thought to himself.

Son of a bitch.

THEY LEFT THE HENDERSONS' WITH A RENEWED sense of purpose. It was imperative they looked at the cell phones that were taken from the crime scenes. The goal wasn't to confirm who they belonged to. Reese had no doubt they were the phones of the victims, but he was curious as to the chain of custody that had taken place since they were found.

With Brantley by his side, Reese managed to talk his way to the evidence lockup, but getting past the guard on duty required a little more finesse, so he passed the baton to Brantley, figuring he could get things done faster. He had no problem talking his way through after flashing credentials and informing the officer that they would get the governor on the phone but he would be the one who had to explain to him the problem.

Apparently, Officer Joe Landry had no desire to do that, so rather than interrupt the governor's evening, Landry showed them the way to the evidence they were looking for. The brown box was right where it was supposed to be, but that was about all that would go right for them after that.

"It's empty," Brantley said, tossing the cardboard lid down beside it. "Son of a bitch."

"Before we jump to conclusions, maybe Collins has them for some reason."

"Okay, fine," he answered. "We'll be rays of sunshine and think positively. Let's find the others."

Of course, Reese knew his optimism would be short-lived. The other three boxes netted the same thing: nothing.

"I want the crime scene techs," Brantley grumbled as he marched out of the storage locker, past Officer Landry, through the station, and right to Detective Collins's desk.

The substation was still busy, but as expected at nine o'clock at night, most of these detectives were gone.

While Reese stood back, Brantley rummaged through what was on the detective's desk, looking for the files on the missing women. When that didn't get him what he wanted, he checked the three-drawer lateral file cabinet behind it and still came up with nothing.

"Maybe he—"

Brantley held up a hand, effectively cutting Reese off.

"Don't. No more excuses."

Reese offered a tight smile, then followed Brantley out of the building.

By the time they got back to the hotel, Brantley was steaming mad. Reese took over from there, contacting JJ, Baz, and Trey to let them know what they'd encountered tonight.

"Why?" Trey asked. "Why would he pretend to be an officer instead of the detective on the case?"

"That's the million-dollar question," Reese told him, ignoring the man prowling behind him.

"Okay, so we know that the families of the victims called in to report the women missing," JJ said, her tone cool, calm. "We also know that crime scene techs were called out to the lake in all cases."

"We know that for a fact?" Brantley asked, stopping behind Reese.

"Yes," she said quickly, smoothly. "I was able to get into the electronic files. There are notes reflecting that."

"What about official reports from the techs?"

"Umm … I haven't seen any, no."

So they were going on the word of the detective again.

"Who called them?" Reese asked, watching JJ's expressive face on the screen.

"That's the kicker. It doesn't say who, but I'm not sure it will." She glanced over her shoulder at Baz. "Should it?"

"Depends. Some detectives are good at documenting things. I always noted everything because my memory's for shit. Figured it was best if I kept it all laid out clearly for my reference if no one else's."

"Well, we know this detective is not good at much of anything except bein' deceptive," Brantley grumbled.

JJ met Reese's eyes through the camera and gave a sympathetic smile.

"What else do we know?" Brantley's voice reflected his irritation.

"I would bet my last dollar that Detective Collins was the same officer who went out on the first call and informed the families that someone would be in touch."

"Okay, Trey," Brantley said, "since you're a bettin' man, would you also say he's the one who has the missing cell phones?"

JJ shifted the monitor so that the camera was directed at Trey. "Yes."

"Playing devil's advocate here," Baz said from somewhere, "we know the governor called us in on this case. The mayor's worried, which means someone has decided these cases are related. It's possible someone else is lookin' into it, which would explain where the case files and the evidence are."

Risking Brantley's wrath, Reese said, "I agree. That's a good possibility."

A grunt was all they got from Brantley.

"Let's throw out another theory," Trey said. "We've got four women who are missing, all taken during their jog at the lake. At each one, they found a cell phone and headphones stacked neatly for someone to find. The crime scene techs did their job, logged it into evidence, then Collins comes along, takes over the cases, claiming they're too different to think they're related. He then hijacks the case files, starts making his own notes because, hey, he's the bad guy so he knows what's goin' on. And now that there's heat on him because the mayor got a bug up his ass and called the governor, he's covering his tracks by takin' all the information so it can't be tied back to him."

Brantley had stopped walking, his hand firmly on Reese's shoulder as they watched Trey on the computer screen.

"That's the theory I'm leanin' toward," Brantley said. "My gut's tellin' me Detective Collins is at the heart of this."

Reese interrupted their trial by assumption and spoke directly to JJ. "What else did you find out on the brother?"

"That's what Baz is goin' over now," she said, nodding her head backward. "He's been readin' through it for an hour. From my initial glance, I couldn't find much of anything. I figure it's one of two things."

"What's that?" Brantley asked.

"Either the brother doesn't exist or someone's done a damn fine job of keepin' his existence a secret."

"Hey, y'all," Baz called from somewhere off-screen. "I don't think the detective's the one snatchin' these women."

JJ peered over her shoulder, frowning. "What? Why would you think that?"

"Because it's the brother," Reese said at the same time Baz did.

Chapter Sixteen

BRANTLEY TURNED HIS ATTENTION TO REESE WHILE JJ's voice droned in the background.

"The brother?" he asked.

"Yeah. And Collins is hidin' his brother's crimes. Probably moved to this area in hopes of puttin' it behind him since those cases are still unsolved. Then they started up again, new area. Close to home. Because we've seen reports that CPS was called out, we can safely assume that something transpired in their childhood that required state intervention."

"It's a bit of a leap to assume their hellish childhood was what prompted his brother to start killin' women, though, isn't it?" Trey countered.

"But it fits," Baz said firmly.

"And it also supports the idea that, because of what they endured, Collins is loyal to his mentally disturbed brother."

"Go get him, Brantley," JJ stated from the computer screen.

He took a deep breath, processed what Reese was saying, remembered that their main objective was to locate Jody Henderson and the other women who'd disappeared. Or was it? Was that the only thing he was capable of doing? Finding people? Sure, it was his job. Now. But his elite training and the sailor in him wouldn't allow him to look the other way, to leave it up to someone else to resolve.

"We can't just confront him," Reese warned. "If we tip him or his brother off that we've figured it out…"

"There's a chance he'll kill 'em," Baz finished for him.

JJ sighed. "Good point. So what do we do?"

"First of all, I need all the info on the brother. Dig deeper. Get me a birth certificate, social security number. Something. I want to know who we're dealin' with," he told JJ. "Where did he go to school? How long has he lived with his brother? What does he do for a living? Job history, all that shit."

"Will do," she confirmed.

"The same on the detective," Reese said. "Follow the trail back to when he was livin' with his mother. Find out what CPS knows. There's a record of it somewhere."

"And that sealed juvie record…" Brantley met JJ's gaze on-screen. "Unseal it."

She nodded, understanding he meant by any means necessary.

"Baz, I want you to reach out, see if you can get a feel for the detective. Talk to his superiors, any partners he's had in the past. But be discreet about it. Reese is right, we can't tip him off until we've done our due diligence."

"Got it," Baz said from off-screen.

"If the brother's our guy, we will take him down. Which means we have to cover our asses. But our priority is still to find these women. I need Collins's address. We'll scope it out, see if we can get eyes on the brother. If he's there, we might be able to follow him to where he's keepin' them."

"What if they're in the house?"

"I'd be surprised if they were," Baz said. "Collins might cover for his brother, hide his crimes, but as a sworn officer of the law, I don't want to believe he could condone it happening right in front of him."

"I agree," Brantley said. "So get me the address, plus the tag numbers for any vehicles they own. Reese and I will head over now, sit on the house for a while."

"Will do," JJ answered. "Oh, wait. Before you go…"

The camera angle shifted, then tilted until Tesha filled the screen.

"She's just chillin' with us," JJ said, a smile in her voice.

Brantley glanced down at Reese, noticed he was staring at the screen, a genuine smile that reached all the way to his eyes.

"Thanks for that, JJ," Brantley told her. "I'm sure you'll find a way for us to make it up to you."

"Of course I will."

The video call ended and Brantley closed his laptop, got to his feet, walked over to Reese.

"Anyone tell you your brain works in mysterious ways?"

Reese stared back at him.

"And it's fuckin' hot," he whispered before leaning in and kissing him.

Whether it was the adrenaline that spiked from their mission or merely the overwhelming lust he felt for this man, Brantley didn't know, but something shifted in that moment. And the detour became unavoidable when Reese fisted the front of his shirt, jerked him forward as their tongues fought for supremacy.

Brantley held on just as tightly, gripping the back of Reese's neck, holding him there as they stumbled to the bed, then down onto it.

They rolled a couple of times, neither of them willing to go down easily.

"I'm not submissive," Reese muttered, nipping Brantley's lower lip.

He laughed, remembering Z's comment from earlier.

Pulling back, he stared down into Reese's eyes. "No?"

Those sexy brown eyes narrowed. "You want me to show you just how not submissive I am?"

He held Reese's gaze. "You're damn right I do."

It was a dare, and it worked. Reese flipped them easily. Almost too easily, Brantley realized. Either he was getting lax or Reese was stronger than he'd given him credit for.

Their mouths fused once more, breaths racing out of their lungs as they became a fumble of hands, working to get clothes off. Neither of them gave quarter, and it became a genuine battle for dominance.

Although he considered giving in to Reese, Brantley was unable to accept defeat, which was how he ended up on top, Reese naked and sweaty beneath him.

He stared down into Reese's eyes. "Another round later," he said, his lungs still working overtime. "Right now, I want you to turn over."

"Make me."

Brantley smiled, couldn't help it.

And then he did as Reese instructed. He flipped him onto his stomach, held him in place as he slid his cock along the crack of Reese's ass. He was tempted to fuck him without lube but knew it wouldn't be nearly as good for either one of them. It took effort, but he managed to hold Reese in place while he fumbled for the lubricant sitting on the nightstand. He smacked Reese's ass a couple of times as he attempted to slick his cock and keep the man from getting away from him at the same time.

It worked in his favor, but he figured Reese wasn't giving him one hundred percent.

When he sank into the blistering heat of Reese's ass, Brantley groaned, his body stilling.

"Oh, fuck, yes," he ground out, his fingertips digging into Reese's hips.

Beneath him, Reese began to move, clearly eager for him to get on with it.

With his adrenaline still surging, Brantley jerked Reese's hips back, bringing him up onto his knees. He was close enough to the edge that he managed to shift one foot to the floor then the other while remaining lodged deep inside the man.

Then he fucked him.

Hard.

No holds barred.

With every punishing thrust, he jerked Reese toward him, their bodies slapping together, their guttural groans filling the air as they sated the urge. Despite the fact he knew it was only temporary, that he would be raring to go sooner rather than later, Brantley let himself enjoy this moment the same as he did every time they were intimate like this.

He had never felt anything this good, anything quite so overwhelming. With Reese, their joining was about more than the act, more than the sheer pleasure that came from fucking. And that was what made him crave Reese.

Because he was so worked up and the man beneath him was so fucking hot, Brantley didn't last long. He pushed in deep, again and again, harder, faster, until his balls were so tight and that tingling sensation lit up right at the base of his spine before erupting into a brilliant shower of heat and light within him.

He didn't waste time. As soon as he'd come, Brantley pulled out, flipped Reese over, and took him in his mouth. He figured he deserved the hard grip Reese applied to his hair as he held him there, driving his hips upward and fucking his face. Not long after, Reese war roaring his release, the sound something Brantley would never tire of hearing.

"YOU CAN CATCH A NAP IF YOU'D like," Brantley said, his attention, like Reese's, on the house they were staking out.

"You think I need a nap?" Reese peered over at Brantley. "Should I be worried about you, then? You've got what? Half a decade on me? Maybe bedtime needs to be moved up to, what, twenty hundred? Twenty-one hundred at the latest?"

Brantley chuckled. "Keep it up, smart-ass."

Reese smiled in the dark, loving the sound of Brantley's laughter. He'd never really paid much attention to someone else's laughter or their smile. He had noticed, with Brantley, they were both rare. He was quick to grin and chuckle when he was with those closest to him, those he trusted with his life, but in mixed company, they were nearly nonexistent.

"Four years," Brantley clarified. "But it's my alpha side that keeps me young."

It was Reese's turn to bark a laugh. When he'd mentioned earlier that he wasn't submissive, he'd been joking. Of course, it was true. In this relationship, he didn't see either one of them as the alpha. More equals. He suspected the same was the case for RT and Z, although Reese's brother didn't mind pretending otherwise to get a smile.

"What makes you think the brother's our suspect?" Brantley asked, switching the tone of the conversation.

"I can't put my finger on it. Makes it more difficult since I haven't met him," Reese admitted. Or seen him, for that matter. "But I didn't get the vibe from Collins. I felt like something was off, but I didn't get the impression he was cold enough to kill someone."

"That or he's a damn good actor. Could be he's gotten away with it for so long it's become second nature. He knows how to play those around him."

"Could be, sure." Reese had considered that, too. "No matter what, I think he plays a part."

"You think they're alive?"

That was a damn good question.

"I'm holdin' out hope." It was all he could do.

Based on JJ's information, if they were correct in their suspicions, there were already twelve women who'd died at the hands of these men. And if Collins or his brother was responsible, it could be that Collins was warning them when he'd said the time was nearing.

"Why would Collins give us so much information?" Brantley grabbed his water bottle from the cup holder. "He basically told us we only had a few days to find them. If his brother is responsible, was that a warning?"

"Maybe he's tired of coverin' it up?"

"Or he's taunting us," Brantley muttered.

"You don't think it's the brother?"

Brantley glanced over, the whites of his eyes bright in the dark vehicle. "I don't."

"The detective then?"

"Yeah. I had that same itch when we talked to him, but it's the details he provided that make me think he's fascinated with these women. More so than worried. He's focused on their appearances, not their backgrounds. He refers to them by their first name. Like he knows them. And while he's the detective on the case, he insinuates himself into the case by pretending to be someone else. Why is that? That's the part I just don't get."

"He wouldn't need to dig into her background or get her history," Reese said. "He already knows everything about her. If he's the one who took her, it could be he pretended to be the officer because he's worried someone saw him. Figures keepin' a low profile in the area is the best for the time being."

"Or they're workin' together," Brantley mused.

Reese glanced behind them when headlights bounced off the interior of the vehicle.

Neither of them spoke as it approached and then passed, brake lights flashing as it turned into a driveway.

"That's Collins," Brantley noted.

They watched as the detective got out of his police-issued vehicle. He carried a couple of bags—looked to be fast food—and two Styrofoam cups. He didn't look around as he bounded up the three front steps. Not a care in the world. Screen door opened, then the door, and he slipped inside, disappearing when the door closed behind him.

"Looks like dinner for two. Means the brother's probably in there."

Reese had to think it was possible Brantley was right.

Brantley's cell phone rang, shocking the silence in the SUV.

"Hey, Trey," Brantley greeted after hitting the button to take the call.

"How's it goin'? Learn anything?"

"Not yet." Brantley went on to explain how uneventful their stakeout was.

"I was wonderin' how Collins managed to catch all these cases with so many other dicks in the department."

Reese laughed. "By dicks, you're referrin' to detectives?"

"Take it how you wanna take it," Trey said with a laugh.

Brantley clearly wasn't enjoying the conversation. "What'd you find, Trey?"

"Whether by coincidence or intention, he's always on scene first," Trey noted. "At least in the three other cases we know about. Even when they called someone else in, Collins was there. He's made a name for himself in this department as the guy who tackles the cases that involve little to no reason for disappearance."

"Not a coincidence."

"Definitely not. And it makes sense," Reese told them. "He keeps the details to a minimum, probably blames it on a lack of information available. No similarities between the victims, nothing to tie them together except for the cell phones, which is why I don't think it's him. If he was the one snatchin' these women, why leave behind something to taunt the police with? Collins would simply have them vanish so he could back the theory they're not related. Just unfortunate random acts."

Trey's voice came through the speaker again. "Agreed. So I looked back at the crime scenes he worked at his previous precinct. When he was on a beat. Same deal there. Always the first on the scene, then keepin' himself in the investigation by sharin' as much information as possible with the detective assigned."

"I assume that's why he aimed high, got promoted to detective. He could manage them from a different angle, not chance someone finding out about his brother," Reese said.

Brantley grunted, something that sounded like agreement. "Probably easier when he was assigned to a sector. He knew how to time it."

"Exactly. But it's the women from those old cases who caught my attention," Trey said. "They disappeared at roughly the same times as the current set. All in groups of four over the period of a year."

"Somethin' catch your eye on the dates?" Reese asked.

"Yes. The months of their disappearance change, but they're always taken on the seventeenth, eighteenth, nineteenth, and twentieth of the month. In that order. Those happen to be the days of the month the first four women were born, too."

"He memorializing them?"

"Maybe. And the first woman's body did turn up three hundred and forty-seven days after her disappearance. Every woman since has been the same."

"OCD, perhaps? Not a memorial, a ritual?" Brantley theorized.

"Could be, sure."

"And no one tied that together before?" Reese asked, looking over at Brantley.

"How could they? You've got the man responsible for their disappearances, and possibly their deaths, handling the cases." Brantley directed his voice to the speaker. "Did he stay involved in the first cases?"

Trey was quick to answer. "According to the notes, yes. One of the detectives marked it down as questionable. Seemed put off by how nosy he was. Looked like Collins showed a significant amount of interest and it drew suspicions. Shortly thereafter, another woman went missing."

"He was takin' the heat off himself," Brantley said. "Probably got a little too close when tryin' to cover it up. Realized he had to do something to redirect. Do you think there's a significance with those dates?"

Reese shook his head. "I don't. I'm leanin' more toward it being a tradition he's set for himself. A way to remember the others by."

"Or a goal," Trey said. "He has those dates set in his mind, which gives him something to look forward to. Not sure how he selects a month, though. The disappearances aren't spaced perfectly."

Reese sighed. Just another thing they didn't know for certain.

"You at home?" Brantley asked Trey.

"No. Still here at HQ. JJ and Baz are upstairs, pullin' more information. Figure if y'all are pullin' a late night, we will, too."

"Well, keep at it, Trey. I think you're on to something," Reese told him. "Let us know as soon as you find anything else."

"Will do."

The call disconnected.

"He's comin' out of his shell quickly," Reese told Brantley.

"Just wait. My brother might be reserved but he knows how to get shit done." Brantley reached over, squeezed his hand. "Why don't you catch a couple hours' sleep. I'll keep an eye on the house."

Because they were in it for the long haul, Reese knew he couldn't argue, so he reclined the seat. Within seconds, he was out.

Chapter Seventeen

WHEN TREY DISCONNECTED HIS CALL, BAZ MADE his way down the stairs. He hadn't wanted to interrupt and was doing his best not to insert himself into Trey's research. The last thing the guy needed was Baz providing his opinion when it wasn't warranted. Trey was doing a damn fine job, and Baz wanted him to maintain that confidence.

At his desk, he sat down, opened his laptop, and typed in his password. His stomach growled and he thought about food but shrugged off the thought. Too much to do.

"The brother? Really?"

Baz looked up at the loft, where he'd left JJ, but he was unable to see her. He could definitely hear her, though, and she seemed perplexed about the idea their suspect could be Detective Collins's brother.

"You don't think so?" he called out, spinning around in his chair so he could see her if she chose to come down.

"I mean, maybe," she said, appearing at the top of the stairs, iPad in one hand as she tapped the screen with the other. "I just wanna know how the good detective could cover somethin' like that up."

"Family," Baz mused.

"Nope. No way." JJ shook her head as she started down the stairs. "What about you, Trey? You've got, what? Six siblings? Would you cover up their crimes?"

Baz glanced over at Trey, watched the man consider it.

"I guess it depends on the circumstances. If one of them was a serial killer, no, I wouldn't cover it up."

JJ was still shaking her head. "Exactly. I loved my brother and all, but if he'd murdered people ... I would never cover up somethin' like that."

Baz had never heard JJ so much as mention her brother. Anytime they'd talked about family, it always came back around to his.

"I wouldn't know," he told her. "Only child."

"You wanna go out?" she asked Tesha.

When the dog made a beeline for the door, JJ followed, so Baz did, too.

"What gets me is that he went into law enforcement," JJ said when they were outside, Tesha wandering through the threadbare grass that hadn't quite given up for the coming winter, the area lit by the security lights mounted in the eaves.

"Not all cops are good, JJ. The badge doesn't change the way someone is on the inside."

She turned to face him. "I did not expect you to say that."

"Why not? It's true." Baz leaned a shoulder against the barn while they waited for Tesha to do her business. "Like everything else, not all cops are bad, but not all are good, either."

"What about that whole back-the-blue pledge you guys take?"

"No pledge. I do back the blue. I back the men and women who go out to make a positive difference, who're there to protect and serve. That's the pledge we take. Those who're in it for the right reasons don't see the badge as a free pass."

JJ nodded. "I get it. I do. But what about in this case? Do you think that's why Collins became a cop? So he'd be in a position to cover up his brother's crimes?"

"Only he knows the answer to that."

Tesha wandered back over, stared up at JJ with so much love on her face.

"You ready to go back to my house, little lady?" she asked her, then looked over at Baz. "You have plans for dinner?"

The question surprised him. "No. You offerin' to cook for me?"

JJ's smile only intensified her beauty. "No. But I'm not opposed to orderin' pizza."

"Pizza." He pretended to consider it. No way in hell would he turn down an invitation from JJ. He didn't care if she offered to make tofu. "I can do pizza."

JJ nodded at the barn door. "Let me grab my stuff and say good night to Trey."

Baz followed JJ and Tesha back to her place, carried her bag inside, and set it down where he'd seen it sitting the last time he'd come over.

"I need to feed her first," she called out as she made her way to the kitchen. "Then I'll place the order."

"No rush."

In fact, he didn't care if she waited a few hours before she ordered pizza. The longer it took for dinner, the longer he could be here with her.

Despite what she thought about him, Baz wanted to spend more time with her. And yes, he wanted to take her to bed, to spend the entire night buried deep inside that curvy little body, making her moan and sigh. It was damn near all he could think about. But he'd promised to be patient and he was not going back on his word. If JJ was ready to escalate things between them, he had to believe she would give him some sort of sign.

"Baz?"

He turned around. "Hmm?"

She stepped closer, closer still, until they were nearly toe to toe.

"I don't want pizza, Baz."

"No?"

JJ shook her head and he could see the passion banked in her eyes.

"What do you want, JJ?"

"You."

He felt the word like a physical blow. It stole the air from his lungs, but there was no pain whatsoever.

This was the part he'd been both anticipating and dreading. Keeping her at a distance for her own benefit hadn't been easy. And that was when she'd simply kissed him. He could see the intention in her gaze now. They were taking that step, making that leap. This was not one of those times when he could set her aside and promise more when she was ready. She looked pretty damn ready and he was not about to resist her.

Baz cupped her face, brushed his thumb over her smooth cheek, leaned in. "You sure?"

"Never been more sure in my life," she whispered.

"Fuckin' hell," he muttered.

Then he kissed her.

Hard.

There was nothing patient about the way he consumed her, fusing his mouth to hers, breathing her in while his hands began a hurried exploration. The kiss they'd shared the other day was nothing in comparison to this, and he'd thought it was damn hot at the time. But right now, right here, the only thing he wanted was to strip her bare and make her come. With his mouth, his fingers, his cock. He didn't care in which order, but before the night was over, he would accomplish his goal using several methods.

JJ's fingers twined in the hair at his nape as she held him firmly. His hands weren't quite so PG as they roamed down to cup her ass, jerking her forward, grinding his rigid cock at the apex of her thighs before he curled his fingers around her ass and lifted her off her feet.

Her mouth never left his, not even when he crushed her between his body and the wall.

"Touch me," she pleaded, her lips moving against his. "Baz … I need your hands on me."

He agreed, but his feet were rooted for the moment, his need to taste her, to get his fill too great to ignore. He wasn't taking his time. Neither of them were as they devoured, bodies grinding together, the desperation building.

When he could get his legs to move, Baz relocated them to her bedroom, finding it after the second try. The first door he'd come to was a bathroom, so he bypassed it. Inside her room, he didn't have time to look around because he was too eager to get her naked.

After dumping her on the bed, JJ helped remedy the too-many-clothes dilemma they found themselves in by yanking off her shirt. Distracted by those gorgeous mounds of ivory flesh encased in black silk, Baz managed to toe off his boots and not land on his ass, but he got no further when JJ reached for him, fisting his shirt and dragging him down to the bed with her.

"Condom," JJ mumbled against his mouth. "Nightstand drawer."

It fucking turned him on that this woman was so prepared. She was that way with everything in her life and he found it incredibly hot.

"Now, Baz," she groaned, her nails digging into his shoulders, piercing his skin through his shirt.

When he reached for the nightstand, he didn't make it far because JJ started jerking his T-shirt up. He had to pause so she could get it over his head.

"Holy shit," she said softly. "You're hotter than I thought you'd be."

He couldn't help laughing as he grabbed a handful of condoms from the box, tossed them on the bed, and found her mouth with his again.

This time he rolled so he was beneath her, his hands free to cup her breasts while her hands roamed over his chest. She lifted her head, stared into his eyes, and held his gaze. Once again Baz sucked in air when JJ's fingers slid into the waistband of his jeans, flipping the button free. He had to still her when she started yanking on the zipper.

"Careful," he said with a grin.

"Off," she demanded. "I want you inside me."

Those words from her mouth nearly made him come in his jeans like a damn teenager.

They also helped to spur him as they managed to shuck the rest of their clothes. Baz had no time to admire her, but he knew there would be time for it later. After. After they quelled this overwhelming urge that had been building to impossible levels these last few weeks.

While JJ unhooked her bra and freed her breasts, Baz rolled on the condom, then gripped her hips and positioned her over him.

"Ride me, JJ," he whispered. "Take me inside you."

He gasped when her soft, cool fingers wrapped around his cock, guiding him to the wet heat between her thighs. As she eased down on him, he held his breath, afraid if he moved he would come.

Tight, hot. Fuck.

And then she was moving. A gentle rocking of her hips as he sank deeper inside her. Staring up, he watched raptly as her body did a sensual roll, her nipples hard points that beckoned his mouth.

"Different angle," she groaned.

Baz pulled her down to him, their lips melding as she rocked her hips, changing the angle of her pelvis so he could slide deeper inside her. Impossibly deep.

Heaven.

This had to be heaven because Baz had never felt anything this good in his life. Her soft skin sliding over his, her pussy milking his cock. The tight, wet sheath sending pleasure to every nerve ending.

Baz let her control the pace, let her ride him as they both soared on that intense high that came with two bodies aligning so perfectly.

JJ was the one to break the kiss, sitting up, her hands pressed to his chest as she rolled her hips, taking him deep inside her. Baz could only watch the sensual way she moved, her auburn hair sliding over her shoulders. Gripping her hips, he guided her forward, back, ensuring he filled her completely as the pace increased, her rhythm never slipping.

When her eyes opened, her gaze locking with his, Baz pressed his thumb to her clit, circled the tiny bundle of nerves. Her lips parted, chest heaving with the soft gasps that told him she was close.

"Come for me, JJ," he urged. "Let me watch you come."

She did.

JJ's back bowed, her tits thrust forward, hair hanging down so it tickled his thighs. Her pussy clamped down on him, a velvet fist that dragged his release from him on a strangled groan.

"I knew it'd be good," she mumbled when she fell on top of him, her head resting on his chest. "Just didn't know it'd be that good."

Baz smiled in the dark.

Just wait until she found out what he had in store for her next.

JJ WAS HESITANT TO GET UP, HATING to break the blissful afterglow of phenomenal sex, but she knew it couldn't be helped.

She pressed her lips to Baz's chest, pushed herself up.

"You dispose of that," she said, nodding toward his condom-clad dick, which was, holy mother, still erect and quite impressive. "And I will order pizza."

Baz sat up. "You givin' up on me already?"

"You're tellin' me you're already up for round two?" she countered.

"And three. Four, too."

She narrowed her eyes, studied him for a moment. "How old are you, Baz?"

He got to his feet. "If you wanted to know badly enough, you would've looked it up yourself."

Yes, she would have. But JJ hadn't done it because … well, because she had the sneaking suspicion he was younger than she was. And as long as she didn't know his age for certain, she couldn't use that as her excuse.

"Fine," she said, grabbing his T-shirt from where it lay on top of her pants. "I don't wanna know."

Rather than put her own clothes back on, she pulled his shirt on, ensuring he saw her do it. Two reasons for that, of course. One, it would keep him eager because she had nothing on beneath it. And two, he would have to go shirtless. A man with a body like that should be forbidden to wear clothes.

"Did you bring your laptop?" she called out as she left him behind in her bedroom.

"Yep."

"Good. We need to work."

"I had a feelin' you were gonna say that."

When he slipped into the bathroom, JJ went to the living room, grabbed her bag, and pulled out her computer. She flopped down on the couch, smiling when Tesha joined her, hopping up and settling in at her side.

It only took a few minutes to order pizza. She ordered one large—half with double pepperoni for Baz, half light sauce and all veggies for her—and a side of breadsticks. When that was submitted, she opened her email, checked to see what she'd gotten, and was happy to see there was one she'd been expecting.

Clicking on the attachments, she opened the pdf files and began reviewing them.

"Holy shit," she muttered.

"What's wrong?"

"Nothin'," she said quickly, looking up at Baz. "Well, nothin' more, anyway. We've still got some guy kidnapping and possibly murderin' women."

He was watching her, his eyebrows lifted.

"Remember how Reese asked me to see if there were police reports from the women who went missing?"

Baz came over, took a seat on the opposite side of her from Tesha. She kept her attention on the computer screen because it was difficult enough ignoring him when he smelled so damn good. If she took a moment to truly ogle him, they would both be naked again and the pizza guy would end up beating on the door, leaving their food. It would get cold…

"JJ?"

"Hmm?"

"The police reports?"

"Oh, right." She flipped through the images on the screen, one after the other. "Reese was right. All four of these women filed reports."

"For?"

She pointed at the screen where it noted what the complaint was for.

"Indecent exposure?" Baz leaned in closer. "All four of them?"

"Yep." She kept reading. "Looks like they made the report at the station. A man with a description that definitely fits Detective Collins was doing obscene things at the lake."

"Jackin' off where they could see him?"

The thought made her shudder. "Yeah."

They looked at each other then and in unison said, "That's how he picked them."

"Do you think it was to cover it up? If they went missing, they couldn't point the finger at him?"

Baz glanced at her, that look he got when he was considering it on his face. "Maybe. But more than likely, it was his way of picking them out. With the report, he'd have their information."

"He could find out whatever he wanted to know," JJ stated. "Yes. I bet you're right. He wasn't coverin' up a crime, it was his way of picking his next victim. Whoever would come forward was worthy of his attention."

"And I bet if you look, you'll find more reports filed for the same thing," Baz said. "My guess, he somehow chose his victims based on the dates since we know he's got a pattern."

It was a creepy thought, but it sure sounded more reasonable than him attempting to cover it up.

The rest of the night was spent with the two of them working to put together a timeline of events, determining when the complaints were filed in reference to the disappearances. JJ noted as much detail as she could because she knew Reese and Brantley would ask the question. With Baz's help, they were able to get a full report out via email to the rest of the team but not before three in the morning.

At that point, JJ could barely keep her eyes open.

"Come on," Baz said, holding out his hand for her. "Let's get some sleep."

Without an ounce of hesitation, she put her hand in his and let him lead her to her bedroom. Later, she would wonder at what point she'd decided Sebastian Buchanan was worthy of an overnight stay.

JJ woke with the sun streaming in through her bedroom window. The pillow beneath her head was soft; the blanket covering her was warm.

Everything was normal.

So why did she feel a sudden overwhelming panic?

Had she overslept?

Was she late for work?

Had she missed an appointment?

The fear that she had was enough to have her bolting upright in bed.

Cool air caressed her skin, and she jerked at the comforter, surprised to find she was naked. Her back straightened, her ears perked.

Why was she naked?

Soft breaths sounded from behind her and the events of last night came back with a vengeance.

Baz.

Gorgeous, naked Baz.

Sex.

Incredible, mind-numbing sex.

Oh, God.

Her body warmed instantly from the memories of Baz, of the two of them screwing like rabbits when they made it to the bedroom. They'd finally drifted off sometime around five, which explained why the sun was already up.

Her gaze strayed to the clock. "Oh, shit. I'm late."

JJ jerked the sheet, ready to bolt from the bed when a warm hand landed on her forearm.

"There's no rush."

Glancing over, she saw Baz reclined on the bed, one hand tucked under his head, that glorious muscled chest on full display. His abs—all sleek and contoured—appeared as she tugged on the sheet.

She jerked some more, covered herself. "Then I have to let Tesha out."

"Already done. Twice. And I fed her."

"Why'd you let me sleep so long?" she asked, slightly put off by the fact he'd taken care of things she should've been handling.

"I figured you needed it."

The mattress shifted. Warm breath fanned her shoulder blade.

JJ's first instinct was to kick him out, to pretend last night meant absolutely nothing. Or better yet, that it hadn't happened.

Only, something deep inside her didn't want to let go of it yet. Whatever happened between her and Baz … it had been different. So very different than anything she'd ever experienced, and there was this teeny tiny part of herself that was considering keeping him.

Did it scare her?

Oh, fuck yeah. Made her nervous as hell. Nothing in her life had ever gone well, and she seriously doubted it was going to start now. But damn if she didn't need something positive to help her get through these cold, lonely nights. She deserved that much, didn't she?

"Make you breakfast?" Baz offered. "I can fry up some bacon, scramble some eggs."

JJ twisted to look at him. "You really cook?"

"I've been known to, sure. Not one of my favorite things, but I'm capable in the kitchen."

"The many stepmoms teach you that?"

"Actually, no. That would've been Anna. My nanny."

"You had a nanny?"

"Of course." He smiled. "I mean, who else was gonna take care of me with all those weddin's goin' on?"

She wasn't sure how he was so blasé about his parents' obvious disregard for the sanctity of marriage. JJ would go so far as to say it didn't bother him. Her outlook wasn't much different, she figured. Her parents had made it until Jeremy killed himself. They hadn't been strong enough to last after that. The blame—on each other, on her, but never on Jeremy—had gotten the best of them all and her family structure had crumbled.

Baz reached over, turned her chin toward him. With his fingers lightly grazing her jaw, he kissed her. And right then and there, JJ forgot all about ... everything.

"It's gonna be damn hard to keep my hands off you at the office," he whispered as he pulled her back, his upper body leaning over hers as he tugged the sheet down. "I'll be thinkin' about you just like this."

"Like what?" she asked, staring up into his ridiculously handsome face, the tousled, dark blond hair, those teal-blue eyes.

"Soft and warm. Naked." He dragged his lips along her jaw, his hand skimming her belly and pausing when she spread her legs. "Wet."

JJ moaned when he dipped two fingers inside her.

"Never get enough," he mumbled as he fingered her.

She turned her head, found his mouth with her own. The kiss was slow, a contradiction to the way his fingers began fucking into her, deeper, faster. JJ's breaths labored, her chest rising and falling as the waves of undeniable pleasure crashed through her. Her hips began to rock, meeting him thrust for thrust as she chased the release that would leave her reeling.

"Come for me, JJ," Baz growled softly. "Come for me so I can fuck you."

In any other context, any other cadence, those words would've been crass. Coming from Baz, said in that deep, raspy baritone ... they were enough to trigger her, to send her spiraling.

She had no idea when he'd donned the condom, nor did she care. In one quick shift, he was over her, in her, sliding in deep. Her body acclimated to the exquisite intrusion when she wrapped her legs around his hips. JJ dug her ankles into his ass, urging him to go deeper. He gave her exactly what she needed, their bodies moving in a rhythm that seemed natural, as though they'd been meant for this.

"Oh, God," she cried out, an orgasm taking her completely by surprise, the fierce sensations shredding her as they flowed up from her core, through the rest of her, and out through her fingers.

Baz grunted, lifting his upper body, staring down into her face, punching his hips forward.

Another orgasm stole through her, smaller than the first but no less lethal.

"Fuck yes … JJ," Baz growled, his body stilling as he crested that hill right along with her.

Chapter Eighteen

Tuesday, November 24, 2020

BRANTLEY WOKE WITH A CRICK IN HIS neck and a mild headache coming on. He'd known he would. Sleeping in a vehicle wasn't something he'd done in quite some time now, and his body had gotten used to the comfort of a bed. And the warm, hard body that shared that bed.

Last night, he'd slept alone in the front seat of an SUV, which explained the dull throb in his skull. Not a migraine, thank God, but still painful.

"Got any ibuprofen?" he asked as he pushed the button to bring his chair upright, pulling his sunglasses off his face and setting them on the dash. "Any sign of them?"

"Yes to the meds," Reese answered, motioning toward the floor.

Brantley glanced down, saw the small bottle sitting in the cubby at the base of the center console.

"Come prepared, do you?"

"Figured you might need it. Also brought your migraine meds. Just in case."

Of course he had. Because that was what Reese did. He was the caretaker. In Brantley's life, that role had always been filled by himself. Well, once he'd graduated from high school, anyway. Before that, his mother had been the nurturing sort, taking care of the house and all the kids. But since the first day of boot camp, Brantley had been looking after himself and he would admit, he was rather shitty at it. He never would've thought to bring any medicine.

It was nice to have someone else backing him up on that front.

"As for our suspects, Collins left about half an hour ago. Still no sign of the brother." Reese glanced over. "Figured we could wait to see if Collins intended to come back or if he's on duty today."

"He is," Brantley confirmed. "I called last night, asked for his schedule. You were sleepin'. I was bored."

"Smart."

He stretched his neck, rolling his head on his shoulders. "I try." Bringing his head level, he stared at the house. "Maybe we should make a house call. See if the brother's inside. And then we can check with the neighbors. They might be able to give us some insight."

"I'm game if you are."

Brantley opened the glove box, retrieved the gun he'd stashed there before he drifted off.

Reese started the engine, drove the SUV up to the house, and parked along the curb.

"This way we look like we belong."

"The car, maybe," he teased, opening the door and climbing out.

His body creaked as it acclimated to not being crunched into an awkward position. He adjusted his shirt to ensure it covered his weapon when he holstered it, then clipped his badge to his belt, covered it, too.

Together, they walked up to the door. Just a couple of visitors, casually strolling up. Reese knocked while Brantley stepped to the right, attempted to peek in through the windows. Subtly, of course. The blinds were open. Single room, one couch, a coffee table, and a TV. Nothing and no one else.

"Maybe the brother doesn't live here?"

"Or maybe he's been told not to answer the door." Brantley walked down the steps, peered around. "I think we need to take a look inside."

Reese patted his jacket pocket. "Say the word. It just so happens I brought a key."

Grinning, Brantley nodded, giving him the go ahead to pick the lock.

He was impressed with Reese's time. "You might be faster than me."

"Probably."

Brantley couldn't stop the grin as Reese turned the knob, opened the door a fraction, paused to listen, then pushed it open all the way.

While he waited for Reese to deem it safe to enter, Brantley fought the urge to look behind him, to ensure no one was watching. The point was to look like they belonged. They moved together, slipping inside. Brantley closed the door as quietly as he could, drawing his weapon from its holster, clicked off the safety.

There was an odd smell, one he couldn't place. Not terrible but not appealing, either. Like they sprayed air freshener in a locker room. It put a layer over the mold and body odor combination, but it didn't quite mask it.

Reese backed up to the far wall of the living room, peeked around the corner, then turned back to meet Brantley's gaze. He shook his head, a sign there was no one in that room.

Using hand signals, Brantley instructed Reese to take the rooms on the left side of the house. Brantley would head to the right. One room after another, they worked to clear it of people, not making a sound. When they'd determined there was no one else there, Brantley joined Reese in the kitchen.

Rectangular room with the kitchen setup on one end, the breakfast nook on the other. It wasn't a big space, galley layout, minimal cabinets, small, round table with two chairs and two placemats.

Reese motioned to the items on the table. "Last night's dinner."

He glanced at the empty containers from two meals, mirror images of one another on each side, the Styrofoam cups and paper plates in almost obsessive order. Definitely looked like two people ate there.

"You said no one but Collins left?"

"Affirmative."

If the brother had been there, where was he now?

"Quick scan," he ordered Reese. "All rooms."

They separated, Brantley heading back through the living room, down the hall to the left, taking the first bedroom he came to. It looked to be the detective's. One of those thin, scratchy blankets was shoved aside on the bed, like he'd hopped out and never gave it another thought. The pillow was on the left side of the queen mattress, the indention from someone's head still visible. Beside the bed, a three-legged table stood, an alarm clock on top. There was no other furniture in the room, no dresser, no chest. Not even an extra pillow.

He continued through the small bathroom, noted the razor and shaving cream sitting on one corner of the sink, the other a cup that held a single toothbrush and a tube of toothpaste. Another toothbrush was laid out behind the faucet, still in the package. The medicine cabinet—one of those wooden deals inset into the wall—held a pair of tweezers, some eye drops, a bottle of Tylenol, and another toothbrush, this one with a travel cap. The cabinet beneath the sink had a spray bottle of cleaner, nothing else. Towel closet revealed a couple of washrags and a six-pack of toilet paper. The attached clothes closet held a variety of cheap suits and well-worn shoes.

Brantley searched high and low, ensuring there wasn't something that might give him a clue as to where the brother was.

When he stepped back into the hall, he studied it for a moment. For some reason, it felt like the hallway should go to the right from there, not just the left. He looked down at the floor, saw that the wall was a bit offset, like the carpenter hadn't had the skill to make the corners square.

Shrugging off the thoughts of who might have built this house, Brantley went back the way he'd come, past the doorway to the living room, and into the other bedroom. It held a twin bed that had been stripped of all blankets and sheets. No pillows, no other furniture. With nothing to look at, he pulled the door closed, leaving it the way he'd originally found it, and continued on to the small laundry room, back to the kitchen.

"Any luck?"

Reese shook his head.

"You see a computer?"

"Nope. Guy's smart. Doubt he'd keep anything incriminatin' here. Never know when a partner or co-worker might stop by."

Yeah, Reese was probably right, but it still felt off. Had to be the smell, he thought as he did a three sixty and observed once more.

"I'm good if you are," he said on a disappointed exhale.

Because they'd already been there longer than Brantley cared to be, they slipped out through the back door, locked up behind them. He took a quick peek at the storage shed in the back. Cheap padlock dangled from the bracket, not even secured. Inside, there was nothing worth stealing—only a rusted old lawn mower and a rickety wooden table.

"Now we know watchin' the house won't get us anywhere." They'd been on it all night and evidently they'd missed seeing the brother slip out.

Reese was right. They had to come up with another plan and they needed one fast.

IT FRUSTRATED REESE THAT THEY HADN'T FOUND anything that would help them track down the detective's brother. Not so much as a photograph that gave them an idea of what the brother looked like.

Which was the real problem, he realized.

With Brantley behind the wheel, Reese dialed JJ's number, let the call connect to the Bluetooth speaker.

"What's up?"

"You sound chipper," Brantley said before Reese could tell her his reason for calling.

"What? No. Not... What's up?"

Reese watched as Brantley grinned, that knowing smile that gave away nothing.

Because he had no idea what the inside joke was, Reese got on with his reason for calling. "Something's botherin' me about the brother."

"Hold on. Lemme put you on speaker. I'm at HQ with Baz and Trey. Oh, and Tesha. She's here, too."

A chorus of greetings sounded when the speaker was engaged and Reese could tell JJ was walking, probably making her way downstairs.

"What did you find out about the brother?" he asked, getting right to the heart of the matter.

"I take it you haven't checked your email this morning?"

"Not yet," Brantley said, steering the SUV out of the neighborhood. "We wanted to hear your lovely voice, JJ."

"Whatever. And not much on the brother, unfortunately. I ran a couple of searches overnight and I'm stumped. While some of the case notes refer to a brother, there's no information on him. And I mean none."

"Maybe Collins worked some magic, covered his brother's existence," Trey suggested. "I'm sure it's happened before."

"So there's no social security number? No birth certificate?"

JJ spoke up. "Nothing that confirms so much as the existence of a brother. I even went through some of the hospital records where Collins was born, skipped forward five full years since that's when the parents split up. If they had another kid, he wasn't born in that hospital, and I don't have enough to start hacking all the hospitals in the area."

Reese knew she was right. Couldn't simply start digging into personal information in hopes of finding a person.

"There's gotta be somethin'," Brantley said. "No one exists entirely off the grid."

"Not unless he was born in a commune and they didn't report it," Baz said.

The sound of keys clacking filled the truck.

"Trey, did you come across anything?" JJ asked, her voice directed away from the phone.

"I don't care if it's a yearbook photo or social media," Reese continued. "Something's off about this whole thing."

Brantley went on to fill them in on how they'd made a run through the detective's house. "One bedroom looks like it's lived in; the other's merely storage for a bed. We saw Collins come in last night, carryin' what looked like two meals. Those were still sittin' out on the table, both finished off. But we watched the house the entire night. The brother never left."

"Or if he did," Reese added, "he left through the back and we didn't see him."

It was a possibility and Reese was doing his best to hold on to that rather than to give in to the idea that was forming.

"What's the house like?" JJ asked.

"It's almost like it's a safe house," Reese mused. "Or for appearances only."

"You think he's got another?" Baz asked. "Somewhere he stashes his victims?"

"If he does, it's not in his name," JJ said quickly. "I've already done a complete workup on the guy. Credit score's for shit, but he does show to be the owner of the current residence. He's got three other addresses on his record. The address his parents were at the longest, the grandparents, and then the house the uncle left him. He sold the latter, bought the one he's in now."

"You said the brother's name was Jake, right?" Brantley asked.

Reese held his tongue because that fed right into the off-the-wall theory that was forming.

"Only according to the detective's notes on one of the first cases back in Pleasant Grove. The detective took Collins's statement and the name was noted on there. Can't find it anywhere else."

"Well, keep lookin'," Brantley instructed. "We're gonna swing through McDonald's, grab some food, then hit the hotel for showers."

"Probably need some sleep, too," Baz suggested.

Brantley sounded grim when he said, "Sleep's overrated."

"It'll wait," Reese said. "If what Collins said is accurate, we've got until Saturday before Shelly Masters's time is up. I'm not willin' to let that happen. Which means we've got to find somethin'. He's got to be somewhere."

"We'll keep diggin'," JJ said, her tone reassuring. "Our priority is to find the brother. In the meantime, when you get a chance, check your email. I sent you some information you might find useful."

"No, our priority is to find the women," Brantley corrected. "But we will find the brother and we will nail him and whoever else is helpin' him."

"Understood. We'll hit you back when we know somethin'," Baz said before disconnecting the call.

Brantley glanced over. "What's on your mind? You've got a theory, I can tell. You wanted to say somethin' but you held your tongue."

Reese had no idea how Brantley knew that, but the guy did have a super sense when it came to reading people.

"You no longer think it's the brother?"

Reese stared out the front windshield, let all the information he knew run through his head.

"It's crazy," he muttered.

"Talk to me," Brantley urged. "And go with your gut. I don't think it's steerin' you wrong."

Reese exhaled, dropped his head back against the headrest. "I think we're lookin' in the right place."

"But not for the brother."

This was the weird part. Reese rolled his head to the left, stared at Brantley's profile. "I'm startin' to think we were right in the beginning."

"That Collins is responsible. Why's that?"

Reese sighed, decided to go with his gut. "I don't think there is a brother."

"No?"

"I think they're one and the same."

Brantley came to a hard stop at a red light, his head snapping over. "Are you sayin' he's makin' up the brother? Or are you sayin'…?"

They were both quiet for a second, Reese giving Brantley time to process what he was inferring.

"Based on the house," Brantley said, "there's no reason to think there's anyone else livin' there. And the meals coulda been staged for our benefit. I'm sure Collins hasn't made it this far without bein' astute. Hell, he may be keepin' an eye on us."

"Or the meals weren't staged," Reese said.

Brantley frowned, hit the gas when the light turned green. "I know where you're goin' with this, and I can see it playin' out in my head but can't wrap my mind around it yet."

It was a leap, Reese knew.

"Explains why there's only been mention of a brother, no actual sightings, no record of his existence. At least…"

"Outside of Collins's head," Reese said for him.

"Multiple personalities," Brantley breathed out.

"Dissociative Identity Disorder," Reese clarified. "If this theory's right, Detective John Collins is also his brother, Jake. I'm no expert by any means, but if that's the case, it could be John is the identity that took over to protect them. He became a cop, used his resources to cover up the crimes of the other identity. I've heard that's often the case. The other identities are brought out because of some sort of dramatic incident. Since we don't know what happened when he was a kid…"

Even as he said it, Reese realized it sounded like a far-fetched idea. Something right out of a movie. But it explained so much. How Collins knew about the victims, didn't need to meet with the families because he was the one who took them. Or his other identity did, anyway. Maybe that was something the two identities shared so it could be covered up. Did that make the detective a bad guy? Or a good guy?

"What about the timeline?" Brantley asked, pulling to a stop in the McDonald's drive-thru. "What prompts him to take his victims on those four days of a month?"

"I think you nailed it when you said a ritual. He follows a pattern based on the first women he killed. Those days signify something for him. Baz said those are the days the first four women were born. Perhaps there's some OCD tied in there and this is the pattern he's formed."

"Fucking shit." Brantley pulled up to the ordering screen, rattled off their order.

"Don't forget the coffee," Reese said quickly.

"Can we get two large coffees, also?"

The woman read the order back, gave them the total, and Brantley pulled forward.

"You think we need to bring the FBI up to speed?" Reese asked and watched as Brantley considered that.

"If you're right, this guy has been two people all along. We tip off the FBI, they might take him into custody. Where does that leave the four missin' women?"

He had a good point. "So we find the women then clue them in?"

"It's our only choice. We've got three and a half days left. There's no time to play games with anyone else. We've gotta win this game of hide-and-seek before anyone else can join the party."

Reese nodded, exhaled.

And prayed like hell he was right. Otherwise, they were about to spin their wheels in an entirely different direction while the clock was ticking down.

Chapter Nineteen

ONCE THEY WERE BACK IN THE HOTEL room, Brantley found it impossible to sit still.

After they'd scarfed down sausage biscuits and knocked back lukewarm coffee, Brantley showered, dressed, then headed out to the parking lot while Reese finished up in the room.

His brain was going ninety miles a second, trying to process what Reese had theorized. And it made sense. So damn much sense. John Collins was in fact the brother he claimed to have. One person, two separate identities. Which meant—

He grabbed his phone out of his pocket, dialed JJ's number. She answered on the first ring.

"Police reports," he blurted. "Did these women file police reports?"

He remembered RT mentioning it, thinking it was worth following up on, but he hadn't heard back from JJ on it.

"I told you to look at your email," she blurted.

"JJ, did you find somethin' or not?"

"Yes. God." She huffed and he heard typing in the background. "Hold on."

The call changed to speaker, the clacking of the keyboard getting louder.

"Here it is. And the answer is…"

He could hear her breathing, so he refrained from barking orders at her. He didn't have time for the dramatics, but he reminded himself that wasn't JJ's fault.

"All four reported the same thing, and all out of the same precinct."

"For?"

"Indecent exposure."

"What?"

"Yep. How no one ever found this guy, I don't know. There were numerous reports filed through the months. Not only by these women. Lots of others. Jody Henderson was the last one to file a report."

"When was this?"

"October twentieth," she said. "Exactly one month before she disappeared. She went into the station to do it. Said she saw a man during her morning run. He was … well, you can probably figure out what it was he was doing with his thingy hangin' out."

Thingy? Brantley shook his head, remained focused. "That's the same thing Debbie Struthers reported." He remembered seeing the police report Reese had taken a picture of.

"Correct."

"And the others filed the same report?"

"They did," she confirmed. "And get this, the complaints were filed exactly one month to the day before each of them went missing. November seventeenth of last year, then February eighteenth, June nineteenth, and October twentieth. Like I said, there were other reports filed, but not on those same days of the month. We're thinkin' he was waiting for reports filed on those days."

"Well, we now know how they crossed paths with him." That was something. As well as how he picked his victims.

"Yeah. At the lake. He set them up, then probably stalked them after that."

"Jody's husband didn't mention it," Baz said, his voice moving closer to the phone as he spoke. "Then again, maybe she didn't mention it to him. From what he said, Jody was rather independent. Took care of things herself."

"Maybe she didn't want him to worry," JJ mused.

Brantley agreed. And if any of these women had mentioned it to a friend or loved one, he doubted it would raise any red flags. A nuisance was what it was, something they would likely snicker about after the fact because some pervert was spankin' it in public.

His cell phone beeped an incoming call. He glanced at the screen. Blocked number.

"Hey, JJ. Let me call you back," he said before switching over. "Yeah. Walker."

"Brantley Walker, I've been very interested in talking to the newest player of my game."

He didn't recognize the voice, but it was familiar.

"Game? What game are we playin'?"

"Hide-and-seek, of course. And I'm winning, Brantley Walker. I'm winning. You can't find me." The laugh that followed was almost childlike while the voice was deeper, like that of an adult.

"Who is this?"

"You don't know me, but my brother told me about you. Said you might come looking for me. I think he's scared of you, but I'm not. I'm not scared. I'm supposed to be careful," he said in a singsong voice, another childlike giggle following.

"Who's your brother?"

"Detective Collins." The enunciation reflected pride. "Detective Johnathan Jacob Collins. Recognize the name?"

Jacob. Jake.

Son of a bitch.

"I recognize it," he replied. As well as the voice now. "And you are?"

"That's not important."

"Where's your brother now?"

"He's not here. I didn't want him here. I told him to go away. To quit being a baby."

Brantley turned back to look at the hotel as Reese was walking out. The man looked good when he moved. Long and lean, with just the hint of swagger.

"How'm I supposed to refer to you if I don't know your name?"

"You're not. What you're gonna do, Brantley Walker, is take yourself back to where you came from. I don't want you to play my game anymore."

"I'm actually lookin' for someone," he told the man whose voice belonged to Detective John Collins. The same but different in a way.

"You won't find your friend here."

"He's not a friend," Brantley clarified. "But I think I've already found them."

"No, you haven't. Nope. No way. You haven't found them. I'm too good at this game. You can't find me. Hide-and-seek, you're it!"

Brantley ignored the eagerness of the child and spoke to the man. "I need to talk to John."

"He's not here. He's … he's gone."

"Where is he?"

"Work."

That sounded like a lie.

"And when he's not here, you can't find me. You'll never find me. Or my friends."

Oh, hell. "Who are your friends?"

Reese was staring at him with a questioning expression, so Brantley put the call on speaker.

"You don't know them. You'll never know them. They're my friends. Not yours." The man's words were picking up speed, more and more anxiety mixed in. "And if you don't go home, he's gonna find out, and he's gonna hurt them. I don't wanna hurt them, Brantley Walker, but he does. He wants to hurt them. You have to go away, Brantley Walker."

"Who's he? Are you talkin' about John?"

"No. Not John. He's nice. I can't say his name. I can't. You have to go away, Brantley Walker."

Brantley knew better than to taunt him. He suspected they were right in their theory. This was Detective Collins's alter ego, the one he referred to as his brother, Jake. And the alternate personality wasn't an adult, so he didn't rationalize like one. More than likely prone to violence when he threw his tantrums and wanted to put the blame on someone else.

"Okay. All right," he said, placatingly. "I'm not here to hurt you, Jake."

"Hey! You don't know my name," he shouted, his pitch getting higher. "Go home, Brantley Walker. We don't want you here."

"Jake, let's—"

The call ended.

"Was that...?"

Brantley stared at the phone, at the blank screen. "It was."

"What did he say?" Reese nodded his chin toward the phone. "Before, I mean."

"He started out soundin' relatively rational. Called me the newest player in his game. Told me to go home. He mentioned we were playing hide-and-seek."

"You think he was bein' literal?"

"Has to be. Based on our conversation and his responses, I think we're dealin' with an identity that's somewhere between eight and ten years old."

"At that age, games would be fun, right?"

"And they'd be worth winning. But they get old after a while, right? You get tired of playing?"

"Which is why he discards the women after a certain amount of time?"

Brantley honestly had no idea. That was where his mind had been going before that call.

"Maybe John puts a stop to the games," he mused, "takes over so he can clean up the mess, cover it up as best he can. Then Jake has to find another."

"But why women? Why not kids?" Not that Reese cared to think that either was more at risk. It pissed him off all the same. Didn't matter if it was a woman, a child, or anyone else who was vulnerable to a madman.

"Good question. And he said we wouldn't find him or his friends."

"His friends?" Reese's eyebrows lifted. "You think he's referrin' to the women he's kidnapped?"

"I do." Brantley stared out at the parking lot, surveying their surroundings while he considered their next move. "He's agitated. Not my intention, but I think he's scared of what John will do to him. We have to find those women and we have to do it now."

"It's probably safe to assume the detective's not at work," Reese said as they walked around to get into the SUV.

"Doubtful."

"Maybe JJ can see where the call came from?"

"Worth a shot. Call her back. Tell her what happened." He put the key in the ignition, started the engine. "In the meantime, we're goin' back to the detective's house. There's got to be a clue there somewhere."

WHILE BRANTLEY WOUND HIS WAY THROUGH MIDMORNING traffic, Reese called JJ, told her about the phone call.

"I'll see if I can find a location, but if I'm bein' honest, it's gonna be a long shot since it came up blocked."

"Understood."

"Where're you headed now?"

"Back to the detective's house. Brantley thinks we mighta missed somethin'."

"I think you did," said someone in the background.

"Trey?"

"Yep." His voice came closer to the phone. "Somethin's been botherin' me about your initial inspection of the house."

Figuring this was something Brantley needed to hear, Reese put the call on speaker. "How so?"

"Well, Brantley mentioned one of the bedrooms belonging to the detective, right? Another with only a bed."

Brantley glanced at Reese, back to the road, answered with, "Yeah. That's right. So?"

"How big would you say the house was?" Trey asked.

Reese wasn't sure where he was going with this, but he replied with a rough estimate. "Fifteen, sixteen hundred, maybe."

"See, that's the problem. I was able to pull up the tax records on the house. The appraisal shows it to be somewhere close to twenty-five-hundred square feet."

Brantley's forehead creased; his eyes remained on the road. "I thought somethin' was off. The hallway. It cut off in a weird spot. The wall wasn't straight. Felt like that one wall was in the wrong place for the footprint of the house."

"You think he's got some hidden rooms?" Reese asked.

"It's possible."

"It shows to be four bedrooms, two baths," JJ announced. "I've got the tax appraisal right here. Two of the bedrooms are on exterior walls, two on the interior. Single bath in a hallway."

"I only saw one bath," Brantley announced. "In the master bedroom."

Reese noticed Brantley had picked up speed.

"We didn't see those rooms," Reese noted. "Shit."

Brantley's phone rang, buzzing in Reese's hand. He glanced at the screen. "Holy shit. It's Collins."

"Answer it."

Reese tapped the screen to answer, the call going directly to the speaker.

"Walker," Brantley barked.

"This is Detective Collins."

The voice had the same tone and cadence but it sounded more adult-like than the one Reese had heard earlier.

"Where are you, Detective Collins?" Brantley demanded.

"I'm taking care of an issue. I heard you've been looking for me."

"We have. We need to talk to you about the case."

"What is there to talk about? I think you've figured out a few things."

"We still need to talk," Brantley snapped. "We're on our way to your house. Will you be there?"

"Depends." His breathing was labored, like he was moving something heavy. "How long will it take you?"

Reese glanced at the navigation screen. It showed eighteen minutes to destination.

"An hour," Brantley lied.

"I'll be back by then. Just need to drop something off real quick."

God, please don't let it be a body.

"See you then," Brantley said through gritted teeth.

The call disconnected and the SUV lurched forward as Brantley's foot hit the floor.

"Call JJ."

Reese wasted no time dialing the number, sending the call to speaker.

"We're on our way back to the house," Brantley informed her when she answered. "I need you to contact Special Agent Hillary Jones with the FBI. Tell her our suspicions and let her know we're headin' to the house."

"You think he's there?" she asked, concerned.

"He will be. And I think I might've pissed off our suspect." Brantley hit the steering wheel. "Son of a bitch."

"Call her, JJ," Reese commanded. "Now."

Reese disconnected the call as they sped down the busy highway, the SUV weaving between slower-moving vehicles. They had to pass the police station, then the lake before they made it to the detective's neighborhood. Thankfully, Brantley slowed some on the residential streets, but not much. A few minutes later, Brantley hit the brakes, bringing the SUV to a skidding stop in front of the house, blocking the driveway.

"His car's here. You think that means he is?"

"More than likely."

"How the fuck did he get here so quickly?" Reese asked, opening the glove box and retrieving his backup weapon that he'd stashed there earlier.

"He knows what we're doin'," Brantley ground out, his knuckles turning white as he gripped the steering wheel.

Clearly. And it looked like he was one step ahead, too.

"What's the plan here?" Reese asked, nodding toward the house.

"We need to locate the women first. Secure them."

Provided they were inside. Reese prayed like hell they were. "And then?"

Brantley turned toward him, eyes hard and cold. "We're gonna take this motherfucker down."

It was times like this when Reese wished he had a weapon with a little more power and range. But his Sig Sauer would have to do for now.

Because he never knew what he was walking into, he checked the weapon, then holstered it. He did the same with his side piece, securing it with an ankle holster before getting out of the SUV. He met Brantley around the front.

"Those comms would come in handy right about now," Brantley said absently.

Yeah. Yeah, they definitely would. Reese would have to follow up with his brother on that. Since they seemed to continuously get themselves in these situations, it would be good to have a way to communicate with each other and with home base. Sooner rather than later.

"We need to find those hidden rooms," Brantley said as they approached the house. "If those women are here, that's where they'll be."

"And if they're not?"

"Then we find them." Brantley glanced over at him again. "One way or another, we put an end to this, Reese. Today."

Reese nodded, letting Brantley know he understood.

Stepping up on the porch, Reese sidestepped to peek into the living room while Brantley knocked on the door. It wasn't surprising no one answered.

"We're goin' in," Brantley told Reese, his words spoken softly.

Pulling his pick set out of his pocket, he passed it over. Brantley went to work on the lock, springing it in probably half the time it had taken Reese, which was saying something. Reese had perfected the art of picking locks. Evidently, Brantley'd mastered it.

Once inside, neither of them spoke. Reese kept his ears alert for any noises. The refrigerator hummed in the kitchen, but that was the only noise aside from the heater blowing softly from the air vents in the floor.

Like before, they cleared the house, checking all the rooms to ensure no one was hiding. And like earlier, they found it was clear despite the fact the detective's car was in the drive this time.

Brantley's hand signal directed Reese into the kitchen while he went the opposite direction, into the hallway. Between them, there should be two bedrooms and a bath if Trey's information was accurate. The question was, how did they get in and what was waiting for them behind those walls?

Reese felt along the wall, looking for a secret panel or something that blended. He found nothing, moving in the direction Brantley went. Down the hallway, he continued to scope the walls, the floors. Aside from the ill-constructed wall Brantley had mentioned, he found nothing, so he continued. Through the master bedroom, into the adjoining bath. No sooner did he step into the bathroom than he saw Brantley holding up a hand, motioning him closer.

Brantley was focused on the interior of what looked to be a towel closet.

"These shelves were in place before," Brantley said softly, pointing to a stack of wooden boards leaning against the cabinet.

Peering into the closet, he saw that it was empty. The perfect place for a hidden doorway.

Sure enough, the wall had been crudely cut so that the Sheetrock could be set aside. On the floor, the chalky substance had been ground into the white linoleum. Had they known what they were looking for earlier, they probably would've noticed it.

"If he was in there, that Sheetrock wouldn't be in place," Reese noted. "He'd have a hard time puttin' it in position from that side."

Brantley looked at him and nodded. "You see if the women are in there. I'm gonna check the rest of the house. Be careful."

"Always."

With his Sig in hand, Reese traded places with Brantley, pulling the Sheetrock out of its resting spot, setting it aside. On the other side, there was a thin door fashioned from balsa wood, it looked like. Not sturdy, by any means, but it served its purpose of sealing the space off.

Reese pressed his back to the wall at the side of the door in case Collins was on the other side with a weapon. With one hand, he turned the knob, pushed the door open, then peeked in. On the other side of the door, he was greeted with darkness. The sort that disoriented a person when they were in it for too long. It brought back memories that Reese quickly shoved aside. He would not go there now. He couldn't.

He retrieved his flashlight from his belt, held it in one hand. Supporting the hand holding his guns, he moved deeper into the space.

Reese was greeted with scurrying sounds, and for a second, he wondered if the detective kept an animal. Or maybe rats.

One more step, more scurrying.

Something tickled his face so he reached up, found that it was a string. He tugged on it and a yellow glow filled the space.

No, those weren't animals.

They were women.

Holy.

Fuck.

Chapter Twenty

"COLLINS!" BRANTLEY SHOUTED. "SHOW YOURSELF, MAN. IT'S over."

There was a snickering sound coming from the living room, so Brantley moved that direction, gun at the ready.

"Jake? Is that you?" he asked, keeping his tone cool, that of a parent talking to a child. "We need to talk."

A giggle this time. It came from the far corner of the room.

"We found your hidin' place," he said, shifting so he was moving along the wall, toward the kitchen.

He could see Collins crouched down beside the couch in the far corner, as though he was actually hidden from view.

"You said I wouldn't find it, but I did, Jake. The game's over."

"Nuh-uh," the childlike voice said. "I tricked you."

"Tricked me? How'd you trick me?"

"They're not all here," he called back, another giggle following. "You missed one. My brother took her after he killed her. You'll never, ever find her."

"Son of a bitch."

"Oooh. You can't say bad words." The tone of the voice shifted from jovial to accusatory, his head peeking up over the arm of the couch. "You're gonna be in trouble for that."

"By who, Jake?"

"The mean lady."

"What lady, Jake? Talk to me. Who's gonna be mad that I said bad words?"

Detective Collins, or rather Jake as seemed to be the case now, unfolded himself from the corner, standing tall. He was wearing a ratty T-shirt and a pair of jeans that had seen better days.

"Momma," he answered, his eyes widening as though he was expecting her to appear at any moment. "She's gonna make you pull your pants down."

Brantley watched as horror reflected on the detective's face, his eyes darting to the hallway.

"Does she spank you, Jake? Is that the trouble you mean?"

He shook his head adamantly. "Not only that." His eyes darted around the room.

He honestly didn't want to know the horrors this man might have suffered as a child, but he needed to know what pushed him to do such heinous acts, so he asked, "Does she hurt you, Jake?"

His eyes were wild now, his hands trembling. "She can't find us here, Brantley Walker. We can't let her find us."

"She won't," he assured him. "Your mother won't find us."

"Yeah, she will. She always does."

"What does she do when she finds you?" he asked, keeping his gun trained on the man.

"Bad things."

Christ. They had figured something tragic had happened to make this man regress into a child, but he hadn't considered all the horrific ways she could've inflicted that pain.

"Like what, Jake? Does she not like when you play hide-and-seek?"

He shook his head, lower lip protruding in a pout. "No."

"Why not?"

"'Cause I'm only s'posed to play games with her."

He could feel his gut churn, but he asked anyway. "Like what?"

"The feel-good kind. It's our secret game. I'm not s'posed to tell nobody."

Oh, fuck. "But you don't play those games anymore, do you, Jake?"

The man nodded.

"What does that mean, Jake? You do play them?"

Another nod. "With my friends. I play the game with my friends. To make them happy. It's supposed to make them happy."

"But it doesn't?"

"He doesn't let me play for long."

Brantley frowned, trying to keep up. "Who? John?"

John/Jake shook his head. "Not John. He's nice. He loves me."

Brantley waited, holding his breath.

Again, the detective looked around, eyes wild as though he expected someone to jump out at him.

"Who, Jake? Who's the mean one?"

"Jack," he whispered loudly. "He's the mean one. He doesn't like playin' games."

There was a third one?

"I try to make it better when he's done. I really, really try, but they cry when we play. I don't know why, but they cry."

"Then what happens, Jake?"

The response didn't come, but right before Brantley's eyes, the man's expression shifted, hardened, his posture straightening. Gone was the child, in his place the grown man they'd originally talked to at the police station.

"John?" Please, God, let it be John and not another one.

"You shouldn't be here, Walker."

Okay, good. It was John.

"We're here to help you," Brantley said softly. "We're just here to help."

"They're dead, Walker. They're all dead."

He sure as fuck hoped not. And since Reese hadn't returned, he could only pray he'd found the women and he had called emergency services.

"We know you were protectin' Jake. He told us. That's why you did it, right? That's why you hid their bodies?"

"I had to," he said, his tone adamant. "He doesn't deserve what happened to him."

He saw the man's eyes dart toward the coffee table.

"Don't move, John," Brantley ordered, taking control of the situation. "Don't fuckin' move."

"You can't take him," John stated, his tone hard. "You can't take my brother. He won't survive without me."

"We're not gonna take him. He needs to get help, John. We just want him to get some help."

"They won't help him. They'll hurt him. They always hurt him."

"He said there's one woman missin'," Brantley said, hoping to divert his attention. "Who's missin', John? Where is she?"

John shook his head, glared back. "You need to let this go, Walker. You need to leave. Let it go."

"I can't do that. You know I can't. Those women have families, John. Their families miss them."

"Families are overrated," he snarled.

Brantley figured in John's case that was true. He didn't want to think about what his mother had done to him, what horrific things she'd put him through that had made his brain splinter like that.

In the distance, Brantley could hear the faint sound of sirens. Hopefully they were headed their way.

"She's gone," John said, his tone somber. "I couldn't save her. He didn't want him to play with her anymore."

"Who, John? Was it Jack?"

John's eyes rounded like saucers at the mention of the name. He started shaking his head, a move similar to the way the child identity had. "Don't do that, Walker. I'm warnin' you. Don't do that."

"Tell me where she is," he said easily, trying to stay calm.

"He didn't want Jake to play with her anymore," he repeated. "I had to. I had to." The detective stared at him, eyes cold. "She's gone."

"Where? We need to get her, John. That's your job. It's your job to find them. Help me find her. Tell me where she is. We can save her, John."

"They'll find her soon enough. The water's shallow."

"Water? Is she at the lake?" Brantley pulled out his phone, hit the button to dial, wishing like fuck he had a direct connection rather than a fucking cell phone. "JJ, I need your help."

"Where are you?"

He ignored her question. "She's at the lake," he relayed.

"Who?"

"One of the women. John hasn't told me where, but she's at the lake. Call someone. Have them get over there now."

"Will do."

Footsteps sounded to his left, but they were a familiar sound. He wasn't sure how he knew it was Reese, but he could sense his presence.

"Police are on the way," Reese said, his gun raised and trained on John when he stepped out of the hallway into the room. "They're in bad shape, but they're alive."

"I can't let you take him in," John said calmly, his eyes darting down to the coffee table again. "I can't let them take Jake."

"He needs help," Brantley repeated. "They just want to help him."

Christ Almighty, he hoped like hell backup arrived soon.

"No." The tone of his voice firmed, became harder. "They'll lock him up. Put him in a cage. He can't be in a cage. Never again."

The sirens grew louder, approaching the house now.

"John, the police are outside. They're here to help the women. We need to get them help."

Clearly ignoring him, John took a step forward, toward the table.

"John, I need you to stay where you are." Brantley glanced at Reese, back to John. "We're not done talkin'."

"We're done," he said, taking another step forward.

"John, don't do this."

"I have to. I can't let Jake be taken. They'll hurt him again."

"No, they won't. He can get some help. You both can."

Another step, then another.

Brantley's finger shifted to the trigger. "John, stop movin'. Now."

"I can't do that, Walker. You know I can't."

A few feet away, just out of his visual range, he could hear Reese breathing calmly.

"I'm not gonna hurt you, Walker," John said, his voice odd now. "Jake doesn't want me to hurt you. He likes playin' this game with you."

The detective reached down.

Fuck.

"John, don't do this," he warned.

The next few seconds happened in slow motion, but at a speed Brantley could do nothing to stop. A fist pounded on the front door, startling John. He lunged, grabbing a pistol from under a newspaper on the coffee table. Later, Brantley would question why he hadn't cleared the room, checked for weapons.

In a move too quick for anything but reaction, John lifted the gun...

"Don't do this, John," Brantley shouted, the words still hanging in the air when the gun fired, the detective crumpling to the floor.

Dead by his own hand.

REESE MANAGED TO MAKE HIS WAY OUTSIDE after the officers stormed in, the EMTs following close behind. There was nothing anyone could do for John Collins. The man's brains were sprayed across his living room wall.

Despite all their efforts, despite the fact they had three of the four women alive to see another day, Reese was most disturbed by the news that had been delivered a few minutes ago. Officers had found the naked, severely beaten body of Shelly Masters dumped in shallow water beside a private pier at the very lake she was taken from nearly a year ago.

He wished he could say he was bothered by what had happened, by the fact the detective had taken his own life, but he wasn't. Not after seeing the state those three women were in. Terrified, tortured, and yes, scarred both mentally and physically by what they'd been through. Reese had no idea what had been the motivation behind the anguish Collins had delivered to those women, but whatever it was, it had come out in the form of white-hot rage.

"You okay?"

Brantley's hand touched his shoulder and Reese stopped, turned to face him. He didn't say a word, just met Brantley's eyes. There had been a moment when Collins had gone for the gun that Reese's worst nightmare had arisen. For terrifying seconds, he hadn't been sure what the detective was going to do, but he'd feared that Brantley was going to be the one on the receiving end of that bullet. Reese's finger had been on the trigger, but he hadn't gotten the chance to fire before John had done it for him.

"I'm okay," Brantley said, clearly reading Reese's need for reassurance. "I would've taken him out first."

Or Reese would have.

That didn't change the fact that Reese had been terrified in those few seconds.

"We'll give our initial statements here," Brantley explained. "I told Special Agent Jones they could hit me up for more later. She's meetin' with the mayor. It's a huge clusterfuck since he's a police officer."

Reese could only imagine. Damage control was going to be necessary.

"Have you looked at the rooms where he kept them?" Reese asked softly.

"I was gonna do that now. You can stay out here."

Reese shook his head. He couldn't. "I'll go with you."

He could see the concern on Brantley's face but there was no rebuttal. Reese followed Brantley into the house, past the police and the FBI agents who were processing the crime scene.

When they stepped through the hole in the Sheetrock, Reese took a deep breath, expelled it.

The stench was horrible.

"We're worried about the structural integrity of the house," one of the agents stated. "He took down some of the support walls."

Yes, John Collins had removed the walls separating the two bedrooms and the bathroom to make one large room where he kept the women. The irons that had been affixed to their ankles were empty now, spread across the floor near the twin beds they'd been chained to. From what he could tell, the chains were long enough for them to reach the toilet but nothing else.

There were no windows, no Sheetrock on the walls or the ceiling. It looked as though the detective had sound-proofed the space. Probably to ensure no one heard them. The flooring had been ripped out, leaving only stained and scarred plywood beneath. A sink with a dripping faucet sat just out of their reach. The bathtub didn't appear to work. Based on how frail the women had been, it was likely he fed them just enough to keep them alive.

"How were they when you found them?" Brantley asked.

"They were chained to the beds." He motioned to one of the four beds. "Jody was trying to hide, crouched between the bed and the wall, Debbie was unconscious, and Maria was awake but not lucid. Naked and terrified. Battered. Beaten. Drugged."

"But alive," Brantley said, his voice low, reassuring. "They're alive, Reese."

Yes, they were. Three of them, anyway. As for whether they would be happy about that, he didn't know. They'd been through a horrific ordeal, something they would live with for the rest of their lives. They would see this in their nightmares. God knew he would.

"This is where the smell's comin' from," Brantley noted.

Yeah. Reese figured they hadn't seen soap and water the entire time they'd been here. Probably not much food either.

"We need to get home," Brantley finally said after they'd stood there for several minutes.

Reese looked over at him. "Somethin' wrong?"

"No. It's just where we need to be."

Reese nodded, understanding. There wasn't anything they could do here, and the DPD was competent enough to handle the rest. Since this was an internal matter, it would require some finessing on their part. One of their own detectives was a serial killer.

Fortunately, he was no longer.

They arrived back in Coyote Ridge at seven that night. It had been a long day, but even as exhaustion set in, Reese found himself revived the instant Tesha came running at him when they pulled into the drive.

"Looks like someone's happy to see you," Brantley said as he put the truck in park. "You spend some time with her. I'll take our shit inside."

Reese didn't argue, hopping out of the truck and going to his knee as Tesha all but barreled into him, head-butting his hand for a scratch.

"You miss me, girl?"

Tesha hopped and pawed, yipping a couple of times.

"I think that's the first time I've heard you speak." Getting to his feet, he headed to the backyard, snatching up one of the tennis balls along the way. He lobbed it in the direction of the barn, watched as the dog took off after it.

"Hey," JJ greeted, stepping out of the barn with Baz and Trey behind her. "Y'all made it."

Reese nodded, watched as Tesha pranced around the ball, picking it up, dropping it again. "We did."

"You okay?"

"Will be."

"Anything you need us to do?"

He shook his head. What he needed was some quiet. Some alone time with Brantley where neither of them had to puzzle through information. One night. That was what he needed to regroup. Tomorrow he'd be back to normal.

"All right, then. We're gonna say hi to Brantley, then head out."

"Talk to you tomorrow," Baz said, following her.

Trey stopped at his side, slapped a hand on his shoulder, then squeezed. "Y'all did good."

"We," Reese corrected. "We couldn't've done it without you, Trey."

"I wouldn't go that far." Trey smiled. "But I'll take it.

When he was alone, Reese took a seat on the steps of the back deck. The sun had dipped below the horizon, the twilight beginning to fade into darkness. None of that mattered because the LED spotlights mounted on the house and the barn lit up with motion, so it was almost as though it was daytime.

"Well, that's new," Reese said when Tesha trotted over and dropped the ball at his feet.

Reese had to lean forward to get it, but he did, sending it out into the yard again. Once more, Tesha returned with it, dropping it and waiting.

And that set the tone for the next half hour. Tesha would take a break every so often, wandering around the yard, drinking from the water bowl sitting on the deck. All the while, Reese remained where he was, the images of the day running through his head on a loop. Those women, the detective. He had asked Special Agent Hillary Jones, the one overseeing the case for the FBI, to let him know how the women were doing. She had confirmed that she would be delivering the news to Shelly Masters's family herself. As for the survivors, Jones had texted him a short time ago to say they were all three in the hospital and would remain there for a few days while their injuries were tended to. She had confirmed that Dale Henderson and Alicia Struthers had both arrived, as had Maria Espinoza's parents, all grateful that their loved one was alive.

They would survive, he knew. Time would heal their physical injuries and, if they were lucky, some of the mental wounds as well. Reese knew how that was. He battled his own demons, though he'd grown adept at keeping them bottled up because they were too horrific to reflect on. But seeing those women in that room, chained up the way they had been, it brought some of those memories flooding back.

Tesha bumped his hand, drew Reese back to the present. He forced a smile, figuring if he did, it would eventually stick.

"Probably should make some dinner," he told the dog, getting to his feet.

When he turned around, he saw Brantley standing inside the house, shoulder propped on the doorjamb as he watched him. The concern he saw on his face was understandable.

"Shower with me?" Brantley prompted when Reese approached.

"Then dinner?"

Brantley nodded. "I'll make sandwiches."

Good idea.

BAZ SAT ON HIS COUCH, HEAD TILTED back, eyes closed. He hadn't bothered to turn on the television, didn't even manage to fix himself dinner like he'd planned.

No, from the moment he walked into the apartment, he'd been dead on his feet, the events of the day draining all the energy from his body.

And to think, he wasn't the one who had found those women, freed them, or watched the detective take his own life. Still, it felt as though he'd been right there with Brantley and Reese, not two hundred miles away. Brantley had called, filled them in on what went down, then asked JJ to gather all the evidence they'd uncovered that would help the police and the FBI to close the case up neat and tidy. Along with Trey, the three of them had worked diligently to gather it all together before JJ sent an electronic file over to the special agent now in charge.

He didn't miss it, he realized. Didn't miss being on the front line, seeing the carnage, dealing with the emotional aftermath. Trey had asked him if he would, and Baz had wondered there for a little while. But he didn't and he knew that he wouldn't. He was content to sit on the sidelines, to run the op from behind a computer screen, JJ at his side.

What did that say about him? he wondered.

His cell phone chimed.

Baz shifted as he dug it out of his pocket, checked the screen. It was a text message from JJ, so he unlocked the phone, read it. Smiled.

Getting to his feet, he went to his front door, opened it.

And there she was, standing in the hallway outside his apartment.

JJ lifted a bag, waved it. "I brought dinner." She lifted the other hand, revealing a six-pack of beer. "And this."

Taking the beer from her, he stepped back out of the way, then closed the door when she came inside.

As he'd learned with JJ, her curiosity dictated her movements, and she waltzed right into his apartment, scoping it out from top to bottom.

"A little plain, don't you think?" she asked, pivoting to look at him. "Kinda dark. You need some art on the walls or somethin'."

"You brighten the space up quite nicely," he told her, setting the beer on the end table.

Baz took the paper sack from her hand, set it down, too, then pulled her into him. He cupped her face and stared down at her. "This is a pleasant surprise, by the way. I didn't expect you to show up." He narrowed his eyes. "In fact, I didn't realize you knew where I lived."

She smiled, her green eyes lighting up. "Mad hacker skills, remember?"

"Yes. I remember."

Baz kissed her.

He'd been battling the urge all day, reminding himself they were at work and he had to focus. It wasn't easy when every single thing JJ did made him crazy with lust. He wasn't sure he'd ever met a woman who affected him on this level before. From the moment he'd set eyes on her, Baz had been a goner. She was different. She mattered.

"Are you hungry?" she asked, the words spoken against his lips.

"Depends."

"On?"

"Whether or not you're stayin' the night."

JJ pulled back, stared up at him. "Why does that matter?"

"If you are, then yes, I'm hungry. We can eat, drink a couple of beers, chill. Then I'll take you to bed and ravish you all night long."

He liked that there was a hint of pink that flooded her cheeks. "And if I'm not?"

"Then we'll bypass everything but the ravishing."

"I can probably be persuaded," she said, rising up to meet his lips again. "But the ravishing doesn't have to wait until after dinner."

"No?"

She shook her head. "And it doesn't have to happen in the bedroom."

"Where would you prefer it happen?"

JJ peered around him briefly, looked back up at his face. "The couch looks like a damn fine place to start."

Baz learned shortly thereafter that she was right.

Damn fine place to start.

Chapter Twenty-One

FOR WHATEVER REASON, BRANTLEY COULDN'T SLEEP. HE'D spent most of the night lying in bed, listening to Reese breathe. Every now and then, Reese would mumble something incoherent, his body moving more than usual.

It had him wondering if Reese had nightmares. Odd that they'd slept beside one another for this long and he hadn't noticed. Which he took to mean, if he did have them, they weren't as regular as Brantley's were. Had the events of the past few days gotten to him? He still remembered the look on Reese's face after John Collins took his own life. Completely blank, as though it had no impact on him whatsoever.

Thing was, Brantley knew how he felt. While he had tried to talk the detective down, it was because that was what he was trained to do. Along with hand-to-hand combat, sniper skills, and myriad other special training, he'd also been trained to negotiate. He'd failed this time, but he wouldn't dwell on it. The mental illness had taken its toll on the detective. Anyone could've seen it. Those closest to him should've seen the signs, even if it was only his co-workers.

But that was behind them now. Brantley refused to look back, to worry he hadn't done enough. He'd done exactly what he could, nothing more, nothing less. And now three of those women were back with their families.

No, his failure was not with Detective Collins; it had been Shelly Masters he hadn't come through for. And that he would regret, tucking it away with all the others he'd failed in his life. But he would move on. He would continue to do what was necessary. And while he'd been skeptical about this new assignment, leading the governor's task force in finding missing persons, Brantley knew it was exactly where he belonged.

Reese jerked in his sleep, a strangled cry escaping him. It was enough to have Brantley turning, sliding one hand over Reese's chest.

"It's a dream," he said softly. "Reese. Wake up for me. It's just a dream."

Reese went completely still. His body no longer moved. His chest was barely rising and falling. His eyes opened slowly as though he needed to take stock of his surroundings before he gave himself away in case the enemy was nearby. Brantley knew that feeling all too well.

"Hey." He leaned down, pressed his lips to Reese's shoulder.

"What time is it?"

"Four thirty."

"Early for you, isn't it?"

"Haven't slept much," he admitted, sliding his arm under Reese's head and pulling him closer.

Reese came without complaint, but rather than curl up beside him, Reese apparently had other ideas as he moved over him, his weight familiar and welcome.

A distraction. That was what this was. Whether it was because Reese needed to feel something other than what plagued him in his dreams or because he didn't want Brantley asking questions he wasn't ready to answer, it was a distraction, nonetheless.

Brantley urged him to move atop him completely, their naked bodies aligning. Reese's lips trailed up his neck, along his jaw, back down again. The sensations had his body hardening, his cock throbbing as it brushed against Reese's.

Putting his hands on Reese's hips, he held him in place, ensuring he didn't go too far.

This was what he needed, to be close to Reese, to soothe away the strains of recent events and replace those mental images with something that would get him through the days and nights ahead of them.

"Give me your mouth," he whispered, tilting his head so he could meet Reese's lips with his own.

Their tongues began a leisurely dance that quickly grew more urgent. Brantley kept him close, grinding his hips so the friction of his body glided along his sensitive shaft. He remembered the first time they'd done this. On an airplane, back when Reese was confused about what he wanted. These days, there was no holding back but there had been something incredibly intimate, innately sensual about that moment despite the fact they'd both been mostly dressed.

"Brantley…"

"I'm here, baby. Whatever you need, I'm here."

When Reese lifted up, his hips rocking more insistently, Brantley slid his hand between their bodies, gripping Reese's cock firmly. In the darkness, he could see his profile but not the expression. He didn't need to see, though, because he knew what Reese looked like when he needed more.

"Oh, God." Reese's hips moved faster as he thrust into Brantley's fist. "More. Need … more."

Brantley's grip was already tight but he gave Reese what he asked for, feeling the intensity of Reese's stare as he levered himself up on his hands and drove his hips forward, fucking Brantley's fist like it was a lifeline that might save him from the darkness.

A few grunts and then Reese was coming, his body going stone-still as cum splashed over Brantley's stomach. The sensation had his own cock throbbing, but he ignored it. This wasn't about him. In fact, it was never about him. What he found in Reese was so much more than his own satisfaction.

It was over as fast as it started. Reese crawled out of bed, returned with a towel, and cleaned him off before joining him in the bed once more.

"Let me hold you," he whispered when he felt Reese's hand sliding down between his legs.

He knew he was going to return the favor, but right then, the only thing Brantley wanted was to hold him.

"You sure?"

"Never been more sure about anyone in my life."

"I was talk—"

He pulled Reese close. "I know what you were talkin' about. Now shut up so I can hold you."

There was a soft chuckle. A few minutes later, they were both asleep.

"WHAT'RE YOUR PLANS FOR TOMORROW?" JJ ASKED, hoping the question came across as casual.

"Thanksgiving?"

She quirked an eyebrow. "Yes. Thanksgiving."

"My dad invited me out to his place. Me and my mother."

"Your mom has Thanksgiving dinner with your dad and his new wife?"

Baz offered a one-shoulder shrug. "What can I say? They like each other's company."

"At the expense of their new spouses?"

"My father's theory is, if it's supposed to work out, it'll work out."

"I suppose he's got a prenup."

"Of course. Ironclad, too."

JJ shook her head. "How can he be so cavalier about marriage?"

Baz cocked a hip on his kitchen counter, wiped his hands on a dish towel. "I wouldn't so much say he's cavalier about marriage. More so he's optimistic about love. He loves to be in love."

"And the wedding part? What? He's a stickler for a big party?"

Baz laughed, a sound she adored.

"I never thought about it. But yeah, maybe."

"What about your mother's husband? Will he be there?"

"He's actually out of the country on business. Bigwig CEO. It's the end of the fiscal year or some shit. He'll be back on Sunday. They'll have their own Thanksgiving then." He planted his palms flat on the counter, leaned toward her. "What about you? What're your plans?"

"Don't have any. I did buy a turkey-and-dressing TV dinner if that counts for something."

Baz shook his head, frowned. "No, it does not. You can come with me."

JJ was instantly on her feet. "Oh, no. No, no. I am not havin' Thanksgiving with your folks. No way, no, sir, no how."

"What if I told you he's got an indoor heated pool and a kick-ass hot tub?"

"You cannot bribe me with kick-ass hot tubs, Baz. Just won't work."

He walked around the small breakfast bar. No, stalked was more like it. Before she could run, he grabbed her arm, pulled her into him, and banded his arms around her to keep her from bolting. He seemed to know her pretty well.

His playful expression sobered, his eyes concerned. "Why aren't you havin' Thanksgiving with your parents?"

Her turn to shrug. "They don't celebrate the holiday anymore. Not since Jeremy died."

"You could always invite them to your place," he suggested. "Make them dinner, show them you'd like to celebrate."

JJ tried to push away from him, but he was having none of it. His hold on her tightened.

"Who said I wanted to celebrate?"

"I can see it in your eyes."

JJ closed her eyes. "No, you can't."

Baz chuckled and his lips pressed to hers gently, briefly. "Come to my dad's with me, JJ. I promise, we'll keep it casual. I'll tell them you're a friend from work. How's that?"

Opening her eyes, she mock-glared at him. "What? Am I not good enough to be your girlfriend?"

"You're too good to be my girlfriend, JJ. But I don't want you to feel trapped."

Oddly enough, she didn't, though she had no clue why that was. Hell, anytime a guy wanted to spend more than one night at her place had always made her panic. And she honestly couldn't remember if she had ever slept with a guy in his bed. If she had, it hadn't been memorable.

Yet here she was, still at Baz's, wearing one of his button-downs and nothing more after they'd spent the entire night together. Some of it had even been to sleep.

His arms relaxed, his hands sliding down her backside. Cool air caressed her thighs when he planted them on the backs of her legs then moved them up to her ass.

"Say yes, and I'll do that thing you like."

"What thing's that?" she asked, because yes, he could most definitely bribe her with sex.

He held her gaze, smiled. "Say yes, JJ."

With a sigh, JJ went against every single one of her rules.

She said yes.

And that thing with his tongue … Heaven help her … so totally worth it.

"WELL, YOU HAVE TO ADMIT, TRAVIS HOLDS true to his word," Reese told Brantley as they stood inside the new conference room in the barn later that afternoon.

"That he does." Brantley walked over to the wall, tapped a button. "Question is, did he come up with the fancy electronic system or was that somethin' JJ finagled out of him?"

"My money's on JJ."

"I resemble that remark," JJ called out from the stairs.

Reese looked up, watched as she strolled down.

He couldn't quite put his finger on it, but there was something different about JJ. It was in the way she moved, her smile, even her eyes. She looked … happy.

"For the record, Trey helped me install it," she said, stepping into the room with a coffee mug in her hand.

"Did they get in your way?" Brantley asked. "The construction crew?"

JJ shook her head. "They kicked ass over the weekend. I worked from home most of the time, so no, they weren't a bother. I was impressed at how fast they worked."

"Travis has some serious pull," Reese noted. "So what does this fancy system do?"

"I had it set up so it's easy to transfer any call directly in here from any of our phones. That way, if you're off somewhere and you need us, we're all in one place." She pointed to another switch. "I also talked to a guy at Sniper 1 Security. He showed me how to set up the comms to the phones so there's a direct link anywhere in this building."

"The comms came in?" Brantley looked like a kid on Christmas.

"Yeah. FedEx package arrived yesterday mornin'." She looked at Reese. "I called your brother to let him know we received and that we were super grateful."

"And the computer setup?" Brantley asked, nodding in the direction of the large monitor sitting on the credenza against the wall.

"That was on the governor's dime." She smiled brightly.

"And he knows about that?"

"He does. Gave me full approval." She seemed very proud of herself. "I think Rhonda's startin' to like me."

"Speakin' of the governor…" Brantley turned to face them. "He wants the five of us in his office this afternoon."

Oh, shit. Reese didn't like the sound of that.

"It's not bad," Brantley promised, but he didn't elaborate as to what it was the governor did want.

Reese figured it could be any number of things. Considering what had happened in Dallas…

He pushed the thought away because he needed to stop seeing those women in his mind, the horror that had been inflicted upon them. It pained him still, and he'd never been more grateful to have Brantley than he was right then. The man had been his anchor last night, holding him together, giving him exactly what he needed.

"Where's Baz?" Brantley asked as he headed out of the conference room.

"He went to talk to a guy he knows for one of the positions."

"Police officer?" Reese inquired.

"No. At least, I don't think so." She shrugged a shoulder.

"If we're lucky, we'll get the next few days off," Brantley told JJ. "But keep your phone on you. We get a call, we're on."

She nodded. "Did you happen to check out your new offices?"

Brantley frowned, glanced over at Reese.

Reese did his best not to give anything away. He knew what JJ was referring to because he'd been upstairs to check on the progress already. When they'd come in the house last night, he'd smelled fresh paint, knew they'd been hard at work. What he hadn't expected was for it to be finished. The only thing they had left to do was get the deck installed. According to Travis's email, that would be handled next week starting on Monday. Evidently not even the almighty Travis Walker could work miracles when it came to enough time in the day.

JJ laughed. "He really doesn't go anywhere but the bedroom and the kitchen, huh?"

"Not if he can help it."

"In my defense, I had other things on my mind," Brantley stated. "But I could tell they'd been working."

JJ laughed. "Right."

Reese nodded his head in the direction of the door. "Come on. I'll show you."

He led the way, Brantley walking beside him, Tesha trotting along at their feet.

Once inside, they headed for the stairs. As they scaled the last few steps to the second floor, Tesha darted ahead of them, nose to the ground.

"Holy shit." Brantley stopped at the top.

Reese smiled to himself because there was awe in that tone and he understood why. The entire upstairs had been transformed. It was no longer barren. It now resembled that of an office space worthy of a day's work.

"Who did this?"

"Travis's crew. They started on Friday afternoon, right after we left," Reese explained. "Travis said they finished up on Sunday."

"The same one that worked on the conference room?"

"No. They're good, but not that good."

Then again, Reese knew there hadn't been much to do for this space. Closing up the walls was the hardest part.

"And the furniture?"

"That was all me."

Brantley's eyes darted over to him. "You bought all this?"

"I did. It's my contribution to the household."

"I told you I'd buy whatever you wanted."

Reese laughed. "And you thought I'd be happy bein' a kept man?"

That got him a laugh, and he felt some of the tension drain out of both of them. It had been touch-and-go all morning, and Reese knew Brantley was worried about him. Telling him he didn't need to be would've gotten him nowhere, so he was grateful they had this to come back to. This was part of their new life together.

"Go on," Reese urged. "Check out your office."

Brantley headed across the game room, which was empty for the time being. Reese wasn't sure what they would do with the space, but he figured they'd find something eventually.

A bark of laughter had Reese heading to Brantley's office.

"A couch?" Brantley's blue-gray eyes glittered with amusement.

"I've got one comin' for downstairs, too. A little nicer."

"Reese, I told—"

He held up a hand. "Don't worry. I put that one on your credit card. It was our deal, after all."

Brantley's expression warmed. "This is great," he said, walking around behind the desk. "Not too fancy."

"I thought it suited you."

"What about yours?"

"Mirror image of this one," he admitted. "After I picked all this out, decided I liked it for me, too."

Brantley scanned the space from his seat behind his desk. "They closed in the old door."

"Wasn't gonna half-ass it."

Brantley reclined back, studied Reese. The scrutiny had Reese fighting the urge to fidget.

"You don't half-ass much of anything, do you?"

"Try not to, no." Reese perched a hip on the edge of Brantley's desk, stared at him. "Told you I was all in. I'm tryin' to live up to it."

Brantley got to his feet, walked around the desk, and stopped in front of Reese. They remained like that for several heartbeats, their eyes locked together.

"If you ever wanna talk about it," Brantley said softly, "I'm here."

"I know." Reese reached for Brantley, nudging him forward with a hand on his hip. "Same goes."

Brantley smiled. "Is it wrong that I'm seriously thinkin' about breakin' in that couch?"

Reese returned the grin. "I was thinkin' the same thing, so no, I wouldn't say it was wrong."

A few hours later, they were heading for the capitol.

The trip down to Austin was taken in two vehicles, Brantley driving one, Baz the other. Reese would've preferred to drive because he could've used the distraction. The mere thought of seeing the governor had his stomach in knots. He had no idea whether they were going to get commended or reprimanded for their efforts on the Dallas case. He could see the reasons for either or both, which didn't help his nerves any.

"Did he sound upset when he requested us?" Reese asked Brantley.

"Who?" Brantley glanced over. "Oh, you mean the governor?" He shrugged one shoulder. "Didn't talk to him. Rhonda called."

Well, that didn't help.

"It's gonna be fine, Reese. Whatever it is he wants to say, we're grown-ups. I don't know about you, but I was dressed down plenty of times in the Navy. We can take it."

That was a valid point. Again, it did nothing for his nerves.

By the time they reached the state capitol, Reese was aware of the cold sweat trickling down his spine. Outwardly, he ensured no one saw he was on the verge of an anxiety attack. If he was lucky, Brantley would be the only one who knew how much he disliked being put on the spot like this. If the others found out, he figured he would be in for a lifetime of harassment, so he did his best to look cool and collected.

They made their way up to the second floor where the governor's office was.

"Good afternoon, Rhonda," JJ greeted the secretary with a big grin. "We're here to see Governor Greenwood."

Rhonda looked up, a smile on her face. Looked as though JJ was right, she was starting to like them.

"He knows it was short notice," Rhonda said, "but he's glad you could make it. Unfortunately, he's only got about ten minutes, so this is going to be quick."

Reese damn sure liked the sound of that.

Rhonda picked up her phone, pushed a button, and informed the governor they were there.

"You can go right in."

Brantley led the way, Reese behind him, then JJ, Baz, and Trey. Reese wondered how Baz and Trey were faring. Neither was his normal talkative self.

"Governor," Brantley greeted when they stepped into the opulent office.

Governor Greenwood was on his feet, walking toward them. He held out his hand, shook each of theirs in turn, referring to Reese and JJ by name because they'd been there before.

"Sir, I'd like to introduce you to Sebastian Buchanan and Trey Walker. They're the newest members of my team."

The governor politely greeted them with a firm shake before taking a step back and addressing them all.

"I hate that I had you drive all the way down here, but I didn't think this was something I should relay over the phone."

Reese's shoulders tensed. Here it came. They were being canned because they'd stuck their noses where they didn't belong.

"The Dallas mayor contacted me this morning," the governor continued, his eyes giving away nothing.

"Sir, I take full responsibility for the actions of my team," Brantley said quickly.

"Well, I would hope so." Governor Greenwood met Brantley's gaze. "In this case, especially. The mayor was quite impressed with the work your team did, including the supporting documentation provided on the investigation."

Reese released the breath he'd been holding, as he figured they all did.

"And that's the good news."

Oh, crap.

Brantley stood with his hands clasped behind his back, shoulders squared. "The bad news, sir?"

Governor Greenwood smiled. "I'm being asked to expand your responsibilities."

"To?"

"Not only will you continue to assist on missing persons cases, I've offered up your team to assist with homicide investigations."

"Sir—"

"Only in specific cities for now. Dallas, Austin, and Houston. And only active cases. Depending on how this works out, we'll determine whether that scope will be broadened."

More work. Just what they didn't need.

"I know it's a lot." Governor Greenwood's gaze strayed to JJ's. "But as I recall from your very thought-out presentation, you're up for the responsibility." He turned back to Brantley. "I think you might need to hire a few more people."

A few? At this rate they were going to need an entire department.

"Thank you, sir," Brantley said quickly.

"Don't thank me yet but do keep me updated."

"Of course, sir."

The governor addressed them all as one. "You did a damn fine job with that case. I hope you understand how valuable your assistance was. I had to turn down the mayor's offer to install your team up in Dallas permanently. Told him you've got more than enough going on down here." He nodded, smiled. "Keep up the good work."

A chorus of thank you, sirs went around before they left the office.

Reese expected to feel a hundred pounds lighter now that it was over, but he didn't.

In fact, he might've been tenser now than before.

"We've made a commitment to Travis," he reminded Brantley. "We have to find Juliet Prince."

"It's gonna be fine," Brantley said softly as they headed back down to the first floor. "As a team, we've got this covered."

Yeah, okay. Maybe he was right.

The did make a damn fine team and if he'd learned anything about Brantley, it was that the man finished whatever he set his mind to.

Chapter Twenty-Two

Thanksgiving Day

"YOU READY FOR THIS?" BRANTLEY ASKED AS he strolled into the kitchen to find Reese downing a bottle of water like he'd just run ten miles.

"Maybe you could just bring me a doggy bag," Reese said tightly, not bothering to look his way.

Brantley grinned. "It's gonna be fine, I promise."

"How many people'll be there again?"

"A few."

Reese groaned.

"Let's just say there'll be enough people there that they won't all be starin' at you."

"Not helpin'."

Brantley chuckled. "You've survived Curtis's many family gatherings, have you not?"

"That's different."

"How so?"

Reese looked his way then. "I'm not in love with any of Curtis's sons."

Brantley felt warmth spread through his chest. It had him moving toward Reese, putting his hands on his hips, and stepping in close.

"Have I told you how fuckin' much I love to hear that?"

"I'll tell you a dozen times if it means I can stay here while you go have turkey and dressin' with your family."

"No deal."

"But I do have a surprise. Somethin' that might take your mind off of dinner."

"What's that?"

Brantley motioned toward the back porch. Reese followed, stepping outside with him.

"I've hired someone to put in a fence," Brantley explained. "Not the entire property, but enough to give Tesha plenty of room to roam." He then pointed to the wall behind them. "And I bought those. Figured we could get them installed."

Reese stepped over to the boxes propped against the wall.

"Those are fancy," Reese said, a smile returning to his face.

"Only the best for our girl," Brantley told him. "The dog doors open because of the device that attaches to her collar. That way she can come and go into the house or the barn whenever she wants."

Brantley's cell phone buzzed, then his watch.

"That's the cameras." Reese glanced toward the side of the house.

Tesha had moved to stand at the edge of the deck, her tail still as she stared out into the brilliant sunlight.

The three of them remained like that until JJ came strolling by, heading toward the barn.

"What's she doin' here?" Brantley wondered aloud. "I thought she was goin' to Baz's dad's for Thanksgiving."

"That's what I heard."

"I'll go talk to her."

"And I'll get Tesha ready to go to your parents," Reese said, whistling for Tesha who had run out to greet JJ.

When Tesha headed back to Reese, Brantley started after JJ, calling her name when she kept walking toward the barn.

When she stopped but didn't turn around, he knew something was wrong. The question was: what?

"JJ?" He stopped a few feet behind her. "Why're you here?"

"Work?"

"Are you askin' or tellin', because that sure sounded indecisive."

When he neared, JJ turned around, her eyes darting around him as though she expected the boogey man to jump out at her at any moment.

"Where's Baz?"

She shrugged.

"I thought you were havin' Thanksgiving with him."

Her mouth opened, closed, lips forming a thin line.

"What's goin' on?"

"I can't, Brantley," she blurted. "I can't have Thanksgiving dinner with his family. That's… It's too much. It signifies something … more. Something we don't have. Yet. Maybe not ever." JJ took a deep breath. "We don't have that, B."

Confused, Brantley waited for her to continue. She didn't.

"Why'd you tell him you'd go then?"

"Because I didn't want to disappoint him," she whispered, her eyes lowering.

"But you don't mind now?"

"I doubt he'll even miss me." She lifted her gaze to his. "I left him a message."

For some reason, he didn't believe her.

"JJ—"

She held up a hand. "I don't need a lecture right now, B. I get it. You're all in love and happy but that doesn't mean the rest of us have to be. I like Baz. We … we have fun together. But that's all it's ever gonna be. I know that deep down. No sense confusin' the issue by bringin' family into it."

He wished he could say he hadn't seen this coming, but Brantley knew JJ. She'd been hurt so many times, she refused to open herself up to anyone. It was the very reason she kept all men at arm's length, the same reason she had continued to take Dante the Douche back. With him she never had to worry that he would really want more than she could give, because he was notorious for fucking things up.

"All right," he conceded. "I won't harp on you about it."

"Thank you."

"Nor will I let you sit here by yourself on Thanksgiving. You're comin' with us."

"To your parents' house?"

"Yep."

"Yay! It's been too long since I've seen them."

Why he'd thought she would argue, he didn't know.

Family get-togethers for Brantley's branch of the family tree were not much different than the rest of the Walker clan. The most important thing for them was that they were with family. Every year without fail, Iris cooked lavish meals for Thanksgiving, ensuring every one of her children was going to be there, even if they could only stop in for a few minutes.

Not that any of them had ever done a fly-by on the house when they could help it. And yes, Brantley had been given a reprieve for the years he'd missed when he'd been deployed, but he had always made a point to call home to talk to his parents, ensure they knew he was thinking about them.

Brantley would admit he looked forward to getting together with his brothers and sisters, nieces and nephew, hanging out. His siblings were the same way. Although they all lived nearby, most of them still in Coyote Ridge, they didn't get together as often as they would like. Unlike Curtis and Lorrie, Sunday dinners rarely involved all of them, even though Brantley knew the grandkids usually stopped in to see Grams and Poppop on the weekends.

"Damn, dude, you're cuttin' it close, aren't ya?" Trey asked when Brantley walked into the house, Reese and JJ behind him. "The game's about to start."

The scent of food drifted toward him, his stomach rumbling in response, but he ignored it, in lieu of addressing his brother. Unlike the rest of them, Brantley wasn't a huge Dallas Cowboys fan, so watching the big game on Turkey Day was never a thing for him.

"Reese, please tell me you're a Cowboys fan," Killian said by way of greeting.

"I'm more of a winnin' team kinda fan," Reese said, deadpan.

Trey's eyes nearly bugged out of his head as he shot to his feet. "Blasphemy! We'll have none of it in this house."

And just like that, Reese was brought into the fold. Greetings were shouted along with jokes and laughter as they all met Reese, most for the first time. Brantley had known it would be that way. There were too many people for him to be put on the spot.

Not to mention, Tesha seemed to be a crowd pleasure, immediately gaining the attention from the little kids. Although she remained right at Reese's right leg, Brantley was surprised at how easily the dog settled in with the rowdy bunch. He was happy to see she was starting to trust again.

"Sit," he ordered Reese. "I'll grab you a beer."

"Mind if I say hello to your mom and dad first?" he asked quietly.

Smiling, he led the way to the kitchen, where his mother was working alongside Cal and Sadie while their father sat on a stool and watched them do their thing.

Frank turned, evidently hearing them approach.

Brantley squeezed his shoulder. "Dad."

His father patted his hand, turned on his stool before standing. "Sure glad you could make it," he said to Reese.

"Thank you for havin' me, sir."

"None of that sir nonsense." Frank chuckled as he looked past Reese. "Look who it is, Momma," he called to his wife. "She ain't a little girl anymore."

Iris came around the island, a beaming smile on her face. She first greeted Reese with a hug that had him looking helplessly to Brantley. Then she hurried along to JJ, doting on her as was her style.

Brantley motioned Reese toward the island. "Hey, guys, I'd like you to meet Reese. Reese, my sister Sadie, my brother Cal."

They both nodded and smiled, Cal tacking on a brief, "Howdy."

"I'd shake your hand, but it'd be more hassle than it's worth." Sadie frowned, shook her head. "That did not come out right. Just ignore me, Reese. I meant, you'd get dirty and you'd—"

"He knows what you meant, sis."

They left Sadie blushing from her blunder and Cal working diligently to keep up and returned to the living room.

For the next three hours, Brantley would spend most of his time laughing at his brothers shouting at the television, watching his nephew try to climb Reese like a tree because, somewhere along the way, they'd become best friends, smiling as Ashley and Meghan attached a bow to Tesha's collar. Every now and again, he would hear JJ laughing with the girls from their spot at the kitchen table where they were downing margaritas.

And as he sat there, Brantley would let his gaze stray to Reese quite frequently, a very delicious reminder of just how thankful he was this year.

 STAY TUNED

I hope you enjoyed the third installment of the Off the Books Task Force. There's definitely more to come for Brantley and Reese, JJ and Baz, and the rest of the task force. Each book in this series is a full-length novel involving a new case and the continuation of the relationships between them all. And I promise not to keep you waiting long for each installment.

If you enjoyed *Hide & Seek*, please consider leaving a review.

Acknowledgments

Of course, I have to thank my wonderfully patient husband who puts up with me every single day. If it wasn't for him and his belief that I could (and can) do this, I wouldn't be writing this today. He has been my backbone, my rock, the very reason I continue to believe in myself. I love you for that, babe.

Chancy Powley – You continue to come through for me in every way. You even tolerate my inability to answer my text messages in a timely manner. I will apologize for that now and for all future instances because we all know, I'm horrible at it. Just keep in mind, you are the absolute best friend I have and I am forever grateful for your friendship.

Jenna Underwood — Because you continue to be my friend despite the fact that I am the worlds worst friend. Thank you for always being there for me and for the postcards. They make me smile.

I also have to thank my street team – Naughty (and nice) Girls – Your unwavering support is something I will never take for granted.

I can't forget my copyeditor, Amy at Blue Otter Editing. Thank goodness I've got you to catch all my punctuation, grammar, and tense errors.

Nicole Nation 2.0 for the constant support and love. You've been there for me from almost the beginning. This group of ladies has kept me going for so long, I'm not sure I'd know what to do without them.

And, of course, YOU, the reader. Your emails, messages, posts, comments, tweets… they mean more to me than you can imagine. I thrive on hearing from you, knowing that my characters and my stories have touched you in some way keeps me going. I've been known to shed a tear or two when reading an email because you simply bring so much joy to my life with your support. I thank you for that.

About Nicole Edwards

New York Times and *USA Today* bestselling author Nicole Edwards lives in the suburbs of Austin, Texas with her husband and their youngest of three children. The two older ones have flown the coup, while the youngest is in high school. When Nicole is not writing about sexy alpha males and sassy, independent women, she can often be found with a book in hand or attempting to keep the dogs happy. You can find her hanging out on social media and interacting with her readers - even when she's supposed to be writing.

Want to know what's coming next? Or how about see some fun stuff related to Nicole's books? You can find these, as well as tons of other stuff on Nicole's website. You can also find A Day in the Life blog posts, which are short stories about your favorite characters, as well as exclusive contests by joining Nicole Nation on Nicole's website. To join, simply click ***Log In | Register*** in the menu.

If you're interested in keeping up to date on any new releases and preorders, you can sign up for Nicole's notification newsletter. This only goes out when she's got important information to share.

Want a simple, fast way to get updates on new releases? Sign up for text messaging. If you are in the U.S. simply text NICOLE to 64600 or sign up on her website. She promises not to spam your phone. This is just her way of letting you know what's happening because Nicole knows you're busy, but if you're anything like her, you always have your phone on you.

CONNECT WITH NICOLE

Website: NicoleEdwardsAuthor.com

Facebook: /Author.Nicole.Edwards

Instagram: NicoleEdwardsAuthor

DEAD HEAT RANCH
Boots Optional
Betting on Grace
Overnight Love

DEVIL'S BEND
Chasing Dreams
Vanishing Dreams

MISPLACED HALOS
Protected in Darkness
Salvation in Darkness
Bound in Darkness

OFFICE INTRIGUE
Office Intrigue
Intrigued Out of the Office
Their Rebellious Submissive
Their Famous Dominant
Their Ruthless Sadist
Their Naughty Student
Their Fairy Princess

PIER 70
Reckless
Fearless
Speechless
Harmless
Clueless

SNIPER 1 SECURITY
Wait for Morning
Never Say Never
Tomorrow's Too Late

SOUTHERN BOY MAFIA/DEVIL'S PLAYGROUND
Beautifully Brutal
Without Regret
Beautifully Loyal
Without Restraint

Standalone Novels
Unhinged Trilogy
A Million Tiny Pieces
Inked on Paper
Bad Reputation
Bad Business

Naughty Holiday Editions
2015
2016

www.ingramcontent.com/pod-product-compliance
Lightning Source LLC
Chambersburg PA
CBHW061951170626
46813CB00006B/2607